WON'T TELL

PART
1 *of* 3

MARY KORTE

HAVET PRESS
WWW.HAVETPRESS.COM
KIRKLAND, WASHINGTON

WON'T TELL, PART 1 OF 3

IN THIS BOOK: (1) To emphasize respect for everyone's ethnic heritage, the words Black, White, Red, Yellow, and Brown are capitalized. (2) "Elf" is any person living in the North Pole Region, regardless of height. (3) Santa has five ethnic nicknames. *Soweto* when Black – *Freddie* when White – *Pipestone* when Red – *Hum-Bow* when Yellow – *Otoño* when Brown.

Cover graphic design © 2020 by Matt Hinrichs.
www.matthinrichs.com

Havet Press
www.havetpress.com

Library of Congress Control Number: 2020905907

ISBN: 978-0-9864148-3-1

Printed in the United States of America

◇•◇•◇

TRIBUTE

"Dad, in 1957, while helping you strip corn off withering stocks along a field's outer perimeter to make way for the harvesting combine, you asked, 'Sally, [only you called me Sally] do you think you'll ever *do good* for others someday?'

"Your question annoyed me. At sixteen, my primary agenda was snagging a boyfriend. Doing good for others wasn't. Thus, as I tossed an ear of corn into your truck bed, I mumbled, 'I don't know.'

"At the time, I was too self-centered to realize you — who barely eked out a living as a small farmer — were trying to get me — an abused kid who showed up on your doorstep two years earlier — to look beyond the moment. Yes, that day I honestly didn't know, and I didn't care if I'd ever do good for others. However, dad, you and your wife welcoming me into your home, providing me with love and guidance through my high school years, laid the foundation for me to care about others. So, today I'd say, 'Thanks, Dad, for planting that thought-provoking question into my DNA. Among other things, it was a driving force in bringing my *Won't Tell* series to fruition.'"

<>•<>•<>

ALL LIVES MATTER

It makes no difference

where you fit on the rainbow spectrum.

You are, and always will be,

a gift to be treasured.

—*Mary Korte*

WON'T TELL

PART

1 *of* 3

PROLOGUE

"Shelly Jasselton, the Candy Man's daughter . . . That girl's not one to hold her tongue. Some North Pole Villagers say she acts too big for her snow britches. Thinks she knows more than any elf alive. Fiddlin' nutcrackers. She'll sled-run over you if you got in her way. Whew. Can't count the pickle stews that girl has sloshed through. And she sure sticks it to her little brother. Think she's hated him since the day he was born.

"But, I have to say, she's got one redeeming quality. Morality. Never seen a young elf with such a strong moral streak . . . That is when it comes to others. If she thinks something's not right, look out. She won't leave it be.

"At times, she goes too far. Take, for example, the secret-keeping law. Why that wily whippet wasn't more than seven years old when she started questioning its purpose. A troublemaker if ever there was one. But who am I, the Ghost of Winter, to say except . . . except, I've swirled around this North Pole Region long enough to know the whole story."

"Daddy, that secret-keeping law is stupid. Why do we need it? Everyone who lives here knows Santa looks different every year."

"Why do we need it?" Vic Jasselton, Shelly's father reiterated. Tired after putting in a ten-hour day at his candy factory, but knowing his daughter wasn't one to be easily put off, he laid the evening *North Pole Gazette* aside and lifted her to his lap. "Sweetie," he began, "there's not an elf in the North Pole Region who *needs* that law except Santa. And I'm not sure he needs it. It's . . . it's just something he grew up with. I guess it's a safeguard for him."

"A safeguard? Why does Santa need a safeguard?"

"Oh, how do I explain this? Hmm." Vic hesitated. Thought for a moment. "Okay. You know people from other countries come here to study glaciers . . . and to hunt polar bears . . . and to do some ice fishing. Right?"

"Yeah."

"Well, the problem is, if they learn about Santa's secret, they could tell others when they go back home. And those people could tell their friends and neighbors. Then, before you know it, everyone in the world would know his skin color changes every year. And Santa doesn't want the whole world knowing he's different. So, people coming here to visit, they have to sign allegiance to the secret-keeping law."

"Allegiance? Wha . . . what does that mean?"

"It means if someone tells you something is a secret, or if you find out somebody's secret, you can't tell that secret to anyone else. So, if visitors learn Santa's ethnic secret while

they are here—which fortunately hasn't happened yet—
they can't tell anyone outside this Region."

"Oh."

"It's just a precaution, sweetie. To protect Santa's
secret."

"Santa likes keeping secrets?"

"I guess. And people who live here, they have to pledge
allegiance to the secret-keeping law also."

"Why?"

"Why? So, they won't blab Santa's secret to anyone
when they travel outside our Region. It's like a two-way
street. Both foreigners coming into our Region, and North
Pole citizens going out, aren't allowed to tell."

"But why can't anyone tell Santa's secret?"

"Sweetie, Santa wants everyone to think he's White all
the time."

"But he isn't."

"I know. But that's what he wants people to think. And,
you, young lady, are to honor what Santa wants. End of
discussion. Understand? Now go play with your brother.
Let your daddy finish reading his paper."

Shelly, feeling jilted, shrunk away from her daddy. His
end-of-discussion declaration stuck like a thorn in her craw.
On the spot, she became resolute. "Yeah, daddy. I
understand. You won't discuss it with me anymore. But I can,
and I will discuss it with other elves." And she did. From
that day forth, she blatantly challenged the secret-keeping
law with anyone who, to her thinking, *supported its*

irrationality. Despite rolling her eyes whenever a friend said those infamous words, "You can't tell anyone, because I said, 'It's a secret,'" she, like every other elf in the North Pole Region, knew she was obliged, by law, to never to tell.

Eight years pass . . . Shelly, now fifteen, and a risktaker, had used her growing-up time to refine her wit and beguiling charm for one purpose: to get whatever she wanted. Of late, what she has wanted more than anything, besides a boyfriend, is to expose Santa's long-held secret to the world. "That secret-keeping law. I have to . . ."

Figuring out the *have to* . . . That was her dilemma.

"I can't believe it. Not an elf, not even those Santa works with every day, has ever gone up to him and said, 'Santa, that secret-keeping law . . . It's a dumb law. Don't you think our legislature should expunge it?'

"There's got to be a way to get rid of it. Ho, ho, ho. Wait. There is. Blasted icicles. I can't believe I didn't think of this sooner. It's so simple. Yes. All that has to happen is . . . is someone has to tell Santa's secret. Tell!" The thought, like a lure from the devil himself, widened Shelly's eyes and drew a hand to her gaping mouth.

"Oh. My. God. Would I dare? Of course, I would. Nobody else will do it. But if I do it—No. Make that *when I do it*—I don't want anyone pointing a finger back at me. So, how can I leak Santa's secret to the outside world without *my telling* getting me in trouble? If only I had someone's help. Someone besides me who'd like to stuff that law into a garbage can and bury it under a ton of snow. It's gotta be somebody that's tired of Santa using it as a crutch. I wonder if . . . Hmm. Maybe Mitzi Claus. Yeah. After being married to that secret-keeper for what, forty-some years, it must grate her . . . him keeping that secret under wraps.

"Gotta think about this for a bit. Let's see . . . Mitzi Claus, Mitzi Claus. Would she make a good accomplice? Hmm. Guess I won't know until I check her out.

"Yeah. That's what I was thinking about a month ago. So, I came up with a plan. One that was kinda ingenious on my part. 'Hey, girl,' I said to myself, 'just volunteer at her office. Watch her every move. Gain her confidence.' And so, I did. Fiddlin' nutcrackers. What a waste.

"Of course, I tried talking to her about Santa's secret. I mean, that's the only reason I volunteered there.

"And then there was Mark, her office manager. Nice distraction. Cute. Cute. Cute. He likes me a lot. Even said he loves me. But my dad . . . Oh, well, I sucked it up. Just said, 'Let it go, girl.' Cuz, duh. My reason for being there was to get the lowdown on Mitzi, not to reel him in. But whenever I said something to her . . . You know. About Santa's secret or that stupid law, she'd change the subject. Or . . . or, she'd look at her watch and say, 'Oh dear. I'm late for an important meeting. Bye. See you later.'

"Important meeting, my snow britches. One day I followed her to her so-called *important meeting*. Get this. She met up with a cup of tea in the cafeteria. Just sat there, bored like, stirrin' her spoon in it. Dancin' Prancer. I wasted a whole hour watching her.

"'How was your meeting,' I asked when she got back."

"Fine."

"Her doing that . . . Right then and there I decided she wasn't the one. I mean, if she couldn't even talk about it, I sure in Elk Tundra knew she wouldn't be willing to tell. Nope. Courage is not part of her DNA.

"But Santa keeping that secret. It bothers her. I could tell. Cuz whenever I said anything, she acted so uptight. Probably feels she has to be loyal to him. Yeah. That's gotta be it. Being his wife and all. Sooty bricks. She'll never tell.

"Can't do this alone though. It's too risky. Gotta find someone who'd be willing . . . Hmm. Someone I can trust. Someone who won't cop out on me. A reporter! Maybe I can connect with one, like, down in the USA, one that . . ."

CHAPTER 1

"Shelly. That girl. She's so brazen. Holy walrus turds. What if she were to blab Santa's secret? Yikes. If she did, all that stuff his poppa drummed into his little-boy head would likely come true. What if—"

Hey, girl. What's with you thinking such rubbish?

Mitzi's alter ego, which she long ago dubbed as her nattering Tomacita, often challenged her head chatter, especially when she was in the throes of worrisome thought.

"It's those *What ifs*. They're back pestering me. And my screaming, 'Go away. Leave me alone.' doesn't help. And neither does your butting in." Mitzi, done slamming her nattering Tomacita, fluffed her pillow, then pulled its sides to her ears. A few seconds later, realizing it couldn't quiet her head chatter, she released her grip and stared at the big hand of her bedside clock ratcheting *tick-tock-ticks* toward dawn. "Taffy tarnation. It's not even four o'clock and those annoying *What ifs* are already driving me crazy."

Duh. Of course, they are, girl. It's Christmas Season Blessing Day.

"Dancin' Prancer. Every year, it's *What if this, What if that*. Such nonsense. If only he'd reveal that stupid secret of his. The stubborn moose. Yeah. I used to beg him to tell, but would he listen to me? No. Two years I hounded him. Then I did what any sane person would do. I threw in the towel. One day I said, 'That's enough.' And ever since, on Christmas Season Blessing Day, my anxiety flies like . . . like off the rooftop. Ugh. What a headache."

Face it, girl. Santa's refusal to share his secret isn't all that worries you. Admit it. You're also afraid for *him.*

"Yeah. I am. But must you remind me of that? And the stubborn moose. He has no idea how much I worry. Today, if I were to mention it, he'd dismiss me with a flick of his hand. He'd say, 'Stop worrying, hon. There's no way anyone's gonna find out.' Sooty bricks. It's bad enough ninety percent of the world refuses to believe he's real. But if someone outside our so-called *safety zone* were to find out eighty percent of the time he's not what he makes himself out to be . . . Oh, God, help us if that were to ever happen."

Mitzi turned her attention to the play of window-silhouetted moonlight on Santa's sleeping form. In particular, his stomach rising and falling in cadence with his snoring. "Oh, sweetheart, I'd love to cuddle up to you. But if I did, you'd sense my distress, and then you'd pressure me to get it out. And there's no way I'm opening that can of worms again." She shuddered. Not from the room's chill but from past arguments when, time and again, he stood his ground, refusing to expose his racial uniqueness. "No, sweetheart. I'll not start another fight over that ridiculous secret of yours. And I certainly don't want you worrying about *my worrying* that someone outside this Region might figure *you* out.

"Fiddlin' nutcrackers. If only you wouldn't jet off every Christmas Season to some God-only-knows place just to pretend *you* are *you*. Oh, why? Why every Christmas Season do you have to put yourself at risk like that?"

Girl, you know he loves pretending to be a Santa Claus helper. Face it. It's in his blood. He's got to do it.

"Yeah. I know. He says, 'No one will know it's me.' Blasted icicles. If only he wouldn't do that. Fat chance he'd ever give it up though. He loves kids too much, plus the hype of it all. But watch. Sooner or later, someone's gonna figure out he's not always White. And when that happens, he'll be ducking reporters coming in from who knows where. Yep. Just like his poppa feared. They'll twist the facts. Make him out to be a freak. Wow. That would surely send him up a glacier. If only his poppa didn't have that law passed."

Lying flat on her back, massaging throbbing temples, Mitzi thought about the mantra she had devised thirty-eight years ago, two years after marrying Santa. She often relied on it to ease her anxiety. Lately, though, its effectiveness just wasn't there. Still, she started mouthing it. "I love him as Soweto. I love him as Freddie. I love him as Pipestone. I love him as . . . Shimmering icicles. I wouldn't put it past Shelly to blab his secret to some reporter. Oh, sweetheart, I wish you weren't so secretive."

Wish on, girl.

"Bug off, you nattering Tomacita. I'll handle this."

Mitzi, not one to readily admit defeat, persisted. "I love him as Hum-Bow. I love him as Otoño. I love him as . . . Blasted icicles. If the media in Canada, Australia or anywhere else in the world were to get wind of it, why—"

Knock it off, girl. Stay focused on your mantra.

"Okay, okay. I love him as Soweto. I love him as Freddie. I love him as . . . But if some weirdo scientists showed up at our door and whisked him off to some secret research laboratory . . . Holy walrus turds. I'd never see him again."

Stop it. For taffy tarnation, girl. Stop thinking such rubbish. Concentrate on your mantra.

"Right. Okay. I love him as Pipestone, I love him as . . . Yeah but, with his one-of-a-kind genes, he'd be worth a mint on the black market. Some crooked politicians, out to make a bundle, might—"

Girl, stop. For taffy tarnation, stop this nonsense.

"And you stop yelling at me."

Realizing not another wink of sleep lay in her cards, Mitzi bolted upright. "Why? Why won't my mantra work?" She checked the time. "Frickin' fiddlesticks. It's only four-twenty." Eyeing Santa's splayed-out form, she grumbled, "And why is it sleep never eludes you? You're out the minute your head hits the pillow and you always sleep through the night. Oh, how I wish I could do that."

Minutes later, flip-flopping slippers over hallway carpet, she, still frustrated, spouted, "Why? Why do you have to be such a fraidy-cat? If you'd only reveal that stupid secret of yours, this worry wouldn't haunt me every

Christmas Season. And right now, I'd still be sleeping."

Once comfy in her recliner, she pulled her laptop off the coffee table. Lifting cover, knee-balancing it, she stared at its screen. *ZIP* . . . A stream of incoming emails flashed before her eyes. Spotting one from her dear friend Shooting Star, she clicked on it. Her message shocked her. "What! You've got to be kidding. A temp rise like that. Why that's insane."

Weeding through the latest stream, she answered some, flagged those needing further attention, and quickly deleted every screaming *buy-my-service* ad. An hour later, that chore out of the way, she shut down her laptop and headed for the kitchen.

"Think I'll whip up a German pancake. Maybe top it off with some apple slices dipped in fresh lemon juice and cinnamon sugar. Yeah. Like his momma used to make. And, since I know the recipe by heart, it should be a no brainer. Don't have to think. And today, that's a good thing."

Standing PJ clad at a kitchen counter, mindlessly cracking eggs, Mitzi again relied on her mantra to fight her head's *what if* chatter. "I love him as . . ." Not more than a minute later, she groused, "Pointless. Pointless. That mantra is worthless. I need another diversion."

Robotically stirring dry ingredients into well-beaten eggs, she swept her eyes over her kitchen decor. Her peepers, heavy with anxiety and unsettled as much as her mind, darted from her jasper canister set from India to her framed collection of silver teaspoons, to the antique milk can and butter churn salvaged years ago from cousin Martha's reindeer farm. Most mornings she found the coziness of her kitchen, and all its decorative mementos, comforting, but not today.

For a moment, her African violets, lining the kitchen's east windowsill, garnered her attention. Sometimes she doted over them for hours. "They're a testament to your green thumb," Santa often said. Their sapphire-blue florets surrounded by verdant green foliage usually brought a smile to her lips. Today, as she worked a familiar question off the tip of her tongue, her eyes merely blended their colors into blurry blobs. "Why? Why does he have to be such a stubborn moose?"

Setting her bowl on the counter, staring at nothing in particular, she answered her posed question. "Because he just is. Because he's a carbon copy of his poppa. Stubborn and . . . and dead set in his ways."

Heeding her late mother-in-law's directive for making a delicious German pancake—*First, my dear, preheat the cast-iron pan*—she slipped the weighty hand-me-down into the oven and set the timer. "Hopefully, it'll be hot enough to sizzle butter in fifteen minutes."

Leaning into the nearest counter, dropping chin to chest, she stared at her apron's daisy print. The flowered pattern, depicting a field of yellow and white posies, pulled her back in time, to when happiness was such a rarity, she cherished every joyful moment that came her way.

<>•<>•<>

During her recall, she saw her little six-year-old self, sitting in her woodland hideout, plucking petals off her last daisy, chanting, "Does she love me? Yes, she loves me. Does she love me? Yes, she loves me. Does she . . . Ut-oh. All gone."

Rising, meandering through the weedy field behind her blended family's century-old farmhouse near Somerset, Kentucky, she, on the hunt for more daisies, spotted the biggest, the reddest, the most beautiful flower she had ever laid eyes on. Its petal-spread, nearly matching the roundness of her little face, seemed to beckon, "Come closer. Gaze upon me." Staring at it, she didn't know its bulb had been yanked, along with a tangle of noxious weeds, from her stepmother's flowerbed and dumped there the previous fall. To her, it was *a pretty*, and she was starving for *pretties*. Running to it, she bent down and snapped its fat stem from its lifeline. Almost prayerlike, she pressed her face into its softness *and said*, *"My pretty."* Laying claim to it, whiffing its fragrance, lifted her spirits, but not for long. Fear that her stepmother would accuse her of picking it from her flower garden crimped her excitement.

"Is she looking? Did she see me pick it?"

Mitzi's fear was real. If the redhead sighted the flower in her hand, she would march toward her screaming accusations and threats. Always, her stepmother processed her truth-telling as lies. When confronted with such terror, Mitzi knew better than to run. Running, she knew, always ended in a harsher beating.

Imagining the worse, and now anxious, Mitzi darted her

eyes from window to window on the backside of the farmhouse. Spotting no angry face glaring at her from any pane, she breathed a little easier. Still, fright lingered. Looking down at *her pretty*, she mumbled, "Gotta run. Hide. Before the redhead says I picked you from her garden and starts yelling and hitting me."

Barefoot, wearing only scant underwear, she, smoothly like a garter snake slithering through tall weeds, quickly put distance between her and the old farmhouse, a farmhouse so hewn in by nature's reclamation, newcomers had difficulty finding it.

If satellite surveillance had existed in the late 1940s, it would have shown a dilapidated fence bordering an unkempt apple orchard east of the farmhouse. To the west, it would have highlighted an entanglement of underbrush shoring up a thicket of old, gnarly trees. This *thicket* lined and nearly obliterated the quarter-mile lane linking the farm to the gravel road leading into Somerset.

To the north, the satellite's powerful lens would have captured an old barn, but not the hay rotting beneath its sagging roof. Sadly, until time reduced it to nothingness, the fodder would serve only to incubate baby mice for hungry snakes lying in wait.

To the south, the satellite's lens would have surveyed a mammoth, weed-choked strawberry field which, sadly, hadn't seen the till of a plow or the planting of new starters in more than twenty years. Mitzi's father had dreams, but they had yet to materialize.

The rundown old fruit farm, a good eight miles or so from town, proved to be a child abuser's paradise. With no electrical wires connecting the house to power poles running parallel to the county road, the few travelers who sped by at fifteen-to-twenty miles per hour were oblivious to its existence. Mitzi's stepmother hated the inconvenience of *no* electricity, but she loved that *not a soul* could hear her young victim screaming.

Flower in hand, seeking reprieve from her stepmother's wrath, and the sweltering heat, Mitzi glanced back to see if stepsister Karen and half-sister Janice were following. Relieved they weren't, she settled into a slow trot.

Shortly after the man called Daddy jerked her away from loving relatives and plopped her down in his chaotic blended family, she learned the folly of trusting either sister. From the day she arrived, she shouldered the blame for their misdeeds. All they had to say was, "Mitzi did it." Little protégés of their mother, they often taunted her with hateful ditties. Ditties meant to demoralize her.

Many evenings, when her father worked his four-to-twelve coal-mining shift, and she, sentenced to chair-sitting, they, along with their mother, would prance around, nose-thumbing and belittling her with sing-song putdowns. "You're a stupid idiot, a scumbag, and a bowie-hunky too. You're a nincompoop, a sneaky kraut . . ." Such denigrating remarks not only solidified her scapegoated role, they often reduced her to tears.

As Mitzi ran along the narrow footpath, weedy barbs easily snagged her skin, drawing blood. But little scratches never deterred her from reaching her wall-to-wall (so to speak) moss-blanketed paradise which lay between an old tinder-dry fruit shed and a dilapidated fence. Overgrown briers and a canopy of low-hanging hickory-tree branches hid it well. Her secret place had all she needed: a rock to crack hickory nuts and a sprung bobby pin to dig out nutmeat.

Finding safety in a woodland niche her stepmother never treaded, she, leaning against the old fruit shed, would while away time plucking petals off daisies, chanting, "Does she love me? Yes, she loves me. Does she love me? Yes, she loves me."

Usually, when her hunt for more daisies proved futile, she would return to her hideout, close her eyes, and will herself into her birth mother's arms. Imagining her tender touch, she would beg, "Please, Mommy. Please come get me. Please take me away from these awful people. Please."

On this day, looking down on her beautiful flower, she pictured herself gifting it to her birth mother and receiving a big hug in return. As she imagined this, an insidious scream intruded on her fantasy.

"Bohunk, where the hell are you?"

Every time those words singed Mitzi's ears, she would jump to her feet and run like lightning until she was standing submissively in front of the redhead, awaiting her fate.

"Oh, how many times did I sing that wishful ditty when sitting by that shed? Always, I said, 'Yes. She loves me,' because I couldn't bear the thought of my birth mother not loving me. And too, I clung to the belief she'd magically appear one day and whisk me away from my hellish predicament. But she never came. I was clueless until I became old enough to understand death. Even then, I longed for her to swoop down from heaven and whisk me away. Sooty bricks. I didn't even know her name. Nobody talked about her. And I didn't dare approach my dad. The redhead made it clear that I was not to go near him."

Mitzi, pulling herself back to the here and now, said, "Okay, dearie, enough with the woeful tales."

Stirring pancake batter, she again chanted, "I love him as Soweto. I love him as Freddie. I love him as . . ." Sadly, it didn't help. Despair, and more *what if* chatter—"*What if* people taunt him? *What if* they make him out to be a freak? *What if . . .*"—rendered her mantra ineffective.

She thought about smacking the counter with her wooden spoon; but, knowing the ensuing racket would likely wake Santa, and also spatter batter everywhere, she merely tightened her grip on it.

"Dancin' Prancer. His secret makes him so vulnerable, and there's not a thing I can do to protect him."

Hurriedly, she poured pancake batter into her pre-heated pan, then slid it into the oven. As sobs rose in her chest, she watched a trembling hand—one that seemed detached from her body—lifting a corner of her apron to wick away tears.

Every Christmas Season Mitzi fought both the *What if* chatter in her head and her ensuing anxiety. Much to her dismay, not until her husband completed both his Santa Claus helper stint and his Christmas Eve run did her worries lessen.

Most days, she kept her *what if* chatter at bay by focusing on her work as production coordinator. But always, the morning of Christmas Season Blessing Day, she couldn't shake the blitz. A good cry, long before Santa rose from slumber, usually brought some release.

Her dear, dear husband . . . He didn't know this worry weighed her down every Christmas Season. Nor did she want him to know.

"All these years of marriage and never a Christmas Season without worry. Why? Oh, how I wish I didn't know the answer to that question, but I do."

She set the oven timer for forty-five minutes. To break anxiety's hold, she stiffened her arms and plunged her fists deep into apron pockets. After twisting her neck back and forth a few times, she started venting as though Santa were standing in front of her.

"Whenever I suggested you make your secret known to the world, you'd turn into a riled bear. Never would you listen to reason or even consider the merits of revealing it. Taffy tarnation. What's it been? Forty years of marriage and still the futility of it haunts me. Every time I pleaded, 'Please, dear. Please tell your secret,' you'd throw your head back and yell, 'No. No. No. I'll never, ever tell.' And then, seeing your face reddening up, I knew better than to press the issue. Oh, why, why do you have to be so stubborn? Why are you so hellbent on keeping your racial changes secret forever?"

Girl, why are you working yourself into such a dither?

Mitzi's nostrils flared. "Listen, you nattering Tomacita. Yes. I know I *need* to tone down my anger. So, am I going to? Sure. When I'm good and ready. And for your information, I wouldn't be so steamed if those *What ifs* hadn't robbed me of a good night's sleep. And you and I both know they wouldn't be hounding me if it wasn't for you-know-who's dumb secret. Frickin' fiddlesticks. Who knows why he insists on hiding his racial changes? I certainly don't."

Thinking on that, she said with less intensity, "No. That's not true. I do know why. Sweetheart, you made that stupid promise to your poppa. You promised to never, ever tell. Lord knows, every time I pushed you to break *your little promise*, you fought me tooth and nail. Seems like all my urgings ever did was turn you into a riled bear. And then, what did I do? The only thing I could do. I let it go. I finally realized I was wasting my time. Prancing Dancer. No matter what I said, you wouldn't budge. So, I clammed up. 'Subject

19

closed,' I said, vowing to never mention it again."

Much like her commitment to the secret-keeping law, Mitzi vowed to keep her lips sealed forever. Yet, in doing so, she unwittingly created a breeding ground for those nattering *what-ifs*. Every November first, like hordes of insects descending in a breeding frenzy, they invaded her mind with a vengeance. *What if this . . . What if that . . .*

She checked the minutes left on the oven timer.

"Blasted icicles. Today, the world would go crazy if anyone blabbed your secret. Yeah. I can see it. If it were revealed now, reporters would hound us relentlessly. Oh, what a mess that would be. But even so, sweetheart, I've always thought it would be better if you told rather than taking the risk of someone exposing it.

"Sweetie, you don't know it, but to be honest, there are times I find myself wishing someone would *out* you. I even thought about spilling my guts to Shelly last month, when she was asking so many questions. But, I held my tongue.

"Mark my word, Mr. Hum-Bow Claus. Someday, someone will tell. Yeah. You think that law your poppa had the Senate pass years ago will protect you forever. Hey. I've got news for you. People don't always keep secrets. Oh, they intend to, but the best of intentions can and do go by the wayside. Just watch. Someday, someone here will *out* you, or some outsider will figure it out. And then what?"

A glimpse of the wall clock told her Santa would likely rise within the hour. Hurriedly gathering her gummy baking utensils, she said, "I've got to get this place cleaned up and myself calmed down before he wakes up."

A self-pressured sense of urgency—only because she was a bit neurotic about keeping things tidy—set her to rinsing and stuffing her baking utensils into the dishwasher. Once done, she cupped her hands under the faucet and doused her eyes several times. As near-freezing water eased their puffiness, she wished it would also ease her worries.

Resolutely she mumbled, "I need to . . . No. I want to look cheery before he gets up. Like I'd never been crying." Grabbing a towel, patting her face dry, she said, "Now to do some pushups, stretches, maybe lift some weights. Gotta get rid of this headache."

A few minutes later, stretched out on her exercise mat, she pulled her knees to her chest. First one, then the other. Then both together, again and again. No chanting. Just slow, yoga-like breathing.

After her workout, she, feeling a little less distraught, fixed herself a cup of hot cranberry tea. Sitting at the kitchen table, squinting to read the thermometer tacked to the outer window frame, she almost screamed, "Holy walrus turds. It's twenty-two degrees out there. I can't believe it's gone that high already."

Rarely did Mitzi give a rat's tail as to where that mercury line stood. Seldom did she check it. Today, as she stared at it, the gist of Shooting Star's e-mail popped into her head.

Caught the late-night news. They said the temperature will rise from forty-three below to fifteen above by 6:00 a.m. and it's supposed to climb even higher. Might reach thirty-

21

five above by early afternoon. Can you believe that?

"No, I can't believe that, Shooting Star. And I didn't believe it when I read your e-mail earlier either. But now . . ." Hesitating, lifting her mug to her lips, she blew ripples across its steamy surface. Then, whiffing its fruity aroma, she took a sip and said, "What a fluke. Never has this happened before. If this keeps up, we'll soon be saying *dripping icicles* instead of *shimmering icicles*."

To get an update on the weather, she twisted at the waist and turned on the radio counter-bound behind her. Rotating back around, she glimpsed the wall clock across the room and let out a whispered scream. "Sooty bricks. It's almost seven-thirty. I've so much to do before I—"

Dancin' Prancer, girl. Stay put. Enjoy your tea.

Her nattering Tomacita's intrusive remarks had her rethinking her intention.

"Yeah. You're right. I should stop frettin' so."

Slumping against her chair's back, consciously drawing in a deep breath, she became cognizant of the rich cinnamon scent permeating the whole cottage. The spicy aroma not only brought a smile to her lips it also set her to picturing Santa lying in bed, mouth wide open, snoring loudly. "Ah, sweetheart," she playfully said, "I bet the aroma of my German pancake is sending your Hum-Bow nose into a twitching frenzy." Sighing, grateful the worst of the Season's *What-if* emotional assault was behind her, she lifted her mug to her lips and savored another sip of tea.

<>•<>•<>

Chapter 2

Whiffs of Mitzi's German pancake were luring Santa toward wakefulness. With his mouth salivating for the breakfast treat, he, sliding tongue over dry lips, willed his eyelids to rise to half-mast. "Yum, yum, German pancake. My favorite. Guess that ruins my plan to catch some extra winks." Revisiting what he just said, he popped his eyes wide and said sarcastically, "Yeah. Right. As if I could get in some extra winks on *this* day."

As nighttime grogginess dissipated, his thoughts turned to Mitzi. "I'm so lucky to have her for a wife because she sticks by me no matter what. And I've never doubted her faithfulness. No. Wait. There was that one time. Let's see. When was it? Eight years ago, I think. No matter. We ironed it out. Anyway, I guess, just like other couples, we've had our ups and downs. Much as I hate to admit it though, she sure taught me . . ."

Stopping mid-thought, he patted his tummy and grinned. "Yeah, Mitzi. I remember when you let me know, in no uncertain terms, that you'd no longer tolerate me taking you for granted. Back then, I was clueless. Yes. All through our first thirty-two years of marriage I had no idea

I was expecting you to wait on me hand and foot like my momma always did. Sooty bricks. It never hit me until you went berserk on me. Yeah. Not until you ran away eight years ago, did I realize how good I had it. And yes, what you put me through back then was hell. Today though . . . Hey, it sure makes for good daydreaming."

Curling up on Mitzi's side of the bed, he muttered, "Oh, to squeeze in some extra winks or maybe do a little daydreaming." Fighting the urge to succumb to either, especially the latter, he scolded himself. "Listen, ya old bloke. Now's not the time to get caught up in a daydream. Especially the one about Mitzi's charade. No. No. Not today, mister. That one will have to wait for a stroll through the ice sculpture park when I've time to spare. Now, buddy, stop your stalling. Move your butt out of bed. Get out there in the kitchen and enjoy Mitzi's German pancake while it's still hot. And you'd better show her some appreciation for getting up early to make it too."

Off flew the covers.

Rolling onto his back, dangling feet over his side of the bed, he pitter-pattered the floor, seeking his slippers. After finding one, then the other, and wiggling his feet into them, he, still reluctant to get up, linked his hands over his well-endowed tummy and started singing. "Oh, it's Christmas Season Blessing Day, time to put our play away . . ." Midstream, he switched to a childish tantrum. "But I don't want to get up. I don't want to get up."

Five minutes later, sauntering into the kitchen, still

pajama-clad, his eyes, in cahoots with his nose, zeroed in on Mitzi's German pancake. "Ah. So, there's the culprit that woke me."

"My treat," Mitzi said, topping off her smile with a playful wink.

Santa, sidling up to her side, planted a kiss on her lips. "Smells scrumptious, my love. And thank you. It was so sweet of you to get up early to make it."

"You're welcome, sweetie."

As she spoke, Santa studied her eyes. He didn't know, and he couldn't tell that she had been crying. Still, he sensed, like he had every November first for the past three decades or so, that something was troubling her. In prior years, he said nothing. Nor would he today. He used to. But always, she said the same thing.

"Sweetheart, nothing's bothering me. Really. I'm fine."

Today, even though his heart weighed heavy with concern, he decided not to press the issue. Still, it troubled him. "I wish she wouldn't be so tightlipped. Knowing her though, I'll never be privy to whatever it is that bothers her on this day of all days. Oh why, after all these years, why does she still hold back on me? Trust issues, I guess."

"Bring me your plate, sweetie," Mitzi said, "and I'll cut you a piece. Fixings are on the table, next to your morning paper."

As Mitzi knife pierced the puffy pancake's center, Santa, hovering, leaned back to avoid hot steam in his face. Seconds later, a loaded plate in hand, he marched to the table, cooing,

"Oh, what a treat." Once settled, he slathered the fluffy pancake with gobs of butter. Next came drizzles of maple syrup, a sprinkle of blueberries, and a mountain of whipped cream. His first mouthful of the delicacy bloomed ecstasy across his face. Winking at Mitzi, he said, "Mm, mm. It's perfecto, my love. Per-fect-to."

"Just like your momma's?"

"Yep. U-u-uh . . . No. It's better."

In keeping with his morning ritual, he picked up the *North Pole Gazette* and turned to its back-page comics.

Mitzi, her plate full, sat down opposite him and glanced the paper's front-page headline. Realizing it was the same as previous years, she read it aloud with a sarcastic twang.

"Hmm. *Feasting and Merrymaking to Follow Santa's Blessing.* Okay." Peering over the paper's top edge, she waited for his reaction. When none came, she said tersely, "Whacky walruses. Why do they always print what every elf in this Region already knows?"

Santa, lowering his paper, pithily responded to her question with one of his own. "Taffy tarnation, hon, why do you always have to bring that up?" Angrily whipping his paper outward, he said tersely, "Hon, you know just as well as I do. They print that because it's tradition. Our tradition."

"Tradition!" she shot back. "If you ask me, it's nothing but a waste of ink and paper."

Santa flinched. Arching his brows, glaring at her over the newspaper's top edge, he enunciated his next words with forced calmness. "My dear, a little ink and paper ain't worth worrying about."

"Who's worrying? I just think it's a waste and . . . and stupid. Come on. Snowman up. Admit it. It's really stupid to print what everybody already knows."

Santa, rolling his eyes, retreated behind his paper. Rather than picking up where he left off though, he sat, thinking. "Nope. I'm not giving in. I'm gonna make my point." Lowering his paper, he said decisively, "Like I said, love. It's tradition. So, face it. Some things stay the same around here, like the—"

"Like the weather," she spouted smartly. "Betcha in an hour or so it'll be so warm outside we won't be able to see our breath." Chalking one up to her credit, she crossed her legs and batted her eyelashes at him.

Ignoring her pompous tease, but bristling, Santa countered, "Whadaya mean? Our breath is always frosty when we're outside." Twisting sideways, he glimpsed the outdoor thermometer. Shocked by what he saw, he blinked several times.

"What!" He hated to admit it, but the high mercury line proved Mitzi right. Staring at it, he added, "Well, blow me down an iceberg slide. It says it's twenty-four degrees out there. Don't tell me a falling icicle crashed into that thing and knocked it off-kilter."

"You haven't been outside yet, have you?"

"In PJs? Of course not. But if that thing's right, something's wrong. Do you think some war-crazed country messed up our atmosphere with a nuclear bomb?"

"No, sweetie. Nothing like that happened."

"Are you sure?"

"Yes, sweetheart, I'm sure." Reaching across the table, gently tapping his *Asian* nose with her index finger, she said, "Got an e-mail from Shooting Star this a.m. That girl went on and on about this temp spike. But neither she nor the news I listened to just before you got up, said anything about a bombing causing this. So, stop fretting. Here. Have some more tea to wash down that pancake."

Tipping the teapot, she flicked her eyes back and forth from the stream of steamy tea filling his cup to the shocked look on his face. "Come on, Hum-Bow. Stop worrying. Just chalk it up to Mother Nature. She's probably pulling an old trick. Or, maybe, a new one."

"You think so?" As he watched her set the teapot back on its trivet, he, deciding to leave well enough alone, turned back to his comics.

Mitzi, not about to let him *let it lie*, said testily, "Yes, it's got to be her doing. Mother Nature, I mean. But, why'd she have to pick this day, of all days, to lay a thaw on us?"

Lowering his paper, deep lines creased Santa's brow as he shot back, "What's with you? First, you tell me not to worry. Then, you complain about the nicest day we're about to have in the history of our existence. Of all things. You, a sun lover, upset over a nice temp spike. Why I'd think you'd be jumping with joy." To further make his point, he set his steely eyes on hers, challenging her to a staredown.

Ignoring his invite, Mitzi turned away, saying, "Hey,

don't expect me to buy that argument."

He smiled weakly. "Look, hon, I think this is great weather for our Blessing Day festivities."

She exploded. "Great weather. Bog wash. Us hiking up that mountain in those fur-lined suits . . . Why we'll roast like . . . like pigs in a Hawaiian luau pit."

"Hmm. Those suits are bulky. But hey, if we start early and take it slow, it shouldn't be that bad."

"That bad! My dearest Hum-Bow Claus, take another look at that thermometer. It's climbed a few more degrees since we last looked at it. And don't you think two miles, over half of it up Jingle-Jangle Mountain, is a long way to hike in this thaw? And tell me this. Why in taffy tarnation did you have *that* speech-giving platform built on top of *that* mountain?"

"Oh, love, I don't know. I guess I thought it would be rather novel."

"Novel? It'll be exhausting. That's a long way to hike."

"Come on, love. It won't be that bad."

"Yeah, well, I don't understand why you built it way out there in the boonies. On top of a mountain no less."

"Hey. Wait a minute. I didn't build it. The college kids did with a little help from some high school gofers."

"Yeah. Right. Blame the younger generation. But hey, you're the one who picked *that* site."

Santa, exasperated at this point, slowly exhaled through lips rounded in the shape of a button. Setting his paper aside, he said through a quirky smile, "Okay, love. I confess.

29

I'm guilty. Go ahead. Lock me up. Throw away the key, but—"

"But what?"

"But first, may I please have another piece of your delicious German pancake? Hmm? Pretty please?"

Mitzi, turning to leave, said snappishly, "Help yourself. I've got lots to do before *your* speech-giving hour."

Santa, savoring every forkful of his second piece of German pancake, fixed his eyes on a sun-glinting icicle, eave hanging outside the kitchen's east window. A drip to the sill—an unusual sight in North Pole Region—held his gaze. Minutes later, after swallowing his last bite, he, realizing his overloaded stomach had no desire to move, leaned back, locked his fingers behind his head, and let his thoughts run wild.

"Hmm. With this temp rise, I suspect we'll have us a nice crowd today. Can't wait to set foot on that new platform. And to think, some folks thought I was nuts picking that site. Of course, building it on Saucer Plateau was risky, but I knew those architect students would figure out how to do it.

"Yes. Today I get to do what I've wanted to do for years. I'm gonna give my speech from Saucer Plateau on the very tiptop of Jingle-Jangle Mountain.

"Oh, and did those students ever show those *stuck-in-the-snowdrift* old codgers a thing or two. Got to hand it to them. They didn't let those old farts unnerve them one bit. It was sad though. Those fellows had to make a big ta-do of all that hole drilling. Said it would crumble the mountain. Of course, it didn't. And later, seeing those fat posts cemented firmly in deep wells of fast-drying cement . . . Well, after that, those old codgers went around swearing to everyone they met. They said, 'Hey. Those posts. They'll stand tall for more than a thousand years.' Now, how funny is that?

"And, of course, they had to make a big stink about the high cost of it all. 'Hey,' I told them, 'so, what if it cost a bundle to ship those poles up here from Canada.' Pugh. Who cares about the cost? Yeah. It cost a lot to get them here. But they were needed to make that platform sturdy. And safe. Especially since it rises twenty feet off the ground. Not to mention, that chimney shoots another ten feet up from its center. Ho, ho, ho. Today, I get to wiggle my fat tummy through a thirty-foot-high chimney. Wow. Never before have I climbed through one that tall.

"And the whole Region gets represented. Let's see. Who suggested we carve our community names, one in each of the five outer posts? Wasn't it Pietro? Yeah. It was him.

"Ho, ho, ho. I, Santa Claus, get to strut around a platform that sits right dab in the middle of the world's northern-most spot. Hmm. Maybe not quite, but almost.

"Yep. I'll be able to look east to Sleigh Valley, south to Krisville, west to Rudolphtown and north to Kringleland. All while strutting around that platform. Yahoo. What a day this is gonna be."

Santa eyed the wall clock. The late hour spurred him to

break from thought. "Hey, ya old bloke. Enough dillydallying. It's almost time to leave and look at you. You're not even dressed. And you better check your speech one more time. After all, it's gotta be good enough to foster cooperation a-a-and dampen ornery attitudes for the entire Christmas Season. Ho, ho, ho. What a day this is gonna be."

CHAPTER 3

It wasn't like Hunter Swift Bear, a Sleigh Valley High junior, to volunteer for a task he considered more suited for girls. Yet, he did, for one reason. To get time alone with a girl . . . Shelly Jasselton, a North Pole High sophomore.

Climbing Jingle-Jangle Mountain at the same pace the sun was rising behind it, Hunter thought back to the night he and hundreds of other students had entered Dasher Hall to attend the year's first platform-planning meeting. Shortly into it, his best friend Pietro made his pitch.

"Santa, what if we carved the suburban names and North Pole Village, one on each of the five outer posts? If we did that, the whole Region would be represented. I mean, I think it'd look kinda cool. And . . . and I could do that. The carving, I mean."

"Santa, Santa," came a sweet voice from Hunter's far left, "I think it'd look super rad if we tied streamers to those posts. Long ones. In different colors. And if it's okay, I'll do that."

"Me too," slipped off Hunter's barely moving lips.

The draw was instant. The girl's sweet voice, the sway

33

of her long, blonde tresses, the way she cocked her head left then right, her flirtatious eyes . . . Everything about her tugged at his heart. Not willing to pass up an opportunity staring him in the face, he shot up from his seat. Frantically waving a hand, he shouted, "Santa, Santa, I'll help do that . . . uh, those streamers, I mean. I'll help tie them to posts."

Santa, spotting him, nodded, then said, "Good. Two should be enough for that task."

Hunter, now more interested in the girl than platform planning, turned his obsidian eyes—strikingly infused with longing—toward her. Taken by her beauty, he didn't realize he was staring until she cut her eyes his way, registering his presence.

Embarrassed at being flushed out, he quickly shifted his line of sight to Santa. To anyone looking his way, he appeared to be taking in all the suggestions and rebuttals being voiced around him. Not so. His ears, cordoned off by awakened emotions, heard nothing. Cautiously turning to glimpse the girl again, his eyes—colliding with hers—flared brighter than a deer's, suddenly dazed by on-coming headlights.

Panic, along with excitement and fear, drove Hunter into a duck-down slump. During the past year, he had done a lot of looking, and some longing, but hadn't yet found the courage to approach any girl. Enamored by this young lady, he hoped to conquer his shyness, and his inclination to run.

Knowing he would likely be accused of copping out if he left the meeting early, he settled for slouching down in his seat and jamming his long legs into space beneath the chair ahead of him. Confident he was out of the girl's view, he twisted sideways and motioned for his friend Pietro to lean in close.

Pietro, having witnessed the whole *peek-a-boo, I-see-you* interaction, tilted his head to get the skinny.

"That gosling over there, that blonde," Hunter whispered, motioning with an upward thrust of his head. "Wow. I'd sure like to get to know her."

"What! Her?"

"Yeah, man. She's a knockout."

Pietro's eyes widened. Grimacing, he warned, "Don't go there, bozo. She ain't nothin' but trouble. Big trouble."

"You know her, huh?"

"Yeah. I know her."

"So, what's her name?"

"Shelly. Shelly Jasselton. She's the Candy Man's daughter?"

"Really. That's what she looks like now. Wow. She sure grew up cute."

"Cute! *Estás loco?*"

Hunter, aware they were fast becoming a spectacle, quickly shot back, "Shh. Keep your voice down."

Pietro, rolling his eyes, but complying, said in a lower voice, "*Dios Mío.* Haven't you heard what they say about her at my dad's restaurant?"

"Nope. Haven't heard anything about her, or seen her, since grade school."

"Madre mía! You don't know? Hey, bozo, every guy who catches her eye ends up a basket case." Protective of his friend, he pleaded, "Come on, man. Ya gotta steer clear of her. I'm tellin' ya. She's a heart breaker. And worse yet, she's got a reputation as a nine-some b— Oh, uh . . . uh, I ain't gonna say that word cuz I know you don't like it. But I'm tellin' ya. She's trouble. Big trouble."

"Hey, why ya saying that, man?"

"Taffy tarnation, bozo. Where've ya been? That gosling treats guys like crap. Practiced a lot on her little bro . . . I mean, what she does to him is criminal. Hey, I'll admit. Sometimes I stick it to my little bro. But her? She goes way beyond what's called for. Guess you've never seen her in action, huh? Well, have ya?"

Hunter, face telling all, voiced nothing.

"You're hopeless, man. And *loco en la cabeza.* And me? I ain't sayin' no more. No more ever."

Keeping silent on anything, especially something that grated him, was not Pietro's strong point. Hunter, knowing this, always waited him out. Thirty seconds later, biting his tongue, he muttered, "Look, bozo. It ain't just me sayin' this stuff. I hear it from lots of studs who hang out at our restaurant. She's trouble. Now take her little bro. He ain't got no weight. He doesn't stand a chance. So, my advice. Steer clear of that b— uh . . . I, uh . . . I mean her."

Hunter, amused by Pietro's rhetoric, retorted coolly, "Yeah, well, lots of girls don't get along with their brothers. So, if I get the chance—"

"Chance! Fat chance. Listen. It ain't gonna happen."

"Come on. I betcha I can score with her."

"Hey, dream boy. It's high time you did a reality check. Take a good look at that mug of yours in the mirror. And ya better do it soon too cuz you're not *lily White* ya know. And believe me, that gosling is picky, and getting pickier. Won't give a guy a second glance unless he's more than twenty-one. And right now, let me tell ya. I hear tell she's been layin' them baby-blue eyes of hers on Mark."

"On who?"

"On Mark. Mark Barthlin. Mitzi's office manager. Hey, bozo, where've ya been? Doncha know? That gosling started playin' him last month, as soon as she set foot in Mitzi's office. You know, as a volunteer. And believe me. She's got him pantin' after her like a male husky chasing a bitch in heat. So, why even try? Man, you ain't got no chance."

Hunter, now on the defense, retorted, "Wanna bet. The way I figure it . . ." Sighting Pietro rolling his eyes, he stopped mid-sentence and tugged at his coat sleeve. Pietro responded with a tilt of his head. Hunter, knowing he had his attention, thrust his head toward Shelly and said, "Hey, man, what's wrong with your eyes?"

Pietro, pissed, yanked his arm away from Hunter's grip and let him have it. "My eyes? Hey, bozo, it's you who's blind. I see all them goslings at yer football games. I see 'em checkin' ya out. You goin' out to the field. You runnin' them touchdowns. You comin' off and headin' for the locker room. Them goslings . . . they got their eyes all over ya. They be wantin' to kick ass with ya, and you, what do you do? Nothin'. You pay 'em no mind. What a jerk. Ya could've had anyone of 'em. Easy like. Could've had a steady snow goose by now. A hot one for at least a year or more. Frickin' fiddlesticks. If only I was so lucky. Wish I had goslings pantin' over me like that. Can't figure it. Why ya pay 'em no mind. Not a one of 'em. Hey, they were all pretty nice. Hot lookin' too. Know what I'm sayin'?"

Hunter bore his eyes deep into Pietro's.

Pietro, matching his stare, yelled in a high whisper, "Hey, doncha go lookin' at me like that." With less intensity, he added, "Listen, bozo. I'm just tryin' to be on the up 'n up with ya. I know you're gonna do what you're gonna do. But ya can't say I didn't warn ya. Just remember. I'm tellin' ya this. You're gonna get into a heap of trouble if ya hook up with that gosling. Ya ask me, you oughta turn them hormones of yours off or, at least, direct them to some other señorita. One that's been runnin' after ya. One that'll show ya some respect."

Disgusted, Pietro kicked the rung of the folding chair ahead of him. The elf sitting there turned around and glared at him. "Oops. Sorry." Pulling his leg back, he cocked it over his knee. Still steamed, he said, "You're hopeless, man. Hopeless."

Hunter, aware he had upset his buddy, reached over and tugged his coat sleeve.

Pietro, reluctantly giving in to his beck and call, tilted his head sideways.

"Stop your fretting, man. I'll be okay. You know I like a challenge. Anyway, I can take care of myself. Always have, ya know."

Pietro laughed derisively. "You've just been ignorin' me, huh? I've been wastin' my breath. Okay. Go ahead. Ask her out. But I'm tellin' ya, bozo. Fat chance she'll accept. It just ain't gonna happen."

"Betcha five it will."

"Easiest five I'll ever make." Pietro, grinning, stuck his hand out to Hunter. The sound of their hands connecting, sealing the deal, cracked in the air.

"And hey, bozo, I expect you to ante up with a date. One that's soon. Not like sometime next year, cuz I ain't gonna let ya drag this thing out forever. So, pick a date. Tell me right now. When ya gonna make this happen?"

"Christmas Season Blessing Day."

"Yeah?" Pietro's face bore a look of startled surprise. "Wow. That soon, huh?"

"Yeah. I think I'll ask her to the festivities."

"Like I said, bozo. Fat chance." Pietro, eyes full of skepticism, folded his arms and rested them atop his rounded abdomen.

Hunter, mimicking his posture, oriented his eyes forward. He had egged his best friend on just for the fun of it. As for Pietro's remarks about Shelly . . . He imagined himself kicking them far out into left field. Thinking on it, he didn't want to believe the beauty sitting a few rows back and to his left was stuck up and a heap of trouble, but his

39

cynicism flashed a scene before his eyes of her snubbing him. "Yeah. She'll probably stick her nose in the air at this half-breed and just walk away. Like I don't exist. That would be humiliating. No. That would be racist."

In a meeting hall lively with debate, Hunter, turning contemplative, retreated into a cocoon of hushed silence. While luxuriating in thoughts of kissing the pretty blonde, he pulled his long braid forward and absentmindedly brushed its bundled end back and forth under his chin. A glimpse of its beaded sheath—a reminder of his Indian heritage—triggered thoughts that intermingled with his longing. "I'm not one hundred percent Indian, but I look it, and I'm not ashamed of it like my dad is. Hmm. Wonder if she'll hold that against me? Maybe snub me? Sooty bricks. Dad was so afraid of that, but I'm not. Take my hair . . .

"Grandpa, dad used to make me get those ridiculous haircuts. But after you passed, I stood up to him. I flat out refused to step inside a barbershop. And oh, as my hair got scragglier and scragglier, you wouldn't believe the killer looks he gave me. Finally, when it was long enough to braid, I twisted it into a short nub. Then I looked in the mirror and said, 'Now, bozo, you look just like grandpa.' And dad got over it."

From that day forth, Hunter proudly displayed his Indian heritage by braiding his hair. Still, knowing his grandpa had broken tribal tradition by marrying a freckled, redheaded immigrant from England, he knew his blood carried White man genes. He also knew his English grandma, who died when he was an infant, had had a reputation for being quite outspoken. Their firstborn child, Samuel—Hunter's father—had inherited his mother's red hair, fair skin, and freckles, plus a yen for White man's ways, but not her feisty attitude. Now, reflecting on it, he was glad his genes had flipped back a generation.

"Yes. I can only lay claim to a fourth, even though many say I look full Indian."

On his uphill trek to Saucer Plateau, Hunter kept revisiting the events of that first platform-planning meeting where he, after catching sight of Shelly, sat mesmerized by her fetching smile and flirty blue eyes. Enamored by everything about her, he hardly heard another word being said around him. The meeting dragged on and on, giving him ample time to sneak-peek glimpses of her. Taking in every aspect of her, he wondered if he had made a poor choice about his hair. Following that thought, words his late Grandpa Swift Bear had drilled into him since he was a toddler popped into his head.

"Hunter, always be proud of your Indian heritage, and don't forget to respect everyone else's."

"Sooty bricks, Grandpa, I am proud, but look. Over there sits a girl I want to hook up with. A girl who probably doesn't even know I exist. And maybe, just maybe, my Indian heritage, and this braid, are in the way."

That night, submerged in a sea of platform planners, Hunter reflected on how hurt his grandpa would have been had he voiced such cultural negativity directly to his face.

As he considered the consequences of such an act, he squirmed. Attempting to hide the heat of shame creeping up his neck, he lifted his coat collar, closed his eyes, and willed all thoughts of his grandpa to go away. Still, his grandpa's spirit was strong. Even though he didn't want his nearness or his wisdom, he could feel his vibes and almost see his look of all-knowing.

Wedged between Pietro on his left, who wasn't small, and a heavy-set guy on his right, he stayed slouched down in his chair, toying with his braid until Pietro's backhand swat to his thigh startled him.

"So, bozo, when ya gonna ask her to the festivities?"

"Huh? Oh, I don't know. Probably soon."

"Yeah. Right."

Now, approaching Saucer Plateau, when and how to ask Shelly consumed him. "Will I work up the courage to ask her before time slips away? I sure hope so. But what should I say? Everything I've rehearsed seems quirky. If only I had something down pat, but I don't. Guess I'll just have to wing it."

Winging it did not fall within the parameters of Hunter's comfort zone. "Blasted icicles. She's up there already. Okay, bozo. It's either now or never."

CHAPTER 4

"What's that noise?" Shelly, on her knees, cutting streamers, listened intently. "It's footsteps. Oh, oh. He's here. Yes. Yes. Yes." Her elation spiraling, she not only wanted to jump up and down, but she was also itching to scream her lungs out. Thinking, "Can't do that. Gotta curb my excitement," she sat rigid, holding her breath.

By the time Hunter scurried up the ladder and planted his feet on the platform, she had her emotions in check. Still, her eyes glinted serious intent to play him. Popping to her feet, she greeted him smartly. "Hey, where've you been?"

Hunter, breathless not only from his long trek up the mountainside but also from the sudden onslaught of her beauty, refreshed his lungs with a deep breath before answering her question with a question. "I'm not late, am I?"

"No. I just wanted to get an early start."

Her tart tone brought a grimace to his face. "Yeah. She's stuck up all right. Maybe I should forget about asking her to go with me to the festivities. Sooty bricks. I've certainly got enough information to do so without losing face."

Chewing his lower lip, fighting the urge to bolt, he

thought back to when he had asked around about her. Many of his friends' comments still rang in his ears.

"Shelly Jasselton? Yeah. I know her. She's hot but snooty as hell."

"Hey, man, watch out. She can be downright cruel."

"Shelly? She'll play ya, and then, she'll drop ya. And her brother, Jordan . . . she treats him like crap."

Everyone's description of her as cruel and insensitive haunted Hunter. And each elf he talked to felt sorry for her younger brother.

"What kind of monster is she? Shimmering Icicles. I'd like to get to know her, but . . ."

Day and night, since the first platform-planning meeting, Hunter wrestled with his yo-yo feelings. Despite Pietro, all his friends, even some teen elves he hardly knew, warning him to steer clear of Shelly, he longed to get to know her. Still, other times he felt like bailing.

"Why'd I put money on the line with Pietro? Prancin' Dancer. If I hadn't, I wouldn't be in this mess. Now my honor is at stake. And a bet's a bet. Okay. I can do this. One date. Just one date. Then, if she proves to be like everyone says, that'll be it. I'll drop her. Yeah. Good plan."

Turning his attention to the task at hand, Hunter compared Shelly's dwindled-down pile to his untouched heap. "Fiddlin' nutcrackers. She snuck up here early and divided it in half. Like she decided to stick it to me that she's in charge. So, what's she gonna do after she finishes hers? Stand around? Make me feel nervous?"

Seconds later, dropping to his knees to cut streamers, he chastised himself. "Cool it, bozo. Otherwise, you'll make no headway with her. Headway? Yeah. Right. I don't even know where to start. Pietro, help me."

Knowing he had to do this on his own, he stilled his thoughts. Then it came to him. "Start safe, bozo. Talk about the weather."

One deep breath later he said to Shelly, "Can you believe this crazy temp rise? I mean, it's never been warm like this before. Bet this day is gonna make history, huh?"

"Yeah. And this place too." Popping up from her work, twirling a streamer above her head, she graced his eyes with a sensuous dance routine. Three spins later, a bit winded, she stopped a short distance from him.

Like a fish contemplating a hooked worm, the temptation to respond to her alluring gestures gave Hunter tunnel vision. Seeing nothing but her—longing to hold her in his arms, to caress her hair, to stare into her eyes, to taste her sweet lips—he, emotionally overwhelmed, could not stop shaking. Embarrassed, he turned away from her. On his rise, a cool breeze signaled he had broken out in a cold sweat. He swallowed hard, grasped his knees to steady himself, then leaned into the railing.

Shelly loving the effect her tease was having on him but acting oblivious to it, said, "Wow. It's so beautiful up here. Wonder why Santa never picked this spot before?"

"Don't know," Hunter said, setting his eyes on some distant mountain peaks. Not wanting Shelly to know how

45

much she was turning him on, he looked everywhere but at her.

Shelly, catching his every nuance, stifled a giggle. "Ah, he's shy. But I can tell. He's itching to get close but holding back. Maybe if I tease him some more." A quick spin on her toe set her cavorting across the platform again. Pairing her sexy gyrations with flirtatious glances, she easily drew him in. Slowing her pace, she yelled, "Hey, doncha think this is a cool place for Santa to give his speech?"

Hunter, feeling a little less sweaty, and braver with her at a distance, yelled, "Yeah. It's cool." To himself, he mumbled, "And you're cool too."

As she played him with polished ballet gyrations, he mulled over the negativity he had heard about her. "She can't be as bad as everyone makes her out to be. She can't. Yeah. She comes across as snippy, but there's something about her. For sure, she's a challenge, but she's also smart. And taffy tarnation, she is so-o-o gorgeous."

Hunter, reluctantly turning away from Shelly's one-woman show, glimpsed his pile of streamers. "Whacky walruses. This sure sucks. I'd rather be out there cavorting with her than tying these stupid streamers to these posts." He pulled his foot back to kick them. Thinking better on it, he bent down and grabbed a few instead.

He intended to stay focused. He couldn't. Frequently he sought Shelly's presence. Each stolen glimpse shifted his heartbeat up a notch. It also warned him time was running out. Anxiety over when and how to ask her to the festivities slowed his progress.

Shelly, aware of his sneak-peeking—herself trying to temper amorous feelings—could hardly keep a straight face. Jutting her chin out, projecting disinterest, she asked matter-of-factly, "Hey. Ya think maybe this place might've been sacred Indian ground that just got deregulated?"

Hunter's stomach knotted. The possibility of Saucer Plateau, or even the whole Mountain being sacred Indian ground, was something his grandfather never mentioned. "Deregulated?" he said, his voice full of surprise. "I have no idea. I suppose it's possible. I mean, maybe it was."

His curiosity piqued, and his focus detoured, he closed his eyes and searched inwardly for anything about the mountain his grandpa might have shared. One incident came to mind: himself, hiking up Jingle-Jangle Mountain, working his short legs doubly hard to keep up with his grandpa's long strides. As a little tyke, he had only half-listened to his stories, the remnants of which were now vague. What the mountain had meant to him, or even to his tribe, Hunter didn't know. Neither did he know if it had been registered. However, he did know his gut was screaming, "Yes, bozo. The mountain is sacred."

Bozo. Hunter often referred to himself as bozo when stumped by something. The habit took hold after Pietro anointed him with the clownish name in first grade.

Knowing his grandpa always frowned on self-denigration, he looked around as if checking to make sure his deceased mentor hadn't heard him thinking that thought. Ironically, he started communing with his spirit.

"Oh, Grandpa, right now I don't feel good about this platform being built here. It bothers me. I sure hope we haven't desecrated anything sacred to you or your tribe. And, uh, to my tribe too."

"Hey. With Santa speaking from up here this afternoon, it'll probably be easy for every elf, standing anywhere around this mountain, to see him. Doncha think?"

Hearing Shelly's intrusive voice, Hunter jumped. Recovering quickly, he said, "Yeah, I guess so."

Still bent on reconnecting with his grandpa's spirit, he leaned against a railing and stared at nothing in particular.

"Grandpa, you said this mountain had rumbled once, long ago, before your lifetime. And you first learned about it when you were about five or six when you decided to climb to its top. By yourself. But you didn't go because a tribal elder filled your heart with fear. Remember? You said that he said when he was a young warrior, the mountain scared him half out of his wits. That he was up there, about to set foot on Saucer Plateau when the whole mountain shook violently. And it spooked him so, he ran lickety-split down it with a mess of ice boulders chasing his backside. And you said ever since then your tribe has revered this mountain."

After focusing on that bit of folklore, Hunter closed his eyes and visualized his late Grandpa Swift Bear saying quite seriously, "Son, many moons ago our tribe camped around this mountain, but never on it. And that story about that young warrior almost getting killed? Well, that taught me to respect it. Many times, I climbed that mountain, but never did I set foot on Saucer Plateau."

Blinking away that scene, another, when he was about seven, came into sharp focus.

The hike up the mountain had been exhausting, but the slip-sliding down . . . It was exhilarating. They had laughed till their sides hurt. Reaching the bottom, Hunter had watched and listened carefully as his grandpa lifted his eyes to the mountain and said reverently, "Hunter, our tribe always called this mountain by its Indian name, *Mount Koyukon*. And we respected it. But I guess those days are gone forever." His grandpa's contemplative look, plus the mountain's original name, stayed with Hunter.

"Grandpa, I wonder if this mountain resents having fat posts crammed inside its belly. And who changed its name from *Mount Koyukon* to Jingle-Jangle Mountain? What a blow that must've been. I can't imagine . . ."

Bright sunlight, barreling through a bank of clouds, distracted Hunter. Squinting, raising a hand to shade his eyes, he peered down at the Victory Trees. "Grandpa, something puzzles me. How did Santa know those trees would grow here? Did he somehow foresee that the mountain would protect them? Sooty bricks. I never realized . . . Wow. Look at them. From up here, they look like an arrowhead pointing straight toward Krisville. Know what, Grandpa? Even though I like looking down on them, I don't think Santa should've had this platform built here. To be honest, though, it probably wouldn't be bothering me if Shelly hadn't brought up that sacred Indian stuff. That got me thinking. Hmm. Maybe I'll go down to the courthouse after the holidays. Go through some old records."

Deep in thought, Hunter not only sensed his grandpa's presence, but him speaking as well. "Hunter, listen to your feelings. They run true like our great northern waters. And, son, don't be chicken. Act on them if you think it's the right thing to do."

"Why are you telling me this, Grandpa?"

"Hey, what's up?" Shelly asked, unaware she was intruding into his reverie for a second time.

Startled, Hunter jumped. Turning to face her, he said, "I don't know. I just have a funny feeling."

"Like what?"

"Like . . . like, uh, like something's not right. Especially with the temperature climbing and climbing."

"Hey. With this gorgeous weather, what could go wrong?"

"I don't know. But something could, you know."

"Like what?"

Hunter, reluctant to say any more, but knowing she was expecting an answer, said with hesitancy, "Like . . . like, uh . . . uh, like maybe those college students goofed at putting in these posts. Or . . . or something like that."

Shelly bristled. "Elf Hunter Swift Bear, what in Elk Tundra is wrong with you? To even say that. Or . . . or even think it. Hey. Everyone worked their sled-running buns off and, and dancin' Prancer, we all want a flag up from Santa. Besides, Santa had the Region's best engineers overseeing this project, and they kept good tabs on all we did."

"Yes, but something tells me . . ." Hunter, sighting Shelly rooting her feet in front of him, eyes blazing anger, stopped mid-sentence.

"Hey. What's with this moose malarkey? You know nothing's ever gone wrong before and nothing will this year either."

Hunter, shocked by her gutsy affront, pulled back. As he did, the metal railing, cutting into his lower torso, warned he could go no further. To appease her, he tried reasoning. "Yeah, but . . . but you know, there, uh . . . uh, there could always be a first time. Something could go wrong, you know. Like this mountain could blow or uh . . ."

Shelly, hellbent on curtailing his doomsday thinking, stiffened her arms out behind her and thrust her head forward. In this stance, she strained to meet him eye to eye, but couldn't. Even standing on tiptoe, she was too short to make it happen. But what she lacked in stature, she made up in lung power. In one hellacious rip, anger spewed from her mouth.

"What do you mean, 'There could always be a first time'? You . . . You . . . What are you anyway? Some kind of doomsday jerk out to jinx our most revered holiday? Hey. Talk like that is stupid and crazy and, and . . ." Thrusting a balled fist under his nose, she finished in a clipped voice, "And see this?"

Hunter jerked his head back. Staring at her menacing fist, he wanted to step away. He couldn't. She had him pinned to the railing. Behind him, the solid ground lay far, far below.

Shelly, like an angry tsunami with issues, kept shoving her fist into his face. "Hey, buster, you better stop that doomsday talk, or I'll give you some of this, and don't think I won't do it either. And, and I'm warning you . . . you, you, doomsday jerk. Don't even try pushing your luck with me."

Too rattled to muster an immediate response, Hunter just stared down at her ruffled-peacock stance. Fortunately, she stepped back, giving him room to breathe. And what had earlier rendered him speechless, now bought him time to conjure a plausible comeback.

"Ah, Grandpa, I remember what you taught me to do whenever I didn't know what to do. You said, 'When faced with a bad situation, take time to analyze it, try to see it for what it is. And if that doesn't work, look for the humor in it.' Humor? Yeah. This little mite's blustering is sort of funny. But can't she see? With my football-trained body, I can easily block every blow she throws my way. So, Grandpa, you want me to find humor in this? Well, I see it, and it's just too funny for words."

After reaching that conclusion, Hunter felt like pounding his chest and shouting, "Oh, mighty but cape-less Shelly, you better watch out. This football guy can, and will, prevail."

A force welling inside tipped the corners of Hunter's

mouth into a cryptic smile. He tried squelching it, but it would not be subdued. Turning away from Shelly, he slumped over like a depleted hot air balloon and burst into rollicking laughter.

He did not expect Shelly's reaction.

Like a sparked stick of dynamite, she exploded. "So. You think this is funny, huh? Like I'm kidding? Well, let me tell you, you . . . you moose head. Nobody laughs at Shelly Jasselton and gets away with it. Do you hear me? Nobody."

Hunter, his tidal wave of laughter crushed by her anger, jerked back. "Dancin' Prancer. Pietro said she could go off like a firecracker when you least expected it, but never did I envision this. Wow. She doesn't let up."

Posturing defensively—feet spread apart, palms extended forward—he eyed her guardedly. Pivoting a quarter circle away from the railing, he slid his feet backward. She, like a haunting shadow, matched his steps. The pounding of her clenched fist into the palm of her other hand seemed to overpower his heavy breathing, and hers too.

"Is this little mite insecure or what?" This thought spawned more grandpa wisdom.

"Hunter, when you find yourself in a sticky situation, take time to analyze what's going on before you act. And remember. Things aren't always what they seem to be."

"Good advice, Grandpa. Yeah. It seems like Shelly's deliberately stretching it. To be honest, I think she's trying to control me. But why?"

Hunter had no idea Shelly's hostility mirrored nothing more than her habitual ploys to keep her younger brother Jordan in check . . . to unnerve him, to remind him she was top wolf in their family's pecking order. Nor could he have known his backing off, rather than backing down, had thrown her for a loop. And he had no idea his reaction was having a profound effect on her.

Shelly couldn't figure out what went wrong. Always, guys bowed to her rule, like Jordan always did. Like all guys did. Except for her father. She prided herself at being a master at making guys squirm. Seeing them jump to her command, delighted her to no end. It also heightened her sense of power. But today, her blustery tactic didn't work with Hunter. He turned the tables on her and crushed her intent with laughter. And as he did, a feeling new to her—humiliation—almost took her to her knees. It also made her think, "Is this how my brother feels every time I put the screws to him? Every time I lord over him?"

Hunter, holding his ground, yet casting an uneasy glance Shelly's way, kept trying to figure out what had gotten into her. "There's got to be a reason for her meanness. Why is she acting so bitchy and unreasonable? One thing I know. A physical altercation with this girl is the last thing I want." Anxious to distance himself from her, he quickened his backward steps. As he did, he shifted his eyes from her white-knuckled fists to her quivering jaw. He sensed she didn't know what to do next, and neither did he.

Still trying to make sense of her explosive hissy snit, he

thought about how his father had often reacted to his mom's anger. Not until this moment with himself the target of a female's wrath, did he understand why his father sometimes withered under his mother's rage.

"Yeah, dad. How many times did I catch you walking away from mom without saying a word? Why you did . . . I couldn't figure it out until one day, I saw you staring up at the ceiling, muttering, 'God help me. It must be that time of the month again.'"

Bells went off in Hunter's head. "Yeah. Maybe it's Shelly's time of the month. And if so, my laughing at her was probably too much." Concluding that, he apologized, saying what his father typically said to his mom. "Hey, I'm sorry. Okay? So, just cool it. Okay?"

Shelly, head down, said, "Yeah, well, I wasn't going to hit you. Really, I wasn't. I was just playing you." It was a weak excuse, but the best she could do without losing face.

Hunter, sighting Shelly's hands going limp at her sides, tried reading her eyes. He couldn't. She had tilted her head down. He did notice reddish blotches popping out on her neck and face though. "Hmm. Looks like her blotchy skin is telling on her. She's embarrassed. No. She's more than embarrassed. She's mortified. And me? I'm just glad it's over because I need to get on with this job."

Still wary, he eyed Shelly slinking away. Heaving a sigh of relief, he bent down and grabbed a handful of streamers. His intention was good; but his mind, unwilling to let it go, kept reeling. "What if it wasn't her monthly? What if she has hissy snits like this all the time? Yelping walrus pups. What guy wants to put up with that!"

Making his way around the chimney, heading toward the North Pole Village post, he thought about the bet he had made with Pietro at the year's first platform-planning meeting. "Yeah, man, you're on. I'll bet ya five. And watch. I'll score with her. You'll see."

For more weeks than he cared to count—given everything he had learned about Shelly's snooty reputation—he had sweated over winning his bet with Pietro. Now, after what had just transpired, he toyed with the idea of bailing. "Five bucks. I can afford to lose that. But if I give up, Pietro will never let me live it down."

Seconds later, rising from measuring and cutting streamers, he felt a chill shrouding his shoulders. Not a weather chill, but a chilling sense that someone was standing beside him, trying to hug him. Paying attention to it, he suspected it was his grandpa.

"Okay, Grandpa. I know you want my attention again. So, what are you trying to tell me now, huh?"

Closing his eyes, clearing his mind, he waited. Slowly, a vision of himself at age twelve, sitting by his grandpa's bedside, emerged from a hazy fog. Trusting his grandpa's spirit, he let himself meld into it.

CHAPTER 5

By age twelve, Hunter had seen many animals die. But his grandpa? Ill-prepared for the inevitable, he sat beside his bed, shifting uncomfortably. When his old mentor tried to speak, he leaned forward to listen.

"Hunter, even though I'll be . . . be going away soon to . . . to my happy hunting ground, I'll come whenever you . . . you need me. All you have to . . . to do is . . . is be quiet, close your eyes and . . . and think of me, and . . . and I'll come. And sometimes, if . . . if I think I need to, I . . . I'll come without you . . . you even seeking me. You hear?"

"I know, Grandpa. You're reminding me you'll always be there for me. I get it. But right now, it's this girl. I'm not sure I want to get involved with her. She's so scrappy. So explosive. So spunky. So feisty. Feisty!" That last word had him recalling the last serious, on-the-trail chat he had had with his beloved mentor before death claimed his soul.

"Yeah. That fateful talk happened about four months before I turned twelve, huh, Grandpa? And I didn't want to listen. I remember you started it with, 'Son, I think it's time you learn about girls.'"

"Learn about girls!" Those words flooded Hunter's

mind with anger. Even so, he knew better than to contradict his grandpa. Openly, he could not say anything disrespectful to him. If he did, he would have to live with the shame of doing so for the rest of his life.

Inwardly, he exploded.

"What! You want me to learn about girls? Sooty bricks. Don't tell me I've got to sit through another *birds-and-the-bees* sex talk. No. No. No. First my teacher. Then my dad. And now you? Why? All that stuff about a guy's wiggly sperms fighting to get to a girl's squishy egg to make a baby is yucky. And girls bleeding every month. That's disgusting. If girls do that, I don't ever want anything to do with them."

At eleven, going on twelve, all Hunter cared to know about sex was he had a penis and masturbation felt good. He didn't even know the act had a name, and he didn't care. He and his buddies just called it *jacking off.*

He hadn't always felt good about doing it. Although, it always felt good. Time and again, he had tried to keep himself in check. But his raging hormones always won out. Afterward, he would berate himself, even question his sanity. This back and forth reasoning—"It's okay. No. It's not okay."—went on until his dad barged into his bedroom one day and *caught him in the act.*

Tying a streamer to the post in front of him, thinking about it, Hunter smiled. "Yeah. I'll never forget that day."

He saw himself, one minute in ecstasy and the next, the moment his dad popped into his private sanctuary, he felt like he was sitting in purgatory about to be judged by an angry God. Shocked, he bolted upright and covered himself. His eyes bulged with panic. And his head? It suddenly went dizzy with dread. Fear . . . it, dripping through his veins like battery acid, made him shake and also paralyzed him. Shame moved in too, turning his face crimson red, while embarrassment dropped his head to bowed penitence.

In this stance, lifting his brow just enough to catch his dad's eyes seeking his, his breath froze halfway up his windpipe. He expected the shaming, the berating to begin. It didn't. An uncomfortable silence followed. His dad cleared his throat. Hunter, knowing what that meant, cocked an ear.

"Oops, sorry, son."

Hunter, relieved, slouched his shoulders and expelled air. He couldn't believe he wasn't in trouble.

His dad, having said his piece, stepped into the hallway. Hesitating, still gripping the doorknob, he suddenly swung back around.

"Now what?"

Hunter, eyes focused on his dad's bushy, red whiskers, which lately were graying, could tell his lips—half-buried behind them—were struggling to draw thoughts from his mind. Ironically, had he been an unrelated patient, *doctor-dad* would have had no trouble addressing the issue.

His dad, still red with embarrassment, directed his gaze toward the football banners tacked above Hunter's chest-of-drawers.

Quiet seconds stretched further than Hunter liked.

"Son," his dad finally said, "I don't want you to feel badly or even guilty about what you're doing. All guys masturbate. And girls do it too. It's normal. Quite normal. And there's nothing wrong with doing it as long as you do it privately. And, son, I'm sorry for barging in on you. I should've knocked." Having said his piece, his dad stepped into the hall and closed the door behind him.

Listening to his dad's receding footsteps, Hunter mumbled the new word again and again. "Masturbate. Masturbate. Masturbate. So, that's what it's called."

His chest filled with pride. At first, he didn't know why. After giving it some thought, he figured it out. All his life he had spent far more time with his Grandpa Swift Bear than he ever had with his dad. His dad had always worked long hours, and his grandpa had conveniently been there to pick up the slack. Growing up viewing his grandpa as a pal, his love and respect for him had evolved naturally. Yes. He went to his dad for major decisions. Like, to get permission to do things and to show him his report card. But nothing as weird as this had ever happened.

After their little surprise encounter, Hunter realized he could probably ask his dad anything. "Why now?" he wondered. "What's different?" Lying on his bed, mulling it over, he suddenly brightened. "I've got it. Dad just talked *to* me like a young man, not *at* me like a misbehaving little elfin. Wow. He showed me respect."

His new-found veneration for his dad brought a smile to his lips. That day, little did he realize its importance. In less than a year, death would pull his Grandpa Swift Bear's soul beyond Father Sky, to the spiritual realm of his tribe's happy hunting ground. His death would be a pivotal point in Hunter's life. Without his grandpa, he would have to turn to his dad for guidance into manhood. And this encounter, scary as it was, opened the door for that to go smoothly.

"Come, Hunter," his grandpa said on their last hike up Jingle-Jangle Mountain. Moving at a snail's pace off the trail, he motioned with a shaky hand for Hunter to follow. "Let's sit over here next to this ice boulder, out of the wind. It looks like a good place to do a little powwowing."

Dutifully following his beloved grandpa's directive, Hunter slid his backside down the icy boulder and balanced his weight on his haunches. Even though he could hardly bear hearing the sex talk again, he steeled himself to listen respectfully. His grandpa surprised him. He said nothing about sex. Girls, yes. But no sex talk.

"Son, I know you're not much interested in girls yet, but someday you'll settle down with a woman. I'm sure of it. All I hope is, you'll connect with someone who is kind and loving, and also a bit *feisty*. One who says whatever she thinks, just like your grandma used to do with me. See, women like that, they make the best wives because they're sure of themselves. Take it from me, son. It's that kind of woman who keeps a guy in line. Never allows him or anyone else to walk all over her.

"And son, I hope whoever you hitch up with has an independent streak. Pick someone who's not wishy-washy or sneaky like. What I mean is, I hope you fall for a woman who will put you in your place but won't stab you in the back. Now, if you do hitch up with someone like that, a woman with a feisty streak, believe me, she'll not only be a lot of fun, she'll bring fire to your life just like your grandma did to mine. Now your grandma, she was one fine woman. Feisty, but also tender and caring. And very wise too . . ."

As his grandfather paused, Hunter sought his eyes. His far-away look told him he was recalling a past moment.

"I'll tell you this, son. Your grandma, she kept me on my toes. But we had us some fun." Turning, placing his gnarled index finger in the middle of Hunter's sternum, he finished with, "Now, son, you just tuck all that away in there. In your heart. Okay?"

"Yeah, Grandpa. I tucked your advice away in my heart all right. So deep, I forgot all about it. That is, until now." Chuckling, he added, "And I bet you're happy Shelly is proving to be the type of young lady you encouraged me to find. Feisty and outspoken. So, Grandpa, you win. I won't give up. I'll step back into the fire. Watch me."

CHAPTER 6

After their little tiff, Shelly, convinced Hunter viewed her as the wackiest girl ever, fought back tears. Too embarrassed to look his way, she leaned against the Rudolphtown post, trying to muffle sobs. The truth was hard to accept. Her mean streak, which she had nurtured and honed to perfection, had reared its ugly head and ruined her plans to hook up with this terrific-looking guy. On top of that, guilt, triggering one awful memory after another, was forcing her to revisit many of her parents' chastising remarks.

"Shelly, why do you have to be so smug, curt, bossy, arrogant, demanding, and cruel to your brother?"

In past years, she and her parents frequently locked horns over her meanness toward Jordan. To her, it was a game. Again, and again she heard, and always ignored, "Shelly, stop being so nasty to your brother." – "Shelly, can't you just once, just once in your life say a nice word to your brother?" – "Shelly, give Jordan back his cell phone." – "Shelly, stop tormenting your brother. Now!"— "Why, Shelly, why? Why do you have to be so spiteful to Jordan?" Every day, since *the cute little intruder* had arrived on the scene thirteen years ago, remarks like these had bombarded her ears, and she had ignored them all.

Despite Jordan learning at an early age to avoid her, she continually went out of her way to make life miserable for him. She loved the game. Harassing him. Setting him up. Manipulating him. Cornering him. Making him squirm. Year after year, she chalked up point after point in her little book of nasty endeavors. However, never in her wildest dreams did she anticipate that she would fall victim to her own vindictiveness.

"Whacky walruses. Am I destined to turn off every cute guy that comes along by hissing at him as I have at my little brother all his life? Is this a wakeup call? And Jordan? Mom and dad keep harping about how fast he's growing lately. Even rubbing it in that he'll soon pass me up. That he's getting taller and a lot stronger too. Stronger? Oh no. No. No. No." Visualizing the muscle mass that had popped out on her brother's arms and chest lately, she shuddered. "Blasted icicles. He could turn on me. He could start lording over me. Wow. That would be scary. No. No way will I ever let that happen. Gotta stop it. But how?"

As if by telepathy, she heard her mother's voice. "Shelly, you'd better start changing. And soon."

"Me, change? Hmm. Me, be sweet and loving rather than mean and hateful to Jordan? And start *growing up* like dad's been harping at me to do all these years? Okay, you guys. Watch me. I'm gonna do a three-sixty. I'm gonna *kill* Jordan with kindness. I'm gonna love him with all my heart.

Yeah, Dad. Just like you've wanted. I'm gonna stop treating him like he's nothing but a dirty rug under my feet. Guess you won't be throwing that in my face anymore, huh?"

Realizing her excitement had pushed her voice up a few notches, Shelly turned to check on Hunter's whereabouts. Spotting him on his knees, cutting streamers, she expelled a sigh of relief. "Didn't hear me, huh? Good."

Still eyeing him, she studied him in motion. It wasn't long before a mixture of longing and sadness wilted her body into a ragdoll slump. She blinked back tears. Turning away from him, shifting her thoughts to Jordan, she resolved, "I will do this. Yes, little brother, [sniff] from now on I'm gonna be kind instead of cruel to you. And . . . and [sniff] since it's me who's doing the deciding, that'll be okay.

"Whew. What a wakeup call," she mumbled, fanning a hand in front of her face as though that would help suppress her pressing tears. "I've probably lost my chance with Hunter, but [sniff] I'm gonna act better with the next guy. I will get this meanness out of my system. Yeah. Starting today, Daddy dearest, I'm gonna love my little brother just as much as I've hated him. No. Wait. I'm gonna do better than that. I'm gonna be the best sister ever. Holy walrus turds. I've hated him forever. But not anymore."

Shelly's strong self-talk dredged up horrific scenes, which, in turn, triggered guilt, guilt she did not want to face.

"I need something to do."

Scanning the platform, sighting a flutter of streamer scraps, she dropped to her knees, mumbling, "Guess it's cleanup time." The irony of those words, hitting home, produced a faint smile. Crawling around, gathering and stuffing streamer scraps into her pockets, she felt almost as if, for penitence, she was collecting the many thorns she had inflicted on her brother over the years. Yet, it was Hunter, not Jordan, who dominated her thoughts.

"What are my chances now? I want him to notice me, but after the way I acted earlier, he'll probably never speak to me again. Maybe I should apologize. Apologize! Me? No. No way am I going to crawl on my hands and knees to any guy." Yet, without realizing it, she was doing just that.

On rise from cutting streamers, Hunter caught sight of Shelly crawling his way. The wind, catching and flipping her hair, constantly reframing her face, set his heart racing.

"Taffy tarnation. How could such a beauty acquire such a rotten reputation? She's got good parents. So, what went wrong? Maybe if she had had a grandpa like mine. Yeah. There were times when he was tough on me. Like, when I came home from school one day, bragging about getting the best of a kid who had angered me. 'I showed him, Grandpa,' I said, expecting him to say something like, 'Good job, son. I'm proud of you.' Instead, he laid into me."

"Son, never spit back when someone spits at you. Instead, *Be* kind. *Be* gentle. *Be* patient. And if you keep those three *bees* buzzing around in your head, you'll make more friends than enemies."

"But, but he—"

"No *buts* about it. I expect better of you. Hear?"

"The three buzzing bees as you called them, Grandpa. *Be* kind. *Be* gentle. *Be* patient. Well, at eight, I couldn't understand why you expected me to be kind to someone who was so mean. Now, those three buzzing bees make sense. Believe me, I'll use them."

Hunter, gazing longingly at Shelly, felt a sensation in his chest only one word could describe: *yearning*. He yearned to hold her close, to stroke her golden hair. And more than anything, he yearned to kiss her.

"Blasted icicles. What's it gonna take to get hooked up with her? And those lips . . . I'd love to kiss them. Kiss them! Yeah. When will that ever happen? Probably never. And that gorgeous hair. Oh my gosh, she's crawling this way. Hmm. Wonder if I can touch a few wisps of it without her noticing."

Shelly, head down, deep in sorrowful thoughts, had no idea she was nearing Hunter. "I sure screwed up. He'll never look at me or even speak to me again." Bouncing up, seeing his face not more than fifteen inches away from hers, she gasped audibly.

Caught off guard by her sudden rise, Hunter's eyes flared wide and his heart fluttered. Hoping she would be none the wiser, he, raising a *guilty* hand to mouth, faked a cough.

"Hey. You okay?"

"Yeah. Yeah. I'm, [cough] I'm okay. But, [cough] but I, uh,

[cough, cough] uh . . . I was just thinking. Uh, why don't you start down the ladder while I tie these, *[cough, cough]* uh, these last few streamers to the Kringleland post?"

Hunter didn't expect to hear, "Okay," in a surprisingly sweet voice. But he did. As he watched her flitting off toward the ladder, he silently mouthed, "Wow. She is . . . is like wow, wow, wow."

He longed to run after her, to pull her into his arms, to kiss her, but fear of being rebuffed held him back. Looking was all he dared to do. And looking he did. Longingly, he took in her wispy blond hair cascading down her back, her graceful walk, the fullness of her hips and her lithe, ballerina legs. As he eyed the toe tip of her right boot reaching for the top ladder rung, an almost audible "Wow" road the stream of his long exhalation.

Shelly, sensing Hunter was watching her, felt a little giddy, and ecstatically happy. "Yes. He's still interested in me." Turning to face him, she shouted with unsuppressed glee, "I'll race you down to the Victory Trees. Okay?"

Shocked by the invite, yet pleased, Hunter yelled back, "You're on. Soon as I'm done here." After knotting his last few streamers, he scooted over to the ladder and peered down at her. She, with hands clasped behind her back, beamed him a coquettish smile.

"Ah. Maybe I still have a chance. Yes. Maybe. That is if my nerves hold."

Grasping the ladder attached to the chimney's backside, he playfully bounced his feet down supporting posts instead of using its rungs. Blessed with agility, he had no fear of falling. Yet, in his hurry, he lost his footing and dropped the last few feet to the ground.

"Glad that's done," he said, popping to his feet, brushing off his pants. Lifting his eyes to meet Shelly's, he was surprised to see he had been talking to thin air. "What? Where'd she go?" Looking around, he spotted her stepping backward, putting distance between them.

"Cool. She's inviting me to be playful. Yes. Yes." Like a carefree rabbit, he loped through snow, yelling, "Hey, wait for me." Rather than waiting, she kept moving further and further away. He, having just cranked his legs to their full momentum, sighted—unfortunately a little too late—a solidly packed snowball flying his way. Caught off guard, he had no time to veer from her missile.

SM-M-MACK . . .

On impact, his neck snapped back, and his face, assaulted by icy slush, bore a look of startled surprise.

Shelly, amazed and amused at hitting her target dead-on, yelled, "Bull's eye." Rollicking with laughter, zigzagging through deep snow, she nearly fell to her knees.

Hunter, staring cross-eyed at hunks of snow ski jumping over his nose and down his chin, looked more forlorn than a wound-down toy soldier. Still, he couldn't hold this look very long. The sight unfolding before him—Shelly, drunk with laughter, stumbling over her feet—tickled his funny bone. As she skedaddled off, glancing his way, his pouty lips gave way to a smile. A quick shake of his head rid the wet residue from his face. Teasingly he yelled, "Hey, you promised not to hit me. Remember?"

Laughing, she yelled back, "Yeah. I remember. And I didn't hit you. The snowball did."

Hunter loved seeing this side of Shelly—carefree, stumbling about, happily succumbing to playful whims.

"So, you're testing me, huh?" Rising to her alluring challenge, he bent down and scooped up a heap of snow. Packing it good, he hollered, "Hey, thanks for showing me this stuff's just right for snowball making. And hey, I bet you didn't know this *ol' Indian boy* loves a good snowball fight."

"Well, this *ol' White girl* loves one too." Stooping down, Shelly gathered the makings for her next missile. Packing and rounding her orb, she eyed him juggling his. "Let the games begin," she yelled. Popping to her feet, she took off running down the mountainside. Peering over her shoulder, she wondered when he would start his pursuit.

Hunter purposely stalled to give her a head start. A few seconds later, loping through snow, he yelled, "Just wait. I'm gonna get you good."

"Oh, I'm sure you will. But hey, I don't care, cuz I got you first. So there."

Their playful words, colliding and bouncing off Jingle-Jangle Mountain, followed them down the mountainside as each tried to outfox the other.

◇•◇•◇

CHAPTER 7

Shelly, the first to reach the meadow below, sought refuge near a Victory Tree. She didn't want to call a halt to their play, but her exhaustion demanded it. Spotting Hunter approaching, she pulled a crumpled streamer from her pocket. Waving it, she begged, "Stop. Please stop. I'm out of breath. I can't—"

"Giving up, huh? Well, since I zapped you at least a hundred times, I guess that's okay."

"Hey, hotshot, I got, *[gasp]* I got in my, *[gasp]* my share of hits too." She peeked around the tree trunk to make sure he was empty-handed. Although gasping, she managed to smile coyly as she stepped into the open.

Hunter, smitten, said with tenderness, "Hey, you really are out of breath. Whadaya say we cool it a bit?"

"Yeah. I'm, *[gasp]* I'm all for that."

"Bet you didn't know you're standing by my tree."

Shelly shot him a quizzical look. Navigating her eyes around its circumference, she said smartly, "Really. Your tree, huh? If that's so, then why isn't your name on it?"

Hunter laughed. "Hey, I'm not kidding. It is mine. I mean, kinda. See, my tribe lays partial claim to it."

"What! Are you crazy? All these trees belong to Santa."

"I know that. Everybody knows that."

"Then why do you call it *your* tree?"

"Because my Grandpa Swift Bear planted it."

"You're kidding."

"Nope. I'm dead serious. My grandpa used to tell me the story all the time."

"What story?"

"About why Santa had these Victory Trees planted."

"Come on. Everyone knows that old story. It goes like this. Santa and Mitzi took a vacation to the States. Uh, back in the seventies, I think. And Mitzi got mad because all he wanted to do was traipse through plant nurseries. And uh, when he shipped eleven saplings up here from . . . uh, from somewhere in the USA, she thought he had gone off his sled rails. And she predicted they'd never grow in this frigid climate. But Santa insisted they would. And as soon as they got home, he picked eleven husky elves to plant them in this V formation. And, of course, he did all that to celebrate the end of World War II or uh . . . maybe it was the Vietnam War. Some war, right?"

"Sorry. Wrong."

"Whadaya mean, 'Wrong?' That's the way I heard it."

"Look. You got it all right except for the last part. Santa didn't have these trees planted to celebrate the end of any War."

"He did too."

"No, he didn't. Listen. That was one of my grandpa's

72

biggest complaints. He used to say, 'Hunter, elves come here and talk about how Santa had these trees planted to celebrate the end of the war, but that's not true and—'"

"Then why'd he have them planted?"

"To represent what should be done to prevent another war."

"I don't understand. What do you mean, 'What should be done?'"

"Okay. See that tree down there. The one at the apex of the V formation? The biggest one."

"Yeah."

"My grandpa said it represents the mediator."

"Mediator? What in taffy tarnation are you talking about?"

"Just listen. Okay?"

"Okay."

"And those trees over there . . . Notice they all lead down to the Mediator Tree. Same as this side does."

"Yeah. So, what?"

"Well, they represent one side of the conflict. And the trees over here, they represent the other side. Now, do you get what the Mediator Tree is about?"

"Yeah. It gets both sides talking. It's the go-between."

"Right. That's why Santa had it planted at the apex of this V formation. And all that space inside there, where it's illegal for us to step ever. Well, guess what it represents?"

"I'll bite. What?"

"The negotiating table. An imaginary one, of course."

"Oh, really."

Hunter felt like saying, "Yes. Didn't you know that?" But not wanting to rile her again, he chose to enlighten her instead. "Look. The way my grandpa explained it was . . . Well, he told me Santa had these trees planted in the shape of a V to represent two warring factions. That the apex represents where they come together to work out their differences and the outer ends of both tree lines . . . Hey, see this tree we're standing by and that one over there just opposite from this one?"

Shelly, tracking his pointed finger, nodded.

"Well, these two trees, the furthest ones out, they represent each warring country's military stuff. You know, battleships, missiles, guns, and stuff like that. And, according to my grandpa, Santa purposely had them planted far apart so they wouldn't have to battle for sunshine. Get it?"

"Yeah. Santa wants warring countries to talk. So, these trees represent peace is possible if countries will just sit down and work out their differences, huh?"

"Yep. You've got it, and . . ." Hesitating, cupping hands over eyes, Hunter looked up at Saucer Plateau. "Know what? I bet when Santa starts his speech—because he loves these trees so much—I bet he's gonna face this way."

Shelly, knowing what he was getting at, chimed in. "And this will be the best spot to watch him from, right?"

"Yep. And hey, you wanna join me?"

"Sure. But we better get going. It's getting late."

As Hunter mulled over what just happened, wow, wow, wow beat rhythmically in his head. "I don't believe it. I popped the question without even thinking and she accepted. Wait 'til I tell Pietro. And hey, that means I won the bet. Yes. He has to pay up."

"Thanks for setting me straight about the Victory Trees," Shelly said, distracting him from his thoughts. "I love adding stuff to my history collection."

"History collection. You collect history?"

"Sure do. Right here. In my power-point brain."

"Ah, then. Do me a favor. How about clicking on your *PowerPoint* to find out why we always have turkey on Christmas Season Blessing Day. Fiddlin' nutcrackers. You'd think they'd change up once in a while. Maybe serve ham or steak, or better still, hamburgers and French fries."

"Are you kidding?"

"No. I'm dead serious. I'd really like to know why we always have to have turkey and those yucky cranberries. I hate cranberries. And turkey is *not* my favorite meat."

"Dancin' Prancer. If you feel that strongly about it, why don't you revolt? Or, uh, at least, organize a protest march."

"Revolt? Organize a protest march? I can't do that." After those words flew off his tongue, Hunter felt torn. "By the way I said that, she probably thinks I'm a wimp. Bet she's testing me. Gosh, I want to work on a relationship with her, but . . ."

Shelly, her face stoic, stared straight ahead.

As Hunter tried guessing her intention, something his

75

grandpa once said popped into his head.

"Hunter, always stand up for what you believe is right. Voice your beliefs, even if they seem off-kilter from what others think. I know it takes courage to be the odd snowman out, but it's important to speak your mind. And if others can't accept you for doing so, look at it this way. They're not, and never will be, your true friends."

As much as Hunter wanted to ignore his grandpa's advice, he couldn't. Deep down he knew he was right. Still, he feared if he held strong to his values, Shelly might bolt. He felt torn. He didn't want to come across as a sissy, but neither did he want to take a pushy, aggressive stance.

"What can I say that'll sound sensible, that won't send her off on another hissy snit? One thing I know. It's gotta be something that'll keep her from changing her mind about attending the festivities with me because I've gotta show Pietro that I can do this. But for me to do as she suggested? Never. So, how can I be *my own snowman*, like my grandpa said, without getting her miffed?" He thought and thought, and then . . . "Ah, I know. I'll do what my father suggested during our last talk. Let's see. How did he put it?"

"Hunter, you've got to learn tact."

"Tact?"

"Yes. Like holding back from jumping to conclusions. Think before saying anything. Get your facts straight before you open your mouth. Your grandfather taught me that. Surely, he brought it up a time or two with you too."

Before losing his nerve, Hunter blurted, "Hey, uh, I

76

don't think anyone in this North Pole Region has ever started a revolt. Generally speaking, all disputes are negotiated. And that's a fact."

Shelly was quick to respond. "Well, if you don't like it, at least go and complain to Santa about it."

"Yeah. Maybe I will," he said flippantly. Yet, deep down, he knew he probably never would.

For the next five minutes, snow crunching under two sets of boots was the only sound punctuating the air. Walking on, Hunter dared to do what he had wanted to do all morning. Raising his arm, he swung it around Shelly's shoulders. The move seemed so easy and natural. To his surprise, she nuzzled in close instead of pulling away. She also broke the silence.

"Don't you know why we always have turkey and cranberries at our Blessing Day festivities?"

"Nope. I've always slept through my history classes."

"Hey, if you'd defrost that icicle brain of yours, I'd tell you," she chided, slipping her arm around his waist.

As she made her move, Hunter gulped. Releasing a stream of air like a camper does when blowing on hot, roasted marshmallows, his thoughts went to Pietro. "Wow. He'll never believe me when I—"

"It's all because of greed," Shelly announced.

"Greed. What are you talking about?"

"Why we have turkey and cranberries on Christmas Season Blessing Day."

"What's greed got to do with turkey and cranberries?"

Shelly turned and put a finger to his lips. "Shh. Just listen. It's like this. About forty or fifty years ago, or something like that, some rich dude down in the States, he decided to get the jump on Christmas sales. So, he stocked his store early and drummed up this Thanksgiving Day parade idea to get people out shopping. And he figured he'd make lots of money if he had a star attraction. You know. To draw a big crowd."

"And that's where Santa came in. Right?"

"Right. And that stateside dude wanted the real Santa Claus for his parade. Not a helper."

"So, what's that got to do with us having turkey and cranberries on Christmas Season Blessing Day?"

"Duh. It's like this. Santa was their guest. So, they had to feed him. And the first time they served him cranberries, he said, 'What's this red sauce?' When they said, 'Cranberries,' he bellowed, 'Well, bless my snowy-white whiskers, I didn't know these little red pearls were fit for human consumption.'"

"Don't cranberries grow all over the Northern Hemisphere? Wherever there's a bog?"

"Yeah. But back then, only wild animals ate them."

"And Indians."

"Oh, we can't forget *the Indians*," Shelly said, flipping her scarf at him.

Hunter, catching hold of an end, stared into her eyes and said blithely, "And then, they fed him cranberries and turkey and Santa liked them so much he said, 'Fiddlin' nutcrackers, we've got to have us a yearly turkey feast like this at home.' So, from then on, it's been dry turkey and sour cranberries every Christmas Season Blessing Day."

"Hey, you tricked me," Shelly yelled, yanking her scarf free from his hands. "You already knew."

"No. Wait. I wasn't trying to trick you. And I didn't know. Honest. It's just that . . . that I figured it out as you were telling it. I mean, it was easy, knowing how much Santa loves cranberries. With turkey, that is."

"Yeah. I hear he can down a quart or more of that sauce at one sitting. That can't be true. Can it?"

Hunter shrugged. "Who knows? Maybe he does."

"You think?"

"Listen. With Santa's ethnicity changing every year, anything's possible. And say, isn't his so-called *metamorphic change* gonna happen soon?"

"Yep. A couple of weeks from now. On his birthday, at the stroke of midnight or a minute or two after midnight."

"So, he'll change from Asian, or symbolic Yellow, as he likes to put it, to what?"

"I don't know. I can't keep track. It's either Black or White. Or, uh, maybe it's Brown. I don't remember."

"You, little Miss History Collector, don't remember?"

"Hey, I'm not perfect. Besides, who cares? Santa's just Santa no matter what he looks like."

"Yeah. I guess you're right."

Hunter, saying no more, found himself mentally communicating with his grandpa again. "Grandpa, you could always read me like a book. And if you were here right now . . . well, you'd know I'd like to kiss Shelly, but I'm a little nervous about trying it yet."

"Hunter, uh—"

"What?" Hunter, immediately attentive, wondered if Shelly had guessed his thoughts. He waited anxiously for her to speak.

"Hunter," she repeated, her voice soft but pensive, "what do you think would happen if someone were to break the secret-keeping law? Like, uh . . . like maybe saying something *accidentally* to a person outside our Region about Santa's ethnicity changing every year."

Hunter, hardly able to fathom Shelly spilling those words at his feet, stopped dead in his tracks and stared cuttingly into her face.

She, feeling the heat of his glare, turned away and crossed her arms over her bosom.

Face scrunched and gripping head between hands, he envisioned grabbing her, swinging her around to face him, then yelling, "What! Reveal Santa's secret? Are you crazy? I know you have a reputation for being bold and sometimes too candid, but I can't believe you'd do such a thing. How could you even think about breaking the law drilled into us since birth, the law folks migrating to this Region have to pledge allegiance to, the law meant to keep Santa's racial changes secret from the outside world forever?"

As angry thoughts kept coming and coming—all overtaking his head like icicles seeking night's chill before melting away—Hunter, picturing his father saying the word *tactful*, thought, "Yeah. I gotta let go of this anger. Gotta be tactful."

Lowering hands to sides, he said in an even tone, "Hey. You're not thinking about doing that, are you? Or, uh, you haven't already done it, have you?"

Shelly, angry, swung the toe of her boot into a snow pile beside their path. As spray pop several feet into the air, she yelled, "No I didn't and I'm not going to either."

"Then why'd you bring it up?"

"Because . . . because I think it's stupid to keep secrets all the time. And even more stupid for Santa to hide his racial changes from the whole world. Especially since being different is no longer a big deal."

"But that's the way it is. It's . . . it's part of our culture. Besides Santa promised his poppa he'd never, ever reveal it to anyone outside this Region. And you know everyone who lives here has to honor that promise. And . . . and, that's just the way it is, Shelly. And, the way it will always be."

"Okay, I accept it. Okay. So, drop it. Okay."

Her huffy response told Hunter he hadn't said what she wanted to hear. Still, he tried reasoning. "Listen. Everyone here has always respected—"

"I don't want to talk about it anymore. So, drop it. Ple-e-ease. Anyway, here's my lane."

Hunter held his tongue. His mind though kept whirling. "Holy walrus turds. Why does she have to get so riled? And what if she were to leak Santa's secret? Sooty bricks. I kinda like her. But if she were to blab his most guarded secret, and, at the same, time tell everyone I'm her snow gander . . . Oh, no. Folks would think . . ."

Shelly, quite astute, knew her opinion—which didn't seem shocking to her at all, just the right thing to do—had upset Hunter. "I should never have confided in him. At least, not yet. But somehow, I've got to win him over. If anyone can help me figure out a way to expose Santa's secret, it's him. He's so smart. But to convince him . . ."

Hoping their date was still on, she said with hesitancy, "Meet you at the Victory Trees at eleven fifteen. Okay?"

Hunter said nothing. Rather, needing a diversion, he fished for his pocket watch. As he manipulated it in his hand, he recalled that it had been one of his grandpa's most prized possessions. Now it was his, and he cherished it. Staring down at its gold casing, he thought back to the day his father handed it to him, saying, "Here, son, I think you're grown up enough to take care of this. Your grandpa wanted you to have it."

Neither said a word as the watch transferred from the hands of one generation to the next. Still, what Hunter remembered most was not *the joy of receiving it*. Yes, he was surprised, and thrilled, that his dad was entrusting him with it. But what stuck in his mind as it was placed in his palm, was the slight tremor that had passed from his father's fingers to his hand.

Keenly observant, as his grandfather had taught him to be, he could see his dad was struggling to hold back tears.

Hearing, "Son, I think your grandpa was much closer to you than he ever was to me," he threw his arms around his dad and held him close. In the moments that followed, he sensed his dad—sobbing quietly in his arms—was not only grieving the loss of his father but also regretting what he hadn't said to him before he died.

Hunter, staring at the pocket watch, stayed with his thoughts. "There's always been a schism between those two. But why? Was it because grandpa didn't like dad passing himself off as one hundred percent White? Whew. That sure grated on his nerves. And one thing about dad. Once he decided something, that was it. And grandpa? He sure clung to his old Indian ways. Yeah. Neither one could see that the other's choices were okay. And me? More than once, I was caught in the middle. Fiddlin' nutcrackers. I like being Indian. And I've no qualms about having both Indian and White blood in me."

Shelly, realizing Hunter wasn't about to initiate further conversation, asked, "Where'd you get that?"

"It was my grandpa's."

"Your grandpa had a watch like that?"

"Yep. Wanna hear the story behind it?"

"I'd love to, but it's getting late."

"Oh. Okay," he answered, forcing a smile.

"But I'd like to see inside that watch."

Happy to show it off, Hunter pressed the tip of the winding stem. As the lid flipped up, exposing an ivory face embossed with golden Roman numerals, she let out a loud gasp.

For a moment, Shelly, taken by its uniqueness—and used to digital clocks—studied the position of the hands. After figuring the time, she blurted, "Well, bless my snowy-white britches. It's . . . it's already past ten."

"And you're gonna meet me at the Victory Trees at eleven fifteen?"

"Yes. I'll make it."

"Well . . ." Hunter, not wanting to mess up their first date, hesitated.

"Well, yourself. I'll be there before you." Thrusting chin high, she stepped backward in the direction of her cottage. As she did, she fished for a long streamer scrap in her pocket. Pulling one out, she looped it left to right in sync with some fancy footwork as she, keeping her eyes fixed on him, flitted along her lane. At the halfway mark, turning, running to her cottage, she sprinted up porch steps two at a time.

Hunter, mesmerized by her performance, didn't twitch a muscle until the slamming of her cottage door rang in his ears. As it dawned on him what he didn't do, he, thrusting hands deep into jean pockets, kicked snow. "Yelping walrus pups," he sputtered, "I missed my chance to kiss her."

CHAPTER 8

Forty minutes later, skis propped against *his* Victory Tree—hardly noticeable—and pocket watch laid open, Hunter checked the time. "Eleven-fifteen. Where is she?" He snapped the lid down on his inherited treasure and shoved it deep into his pants pocket. Shading his eyes, he scanned the growing crowd. "What's keeping her?"

A flapping noise pulled his eyes from Victory Tree to Victory Tree. Colorful streamers, binding them together, had him blinking surprise.

"Crepe paper streamers. Hmm. Wonder who strung these trees together with all this stuff. Ah. I bet Santa sent a crew to do this after Shelly and I left. Sooty bricks. They had what? Maybe a half-hour. Have to say. It does spiff up the place. Wow. Shelly's sure gonna be surprised."

Furtively, he glanced around the meadow. "Shelly. What's keeping you? Come on. You said you'd be here before me. Yeah. Right. I should've known."

To placate anxiety, he pulled his long braid forward and brushed its banded end back and forth under his chin. The repetitive act calmed him some.

"Taffy tarnation. Who strung up all these streamers?"

Hunter's eyes widened. "Shelly. That's her voice."

Stretching upward, he spotted her rounding the Mediator Tree. As he watched her approaching, he funneled a deep breath into a low whistle which, in turn, paved the way for him to say, "Gosh, she looks prettier than any model I've ever seen on TV."

That, she did. Her black leather boots blended so seamlessly with her tights, it was impossible to tell where one stopped and the other began. Her tan leather jacket, hiding all but the collar and cuffs of her crinkled white blouse—so easy on the eyes—brought a smile to his lips. Next, sun glinting on metal drew his eyes to her earrings.

"Hmm. Indian made? Maybe. And those bracelets dangling from her wrists, they're cool but not as cool as her hands. Oh, how I'd love to hold and caress them."

As Hunter took in Shelly's classy look, a warm flush crept up his neck, publicizing his anxiety. "I should've fancied up. But I never fancy up. Sooty bricks. I couldn't fancy up. I don't own anything to fancy up with."

This was true. He had always been satisfied with store-stock blue jeans, tee shirts, and quilted plaid shirts . . . that is, until now.

"Dumb bozo. Why didn't you accept mom's offer to buy you some cool duds when shopping last month? At least, those designer jeans. And now, look. The reason you should've just planted her boots in front of you."

Shelly, back to him, taking in the colorful streamers linking the Victory Trees, didn't know Hunter had spotted her when she had rounded the Mediator Tree. Nor did she know he was now watching her every move.

Hunter, taking in Shelly's appearance, judging her attire as super-mod in comparison to his *unremarkable* attire, felt mismatched. This, in turn, fueled his itch to run. Fortunately, before acting on that urge, he shifted his eyes to the crowds.

"Where's Pietro? Bet he's out there watching to see what I'm gonna do next. Hey, amigo, you'd love it if I bailed, wouldn't ya? Yeah. You'd never let me hear the end of it. Well, amigo, that ain't gonna happen. I'm gonna stay put. And that five-spot? It's gonna be mine. But what in taffy tarnation should I do when she comes over here? Grab her? Kiss her? Sweep her off her feet like I've seen lovers do in the movies?" Hunter, weighted with anxiety, and clueless about what to do next, didn't think to yell something like, "Hey, Shelly. Over here."

Shelly, turning from the Victory Trees, scanned the area. Spotting him, she approached, saying, "Hey, what's going on around here?"

Her question, like an unexpected jolt, loosened his tongue. "What? What do you mean?"

"I mean, who wrapped up the Victory Trees with all those streamers?"

"Beats me. Maybe it was a last-minute order from Santa." Hunter, snapping fingers, added, "Ah. I bet he had it done because of this weather."

"This weather? That doesn't make sense?"

"Sure, it does. Look around you. What do you see?"

"Duh. A crowd. One that's getting bigger and bigger as we stand here."

"Right. And in that crowd are lots of little elfins *because* their parents let them tag along *because* it's such a beautiful day. And if some of them were to wander into those trees while Santa's giving his speech . . . Well, I'll wager—"

"Okay. I get it."

Shelly, paying him no further ado, rose on tiptoe. Shading her eyes, she scanned the area beyond their standing point. "Hey," she yelled, startling him, "look up there."

Directing his line of sight to where she was pointing, Hunter squinted.

"See. See up there. There they are. Mitzi and Santa. Isn't this exciting? They're heading to our new platform in the sky. Wow. Are they ever gonna be surprised."

Spotting two red-suited figures trudging up the mountainside, Hunter said flatly, "Yeah. I see them. So, who's gonna be up there with them?"

"Nobody. Just them."

"Just them? But who's gonna run the sound equipment?"

"Mitzi."

"Really. How do you know that?"

"I found out when I volunteered at her office last month. Mark told me. You know, Mark Barthlin, her office manager."

"Mark, huh?"

"Yeah, Mark."

"You like him?"

"A little."

"Did you ever, uh . . . you know. Did you ever hang with him?"

"Yeah. Kinda."

"What do you mean, 'Kinda?'"

"Well," Shelly said, evasively dipping her eyes. "We talked on the phone some but couldn't get together because of all my volunteer work and dance classes."

The dramatic drop in Shelly's voice, and her turning away as she finished speaking, told Hunter he had overstepped his bounds. Realizing she needed time for private thoughts, he decided to say no more. As he shifted his eyes to the crowd, trying to spot Pietro, little did he know his questions about Mark had triggered a replay in her mind of a recent tiff she had had with her father concerning her crush on him.

"Get out of my face and stop telling me what I can and can't do. You're always treating me like a baby, and I'm sick of it."

"Shelly, Mark is twenty-six and —"

"And I'm only fifteen. Right? That's what you were gonna say. Right?"

"Shelly, for fiddlin' nutcrackers, I don't mind you dating. Just pick someone your own age."

89

"Get with it, Dad. This is the Twenty-first Century. Girls date older guys all the time."

"I didn't say you couldn't go out with older guys. But, eleven years older is *not* acceptable to me."

"Eleven years older is *not* acceptable to me-e-e. Eleven years older is *not* acceptable to me-e-e. Eleven years older is *not* acceptable to me-e-e," Shelly mocked, pushing the envelope to the nth degree.

"That's enough, young lady!"

Determined to castrate her father's parental authority, she dug in her heels and fired her next missile. "I don't care if Mark is twenty-six and I'm only fifteen. I'm going out with him and you can't stop me."

To her surprise, her father's usual mulish challenge, "You wanna bet," never left his lips. Instead, he hit her with an ultimatum that sucked the wind out of her sails.

"Okay, Missy. Go ahead. Go out with him. And every time you do, it'll be another three months before I'll sign for your driver's permit."

"What!"

"Oh yeah. And if you plan to test me, you can kiss that cell phone of yours goodbye too."

"You wouldn't dare."

"Try me."

"But . . . but . . . You, you . . . you can't do that."

Vic Jasselton looked up from his paper. Doing his best to keep a straight face, he raised his brow and said evenly, "Sweetie, you're living in my house. I pay the bills. And turning off that cell phone you're clutching so tightly there . . . No problem. It's just a phone call away."

Shelly, eyes pulsing enough venom to kill a herd of elk, screamed, "What! That's . . . that's so unfair. You can't shut off my phone. You, you . . ."

As she hesitated, the walls in the room, having been bombarded time and again by her fiery wrath, echoed deep silence. That is until Vic snapped the pages of his newspaper to its full spread.

Shelly stared at the barrier her father had erected between them. Stiffening, readying herself to blastoff into another tantrum, she leaned into his paper as much as she dared and screamed, "You. You are . . . You are the worst. The very, very worst father ever."

Vic, having resolved to say no more, merely stared at his paper, waiting for the expected. It wasn't long before he heard his daughter stomping off to her bedroom, hissy fitting back at him. "You're cruel and mean and . . . and I hate you. I hate you. I hate you."

Deep down, Shelly didn't hate her father. What she hated was his upper hand. Never could she conquer it. Stubborn to the nth degree, she always held out or pushed him as far as he would allow. She wouldn't give in to his firmness nor would she ever admit he was right. Always, after dramatizing what she viewed as unjust, she would retreat—with a screaming encore—usually to her room, where she could privately wind down her fury with a torrent of tears.

BAM . . . The slamming of her bedroom door set her window to rattling, which she was too angry to notice or even care. Plopping across her bed, fist-pounding her pillow, she screamed, "I hate him. I hate him. I hate him. He's so mean and . . . and unfair. Well, I'll show him. If he won't let me date Mark, I won't date anyone else for the rest of my life. Or . . . or, at least until I turn eighteen."

Slowly her anger gave way to sobbing resolutions. "I'll show you, Daddy dearest. I'll get my driver's license. And there's no way in Elk Tundra that I'm giving up my cell phone. And, *[sniff]* and if you won't let me date Mark, I won't date anyone. You'll see. Mark will wait for me. He loves me. Yeah. And when I turn eighteen . . . *[sniff] Daddy dearest,* I'll be of legal age and . . . and then there won't be a thing you can do to stop me. Oh, Mark, I, *[sniff]* I . . ."

It was a resolution she intended to keep and did keep, for a whole week. That is, until . . .

Sitting with girlfriends at a platform-planning meeting, Shelly spotted a looker seated several rows ahead and to her right. As she took in his features, all she could think about was getting time alone with him.

Never did she expect *the how of that* to happen so fast. His volunteering to tie streamers to the new platform posts shortly after she did, played right into her desire. And Santa, dear Santa. When he said, "Two should be enough for that task," she exploded with, "Yes. Yes. Yes."

Afterward, certain he was eyeing her, she pretended not to notice. But she did notice. Especially his awesome black braid. Like magic, her double-barreled charm kicked in, erasing all thoughts of her no-dating resolution.

An expert at whetting a guy's interest, she squirmed about, repositioning herself into one flirtatious pose after another. A forward thrust of her head sent a veil of hair cascading over her eyes. A fast jerk upward and her tresses flew backward, exposing a *hoity-toity, disinterested* face. Another forward thrust and her hair fell into a peek-a-boo curtain over her eyes. Her veiled-vantage point thrilled her.

"Oh, oh. He's looking my way. And wow. He's so darn cute."

To discourage competition, she twisted left to right, giving the girls around her the feral eye. They got her message: "Back off. He's mine."

Now, dealing with emotions Hunter had stirred by grilling her about Mark, Shelly pulled her foot back and jabbed the toe of her boot into the nearest snow clump. As she watched the ensuing spray landing on his ski boots, anger flared in her eyes and exploded from her lips.

"Ski boots! You skied over here. Why ya sneaky little weasel. You know skiing to holiday events was outlawed a few years ago. Remember? Of course, you do. Everyone remembers when that skier came bombing past that ice boulder just outside North Pole Village and pow . . . Old Jim Kuntz didn't know what hit him. Poor guy nearly died. So, ye grand community-minded one, why'd you do it, huh?"

Shelly, eyes aflame with fury, stepped back.

Hunter, head hung low, started explaining. "I . . . I did it because—"

"Because you cheated," she yelled.

"Cheated! What do you mean, cheated?" Hunter, bewildered, couldn't imagine what he had done to merit such an accusation, especially since he wasn't her snow gander. At least, not yet.

"Moose malarkey. Moose malarkey. Moose malarkey," Shelly spat emphatically. Turning away from him, she ran her eyes up and down the line of Victory Trees. Squinting, making out a lone pair of skis propped against the top one— *his* tree—she turned and thrust an accusing finger at him. "You . . . Why it took me nearly thirty minutes to hike over here. But you? It probably didn't take you more than five minutes on those speed demons."

Hunter, bowed head professing guilt, brought the flat of his hands together. Lifting them, resting chin on thumbs, he extended his fingers steeple-like. In this pose, he looked like he was about to plead, "Please. Please forgive me." He didn't. Instead, he justified. "Look. It's like this. I . . . Well, I decided to come early. I, uh . . . after I left your lane, I went home. Got my skis. And, and then I came in on a trail that nobody uses. I mean, not much. A-a-and I didn't pass one single elf. Honest."

"Bog wash. You probably took longer to get ready than me. Then you raced over here on skis to beat me. So, that means you cheated."

Hunter, quick to protest, yelled, "No, I didn't. Listen." Reaching out, catching hold of her forearms, he sought her eyes.

She shied away from meeting his.

"Shelly, please. Please listen to me. Look. It's not what you think. To be honest, I decided to bring my skis . . . Well, I decided to bring them just in case something went wrong."

"Oh, please. Not that doomsday stuff again." Pulling away from his grip, she blasted him with an icy stare. Then she turned away.

Hunter, caught breaking a safety rule—something he wouldn't normally do—struggled with his feelings. Whatever his options, he felt damned if he did and damned if he didn't and terribly indecisive about whether to run or to stay put. His guilt showed in his posture—head hung low, hands jammed deep into jean pockets, torso swaying to and FRO.

As always, when at a low point, even though he couldn't physically be with his grandpa, he would turn to him in thought. "Grandpa, I know I was going against Santa's rule, but you're the one who told me to listen to my feelings. So, I did. And now look at the mess I'm in."

As stubbornness ricocheted between the two, silence ate up several minutes. Hunter, glimpsing the crowds, noticed some of his classmates were slyly watching their drama. "Holy walrus turds. Strangers staring at me is bad enough. But my friends?" The mere thought of them seeing him in a pickle stew upped his embarrassment tenfold.

"Too bad there's no bear den around here. I'd sure like to hide in one. Yeah. I know, Grandpa. Running solves nothing."

He flicked his eyes to Shelly. "Hmm. Giving me the silent treatment, huh? Fine. Be a snob. See if I care. And, Grandpa, I've had it. This girl's more than I want to deal with right now. I'm out of here."

Turning to leave, the earth beneath his feet seemed to rise up, delivering a hard slap to his face. As the emotional impact of that imaginary slap jarred loose one of his grandpa's wisest teachings—*In order to win, son, sometimes an elf has to be willing to lose*—he reeled back on his heels.

"Grandpa, what are you trying to do? Knock some sense into me? Yeah. I know. The manly thing to do is to admit guilt, to offer an apology. Oh, all right. I'll snowman up." Turning to Shelly, he blurted, "Hey. You're right. I cheated and I'm sorry. Okay?"

Shelly, back to him, arms looped tightly across her bosom, held true to her impish nature. A nose-in-the-air gesture and a flutter of eyelashes signaled her intent to watch him squirm.

"Fritterin' fiddlesticks. Is she going to stay mad at me forever? Man, what else can I do? Well, I know one thing. I'm done trying to please her. I'm just gonna be me. That's it. And if she leaves, fine. Hey, Grandpa, what do you think of that decision, huh?"

After mentally blowing off steam, Hunter didn't know if it was his grandfather's doing or what, but for reasons beyond him, he started seeing the humor in the situation which, in turn, relaxed him some. Deciding to try another tactic—to lighten up, like his friends often encouraged him to do—he pulled a white streamer from his coat pocket and playfully dangled it over Shelly's head. She, in turn, swung at it, play-taunting him while trying her best to keep a straight face. She couldn't. Head tilted back, lips stretching into a telling smile, she drilled her eyes into his and said with a tantalizing smirk, "So, the defeated toy soldier waves his white flag and surrenders, huh?"

Hunter, grimacing as if her words had mortally wounded him, doubled over, gyrated his head sideways, and locked his sad-clown eyes with hers. His facial expression was enough to melt anyone's heart. Even hers.

"Wow. It worked. She's caving. And she's grinning." Eyes still connected with hers, he opened his arms and beckoned her to come forth.

"I'm sorry," she said, falling into his arms. "But you see, my dad says I have a bad temper. Just like my mom's."

"You do?" he stated, widening his eyes as if surprised. At that moment, holding her close, feeling nothing but passion, he could care less about her temper. What intrigued him, what held his attention, were her sensuous lips, which were now parting to speak.

"Yes. And, of course, my mom blames my grandma. She says I inherited it from her."

"It's okay, my little snow goose. You don't have to explain."

97

Hunter's heart beat wildly. He didn't care that they were standing in the middle of a crowd. He could wait no longer. Tenderly cupping Shelly's chin in his hand, he drew her in close. As his quivering lips found the softness of hers, he felt transported to a place he could only liken to a Heaven lit up by a fabulous display of fireworks. Seconds later, with reluctance, he pulled away.

"Wow. What a way to make up."

As those around them started clapping, both noticed the other's face sprouting colorful blotches. Embarrassed, hiding faces behind hands, they giggled.

CHAPTER 9

BO-O-ONG . . . The Green Holly Bell, majestically swinging in the heart of North Pole Village, began its high noon peal. BO-O-ONG . . . BO-O-ONG . . . The striking, signaling the beginning of the holiday's festivities, was telling everyone, "Hush. Pay attention." By the time the last high-noon bong bounced off Jingle-Jangle Mountain, the crowds had muted their chatter and were lifting their eyes to the most impressive platform ever built for the holiday.

On Saucer Plateau—named such because it looked like a saucer sitting atop the rocky cliffs of Jingle-Jangle Mountain—Mitzi, sitting twenty feet below Santa's *Blessing Day* platform, tapped her microphone. "Testing. Testing. Testing. Santa is about to begin his climb. Shout when you see him pop through the chimney top."

Turning from the mike, she blew him a kiss. He, about to stick his head into the fireplace, paused to catch it. After pressing it to his lips, he blew her a smooch. Then he began his ascent to the sky-high platform. Below, in snowy meadows surrounding the mountain, hundreds of elves, anxious to sight their beloved toymaker popping through that chimney top, looked on.

Methodically, at a snail's pace, Santa climbed one soot-free brick after another. The world's fastest chimney popper, the only man alive who could ascend and descend chimneys faster than any rocket blasting off to the moon, slowly worked his way up the freshly built chimney. As he did, he ran his fingers over brick after brick. "Beautiful. Beautiful. Oh, how I love bricks, and if there's a bad one in this stack, I'll find it."

The elves below were waiting anxiously. If Santa went in, they knew he had to come out. There wasn't a chimney in the world he couldn't ascend. Anyway, that's what they thought until now. Minutes ticked by. Impatience showed in their mumblings.

"What's taking him so long?"

"Did the college students mess up?"

"Did they make the chimney too small?"

"Is he stuck? If he is, how will we get him out?"

Ten minutes of worrisome goggling passed before a young elfin, straddling her poppa's shoulders, shouted, "There he is, Poppa. I see him. There's Santa."

All eyes converged on the chimney. Sure enough, Santa was popping through its top.

Twenty million decibels of hooting, hollering, whistling, and clapping shook each niche and crevice of the mountain. A faint quiver coming through chimney bricks—reminiscent of a vibrating chair—delighted Santa. He chalked its cause to the sheer volume of cheering pelting the mountain.

"What a treat. I'd sure love to sit here for a while. Can't though. Have to get my eyes adjusted to this light. Then I've gotta get moving." He blinked and blinked. Finally, able to keep his eyes open without squinting, he lowered himself to the platform and began trotting around it. At each post, he paused. Thrusting his arms high into the air, he turned left and right, acknowledging those cheering below.

After completing his first round, the crowds, in response to the band conductor's cue, began singing with glee.

"Oh, it's Christmas Season Blessing Day,
Time to put our play away.
Today, it's party time,
All-day we'll wine and dine.
Tomorrow to work we'll go,
Making toy production flow.

"Bright and fresh we'll face each day,
Creating what our plans convey.
Toys, toys, for boys and girls,
Dolls, dolls with pretty curls,
Bikes and skateboards greased and shined,
So, kids can stop them on a dime . . ."

On Santa's second go-round, he lingered longer at each

post, waving joyously to crowds below. And what crowds. For eons, only toymakers had braved gnawing, subzero weather for his blessing. But today, with sunshine pulsing warmth, nearly every worker in the Region had arrived with family in tow. Moms, dads, aunts, uncles, grandparents, teen elves, and hundreds of little elfins peppered every snowy meadow around the mountain.

Midway into his third go-round, Santa, saying, "Shimmering icicles," stopped short. "Shimmering icicles? No. No way. Today our icicles aren't shimmering. Today, they're melting. Yeah. As I recall, one was splat-splatting outside my kitchen window this morning. So, today, I should say *dripping icicles* not shimmering icicles."

Stepping to the railing, smiling smugly, he changed up. "Dripping icicles. What a day. Why look down there. All the meadows are jam-packed. Seems like the whole Region has turned out for my blessing. Hmm. Wonder why. Ah. I know. It's this gorgeous weather. Yep. That's gotta be it."

Pausing, taking in the dips and rises of Rudolphtown's snow peaks, wonderment filled his soul. "Mother Nature, you're a gem. This weather is perfect. Actually, today everything is perfect. Absolutely perfect. Oh, thank you. Thank you, my dear lady. You couldn't have blessed us with a better day."

Chapter 10

In the North Pole Region, two things changed every year: Santa's ethnicity and the Blessing Day's Platform site. Everyone knew Santa woke on his birthday with more or less melanin in his skin. And he always picked a great site for the Blessing Day platform. This year, many questioned not only the expense but also the practicality of building it on Saucer Plateau atop Jingle-Jangle Mountain. However, when completed, with it looking as elegant as a crown of jewels on royalty, doubt dwindled to nothing.

It was also common knowledge that two things never changed in the Land of Icebergs: Santa's hair, snowy-white since birth, and the Blessing Day flagpole.

Nary an elf cared that Santa's hair never had, and never would have, a hue of color. The flagpole though played an important role in the November first festivities. Late October, teen elves would remove it from storage and give it a high shine. This year, anchored to the backside of the platform's chimney, it seemed to shout, "Look at me. I'm the king of Jingle-Jangle Mountain." Still, it would have none of a king's splendor until crowned with the Blessing Day Flag, an honor bestowed upon it by Santa if, and only if, the platform passed inspection.

Strolling from post to post, eagle-eyeing joints, braces, the fitting of seams, the welding of rails, even the platform's overall design, Santa marveled again and again. Like the chimney he had climbed earlier, he found not a flaw.

"Wow. Those students sure did a terrific job. They deserve a double flag-up. And you down there," he said, turning his attention to hushed crowds. "I know, I know. You're all waiting for my verdict. Well, since you didn't disappoint me, I won't disappoint you." Releasing the cord from its anchored pivot, he worked the colorful emblem up the flagpole. As he did, a balmy wind took hold, unfurling its green and white stripes surrounding a circular map of the Region. "Flag," he said, chest swelling with pride, "you're about to cause one fiddlin' nutcracker commotion."

His prediction rang true. Every elf, especially those who had helped build the platform, were waiting breathlessly for the moment. Each, eagle-eyeing the platform, hoped to be the first to sight their beloved flag flapping in the wind.

"There it is," Hunter shouted, taking the honor.

The commotion that followed rivaled nothing short of a stadium of fans cheering a major league football team's winning touchdown. High-fives, catcalls, shrill whistles, and exuberant shouts exploded like popcorn kernels popping in a lidless pot. "It passed inspection. Yea. Santa likes our platform. He gave us a flag-up. Yea . . . Yea . . . Yea

. . ."

Shortly after uncorking their jubilation, the excitement died down and the youth, like their elders, stood quietly, saluting their beloved flag. It proved to be a brief reprieve.

CLANG . . . The striking of band cymbals and the following drum roll echoed from mountain to mountain. On cue, the bandleader, dipping baton to drummers, announced, "Elves and elfins, our Christmas Season theme song. Please join in." Rhythmic drumming, horn-tooting, and joyous singing signaled the start of a festive holiday.

Santa, peering down, voiced heartfelt satisfaction. "How beautiful. Our whole region is singing our Christmas theme song." He closed his eyes and swayed with the music. "Wow. Those vibrations tickling my toe soldiers . . . I love them. How fantastic. This mountain is humming right along with the crowds."

On his next go-round, streamers Hunter and Shelly had tied to posts—fluttering, swatting each other's tails—caught his eye and set him to imagining elfins playing a game of tag, each shouting in turn, "I gotcha. You're *IT* now."

Gazing out beyond the streamers, he drank in the view. Visibility, clearer than a flawless diamond, beckoned him to capture the landscape's beauty for posterity. Taking in cottages, factories, all he could see of North Pole Village, he voiced with a smile, "Ah, like sunbathers on a beach, your windows and doors are soaking up the warmth of today's sun." Slowly hopscotching his gaze to the suburbs, miles out from North Pole Village, he briefly reminisced about each.

"Betcha there's at least a hundred reindeer farms out there in Sleigh Valley. For sure, it has the best bakery in the Region. Oh, and their cheese bread. It's to die for. And Krisville, our software mecca . . . Lots of gadgetry created there, especially at Mod-Toy Electronics.

"Oh, Rudolphtown, I have no idea how many coalmines tunnel through your mountains. But, you can bet your bottom shaft, we'd sure be in a pickle stew if we didn't have you as our heat source. And you, Kringleland. Yes, you. Your sprawling plains are no more than a smudge on the horizon from here. But distance doesn't equal lesser importance."

Reflecting on his efforts to get Blitzen University and Vixen Vocational Center built in Kringleland thirty years ago, Santa's chest swelled with pride.

"Today, with the demand for complicated electronic toys, our young elves need all the education they can get. Yeah. Our Urban Planning Committee was right. Kringleland has proven to be the perfect spot for our airport. Ah, this place is so beautiful. And lucky for me, all who live here are loyal to the secret-keeping law."

The impetus behind that law drew him back in time, to an evening when he—four years old and brown-skinned— had hopped out of bed and scampered toward the kitchen to beg a drink of water. Halfway there, the sound of his poppa's angry voice startled him. Slackening his pace, he tiptoed the rest of the way. At the doorjamb, he hugged the sidewall. Even though he was trembling like a scared rabbit, he stole a peek.

BAM . . . BAM . . .

His poppa, fist slamming the tabletop, popped his eyes wide and set him shaking and hugging the wall.

"Woman, that show was the most inhumane thing I've ever seen. There should be a law against putting people on display like that. And I'll tell you this. Even though our son is different than anyone else in the world, no two-bit circus will ever bill him in a freak show. No sir. Not if I have anything to say about it."

In the seconds that followed, Santa, hearing nothing but heavy breathing, dared another peek. At that moment, witnessing his poppa fist pounding the table again . . . BAM . . . BAM . . . BAM . . . his big brown eyes, unaccustomed to the scary scene, quivered a mile a second right along with the rest of his body.

"No sir. Nobody's gonna put *my* son in a circus wagon for everybody to gawk at. *Not* my Soweto . . . *Not* my Freddie . . . *Not* my Pipestone . . . *Not* my Hum-Bow . . . *Not* my Otoño . . . *Not in my lifetime!*"

Santa, staring wide-eyed, stiffened. Never before had he heard his poppa yelling in rising crescendos, or seen his chest heaving like angry waves on a wind-chopped lake, or witnessed his eyes bulging like a mean badger's.

BAM . . . BAM . . . BAM . . .

Hearing his poppa fist whacking the table a third time upped Santa's heartbeat tenfold. Trembling, he pulled back and flattened himself against the wall.

"Shh."

His momma's gentle admonishment perked Santa's ears. Daring another peek, he spotted her rocking back and forth, working her knitting needles faster than a factory's machinery could drop candy canes into cellophane wrappers.

Thump . . . thump . . . thump . . . thump . . . thump . . . His poppa stomping fury into kitchen floorboards made the cottage shake and sent a quiver up Santa's spine that radiated outward into unstoppable shivers.

Sighting his poppa leaning into his momma's face, speaking sternly, his eyes stretched wide and his breath caught in his throat. Had a mirror hung before him, inviting self-inspection, his own reflection would have scared the Ghost of Winter out of him.

His poppa saying, "Listen to me, woman," spiked his attention. "Nobody's gonna call my son a freak. I'll make sure of it. I'll protect him from every freak-spouting scoundrel that darkens the face of this earth."

"And just how do you propose to do that?"

"How? I don't know. But I'll figure it out."

"Well, you'd better get yourself calmed down before your ranting wakes Santa if it hasn't already."

Santa, hearing his name spoken, and fearful of getting caught eavesdropping, forgot about his thirst and dashed back to bed. Under the safety of his feather-tick quilt, his little-boy body shook in long-john pajamas.

"Freak. Am I a freak?"

◇•◇•◇

Santa had heard the word *freak* for the first time two nights ago at the circus.

Before enjoying the evening's performance in the big tent, he and his poppa, arriving early, decided to take in the full spectrum of the circus. Nearing the *Freak Show* area, they witnessed a young elfin pointing at a man—a man no taller than the lad himself—saying, "Hey, Grandma, look at that funny little man over there. See. In that wagon, making faces at us behind those bars. He looks like a freak."

The lad's grandma, glancing briefly at the deformed little man, showed no hesitation in voicing her opinion. "Hmm. I know he's part of *The Freak Show*, but freak is not the word I'd use. I'd say he's an oddity. Something unusual to look at. Now, you just be thankful you don't look . . . look unusual. Because if you did, somebody might stick you in a circus wagon for others to stare at."

At the time, Santa thought everybody in the circus, even those not confined to cute, tiny-house wagons with bars over windows, must be freaks. Especially clowns with orange hair, fat red lips, and white faces. He noticed they wandered about doing silly things to make people laugh. But people being put on display just because they looked different . . . When his poppa hurried him away from the *Freak Show* area, saying, "No way to treat people," he could tell that troubled him.

The exciting event called a circus, with lots of colorful

wagons, a momma and baby elephant, and a huge assortment of exotic animals was the talk of the Region. When his poppa took him, Santa was awed by everything. The strange animals. All the clowns. The trapeze artists who did tricks on high-up tightwires and swings. The fire eater. The man who got into cages with growling animals and cracked his whip . . .

Wide-eyed, taking in everything, Santa, along with other spectators, laughed and squealed. And he loved hearing all the *Ohs* or *Awes* being voiced around him.

Upon leaving, enamored by everything he had seen and heard, he announced, "Poppa, when I grow up, I wanna be a circus clown."

Back in bed, curled into a tight ball under his fluffy feather tick, with only his Otoño nose exposed to pull in air, Santa's four-year-old mind reasoned, "I must've made poppa mad when I said, 'I wanna be a clown.' Tomorrow I'll tell him I never want to be a clown. Then poppa won't be mad anymore."

That night as he entered dreamland, what he witnessed in the kitchen seeped into his subconscious. Little did he know then how much his poppa's strong words and scary actions would affect his future thinking and actions.

Two years later, sitting in his first-grade classroom, Santa listened intently as his teacher announced, "Elfins, today we're going to learn about a new law. A secret-keeping law that says nobody in the North Pole Region is to divulge another elf's secret. Not ever. Not unless that secret were to bring harm to someone. Now, do any of you know what the word *divulge* means?"

"That was my poppa's doing all right," Santa said, turning his attention to elves singing in snowy meadows below. The last line of the Season's theme song, *Each year's blessing guarantees quality toys under Christmas Trees*, rose up the mountain and faded into oblivion.

"Oh. Oh. That's the end of the song. Good thing I stopped my daydreaming."

Looking down at everyone cheering wildly, Santa began readying himself to bless his toymakers. This moment, he knew—with families from all over the Region standing together, united as one, waiting for him to speak—would be revered today, but nothing more than a piece of discarded time tomorrow. Presently, the moment seemed to wrap ribbons of anticipation around all those waiting for his blessing. His speech, meant to bolster a gripe-free work environment during the Christmas Season . . . Well, knowing merrymaking would commence shortly thereafter, he always kept it short.

"Dancin' Prancer. They're sure having a lot of fun down there. Why spoil it. I'll just go around a few more times."

On his next go-round, Santa lingered longer at each post, waving joyously to everyone below. To him, it seemed the more ruckus they made, the more those lovely tremors soothed the soles of his feet. Likening them to little sparklers—a delight to experience, yet quite harmless—he wanted more.

In normal, subzero weather, he would stroll around the platform a few times then give his speech. Today, enamored by unusual weather, and loving those vibrations soothing his feet, he found it easy to rationalize, "Can't say that it'd hurt to go around a few more times. Sooty bricks. Look at them down there. They're so hyped. Bet no one will give an Elk Tundra if I circle this thing a little while longer. Anyway, it's a perfect day for daydreaming."

Santa had two hobbies. Collecting soot from chimneys around the world ranked second, daydreaming came in first. Every elf in the Region knew he could easily get lost in one for hours. Whenever folks spotted him ambling through the ice-sculpture park on a sun-crackling day, they knew exactly what he was doing. Today, he wasn't walking in the park, but piercing sunbeams were pulling him into a daydreaming tangent.

"Let's see. I want to run through one that has some punch to it. One I can get lost in while enjoying this magnificent day. Ah, I know. I'll do my favorite. *Mitzi's Charade*." Oblivious to time, he trucked toward the next post, rationalizing, "Hey, everyone down there is having a whale of a time. So, I'm gonna have me some fun up here too."

One-finger tap to his Hum-Bow nose was enough to get him started. "Hmm. Let's see. When did Mitzi pull her shenanigan on me? Wasn't it eight years ago when I was Black? Yes. The last year my poppa, bless his soul, got to call me Soweto before he died. Hmm. If my memory serves me right, I'd just come home from work and I was so-o-o tuckered. Yep. That's the scene." Saying no more, he slipped back to that long-ago moment when it all began.

Walking through the front door, dead tired after a hard day's work, Santa expected Mitzi to greet him with a big hug and a juicy kiss. Instead, she thrust her needlework under his then Soweto nose and screamed, "Do you see this sock?"

Startled, flipping his eyes from her sharp darning needle anchored in his sock's threads to her fiery eyes, Santa jumped back. The possibility of his Soweto nose being slashed with that sharp needle drew sweat beads to his brow. He couldn't believe his eyes. For years, his wife had lovingly used that needle to mend his socks. Now, she was shoving it under his Soweto nose like a lethal weapon. He had to face it. His sweet, loving wife, who rarely raised her voice, was throwing a moose-snorting conniption fit.

"Do you see this sock?" she bellowed a second time.

"Yes. Yes, Mitzi. I see it." Trembling, keeping his eyes glued to her needle, he, so intent on protecting his Soweto nose, could hardly think straight.

For several minutes, the two pantomimed a war dance. He stepped backward and she stepped forward. Weaving between and betwixt overstuffed chairs, the sofa, floor lamps, literally everything in his path, Santa found it almost impossible to pull his Soweto nose more than an inch or two away from her darn, darning needle.

His mind reeled with indecision. "If I grab her arm, will that stop her, or will she panic and run that darn needle clear up my Soweto nose? Maybe I should turn and run. No. Better to talk her down." Even though exasperated, he said slowly and evenly, "Mitzi, why? Why in taffy tarnation is it so important for me to see that sock?"

"Because," she snapped, "it's the last sock I'm ever going to darn. I'm sick of sitting around this cottage day in and day out darning your *darn* socks. Do you hear me? I'm sick of doing nothing but *darning* your *darn* socks."

Santa, taken aback by her angry outburst, reeled. "Why? Why, after all these years of blissful marriage, is she going berserk on me? Holy walrus turds. Is it going to be like this from now on? Am I not going to know what to expect from her anymore? Is our marriage doomed?"

Scared and befuddled, he blurted out the first idea that popped into his head. "Dear, maybe you need to do something fun or different or . . . or just get away from here for a while. So, uh, why don't you take a vacation. A nice, long vacation. Just you. By yourself. You could go anywhere you want. Do whatever you want. And you don't have to tell me where you go or what you do if you don't want to. Think about it. Maybe getting away from me, and *my darn socks*, for a while will do you good."

<>•<>•<>

CHAPTER 11

Santa popped out of his daydream to check the crowds. His lean-over-the-railing was greeted by thunderous roars. "Whew. Still going strong, eh? Hmm. Wonder what Mitzi's doing. Bet she's wishing I'd get on with my speech."

Sitting at the control panel below, Mitzi, frustrated, yelled, "Santa, what in Elk Tundra are . . . Are you daydreaming up there?" As if needing to confirm her suspicion, she lifted her eyes to the near-cloudless sky. "Uh-huh. That's what you're doing all right. And there's no telling how long you'll keep it up. And the crowds? Listen to that ruckus. Why they're just egging you on."

For a while, Mitzi mulled over her busy work schedule. With Christmas nearing, she needed more help. Shelly Jasselton had come into her office two months earlier to sign up for volunteer work. Not knowing how well a fifteen-year-old would do, she only let her sign up for October.

"What a mind that girl has. And the questions she asked about Santa's secret. So many. It was scary. I have to say though, she was a good worker. So much so, I'd have kept her through the Christmas Season. But Sleigh Valley

115

Medical Center has her now. My loss, I guess. But what spunk. If only I could've said whatever I thought when I was her age. Yep. Having loving parents makes a big difference. And, we're now living in progressive times. Times when child abuse isn't tolerated like it was when I was a kid."

Santa's boot-clomping drew Mitzi's eyes to the overhead beams. "Yes. I know, sweetheart. You're up there reveling in some old memory. Just daydreaming away with no sense of time. Knowing you, it'll be hours before you get on with your speech. Yep. It's a given. When that old sun comes out, you start reminiscing. Well, since I've nothing better to do, I'm gonna follow your cue and settle into some daydreaming of my own."

Leaning back in her chair, closing her eyes, an indelible memory pulled Mitzi back to Harlan, Kentucky, to a kitchen cozy-warm with love. She saw herself, a happy toddler, sitting on a flower-patterned linoleum floor, playing with A-B-C blocks. Her favorite teddy bear and tattered security blanket lay no more than an arm's length away.

A good distance from her, high above her reach, a squatty enamelware teakettle, puffing steam like an old locomotive, sat regally on the cast-iron cookstove's front-most lid. Easily, it held a gallon of water and was kept full, and hot, at all times. Besides being readily accessible for dishwashing and cleanup jobs, Gramps and Uncle Tom found it handy for softening their shaving-mug soap. As for guests, it was a ready source for hot tea.

Kitty-corner to the cast-iron cookstove, a feed sack

curtain hid the kitchen sink's convoluted drainpipe. It carried nutrient-rich slurry through an outer wall to gramps's backyard garden. Every summer, on property rented from Stonega Coal and Coke, the constant feed produced stunning roses, which neighbors admired and often received, plus hardy vegetables for the family's table.

The family's precursor to electrical refrigeration, an old oak icebox, hugged the outer wall across the room from the hot cookstove. Its three doors had latches Mitzi couldn't reach. One or two times a week the iceman walked in weighed down with a heavy block of ice secured within jaw-spreading tongs. Mitzi loved watching him chiseling off chunks, sizing it to fit its allotted icebox space. Not a sliver of ice was wasted. All, except the piece placed in her waiting hand, was gathered up and dropped into pitchers of iced tea or lemonade. As she sucked on her piece, much of it dribbled down her chin, soaking the front of her dress.

One lazy evening, laughter filled the kitchen as the important people of Mitzi's world sat around the table, swapping stories and downing dangerously hot coffee. From her floor vantage point, she found Aunt Rachel's and Uncle Tom's way of cooling their coffee less interesting than how gramps did his. They just blew across the rims of their cups, but gramps, to drop his coffee's temperature to sipping tolerance, he poured his into a saucer. Mitzi, her awe-filled eyes fixed on his arthritic fingers, held her breath each time he slowly, and shakily, lifted his saucer, brimming with cream-colored coffee, to his lips. Puckering, he'd blow the gentlest ripples across the shallow lake. To her amazement, never did he spill a drop.

On this particular night, midway through gramps' coffee-cooling routine, a screech, a swish, and a loud slam drew Mitzi's eyes—and everyone else's—to the screen door. A hush fell over the room. A strange man, at least strange to her, sauntered into the kitchen, acting like he owned the place. Staring up at him, she, unlike the others, didn't know all hell was about to break loose.

SWI-I-ISH . . .

Scooped up in one swift swoop by strong but gentle hands, Mitzi, coming face-to-face with her Aunt Rachel, heard, "Say 'Hi' to your daddy. Say 'Hi' to your daddy, sweetie."

As the stranger stepped closer, holding hands out, saying, "Come to Daddy," his cavern of off-kilter, tobacco-stained teeth, jawing behind lips buried in a scruffy beard, frightened her. Quickly turning away, she buried her face in her aunt's bosom.

Gramps, asserting his head-of-household position, stepped up to his youngest son, and asked, "Okay, Pete. What do you want now?"

"You know."

Those two words, slipping off an arrogant tongue, had everyone's chest pumping anger.

Gramps, a short, quiet man—long saddled with the aftermath of a broken back acquired in a mining accident— could roar like a lion when riled. Although lacking physical strength to stop this sneaky-by-nature son, he did have it in him to verbally fight for the well-being of his granddaughter. Pointing his cane toward the parlor, he motioned for Pete to follow him into the room reserved for special occasions and private talks.

Not until the parlor's French doors closed behind the two men, did Mitzi pull her face away from her aunt's bosom. Voices. Angry voices, ramping louder and louder from behind those doors, prompted fear, tears, and trembles. Aunt Rachel, holding her close, covered her ears in an attempt to calm her. It didn't help.

Mitzi didn't know the man called Daddy's intent. Aunt Rachel did though. She knew he had come to take her away . . . far, far away from the only home she had known since she was three weeks old, since the death of her mother.

When the arguing ended in the parlor, Gramps emerged with disgust written all over his face. Seems he, who had *no legal rights* had been informed by Pete that as Mitzi's father he had come to exercise *his parental rights.* And, if necessary, he would go find a policeman to assist him.

In the next hour, the screen door's hinges screeched again and again as Mitzi's treasures were toted to the car.

"Going to your new home," Pete announced, moving toward his daughter. With no more empathy than a villain, he wrenched her from his sister-in-law's arms. Like the thief in the night that he was, he quickly carried her outside and plunked her down among the array of dolls and teddy bears piled high on the front seat of his rickety, long-outdated

Model-T Ford. As he did, he paid no mind to the snide objections and name-calling singeing his ears.

Facing the inevitable, Aunt Rachel, Uncle Tom, and Gramps took turns sticking their heads into the car to kiss *their* little girl goodbye. Tears streamed down Aunt Rachel's face. Uncle Tom and Gramps, both eyeing the man called Daddy with disgust, just wore sad frowns.

As they drove off, Mitzi, too young to understand the ramifications of what just happened, sat quietly, listening to the car's chug-chugging when rolling level and to its near-death sputtering when climbing hills. The strange man, steering around bends and up and down hills, said nothing.

After acclimating to the Model-T's interior, Mitzi's eyes drifted to the headlights' luminosity raying wide on the road ahead. As the jalopy's balding tires churned up dust behind them, the country roads, in cahoots with the man called daddy, stole her away from the family who had taken her in, who loved her dearly, whose hearts were now breaking.

When sleep happened, she did not know. It, like the man called daddy, came unannounced.

Hours later, in the dead of night, a room flooded in bright light assaulted Mitzi's sleepy eyes. "What's this? Oh, the strange man called daddy is carrying me into somebody's house." The door, slamming behind them, startled her to full wakefulness.

"Bring her over here. Set her down on the ironing board." The owner of that voice, a redheaded woman, stood back and sized up her new charge. Leaning in, she kissed

Mitzi on the forehead. Never again would she repeat the act.

Moments later, Mitzi found herself kneeling on the kitchen floor, exploring contents of a toybox while the man called Daddy, and the redhead, sat at a nearby table, chatting and sipping coffee.

"It's late and I've got to get up early for work."

"You go to bed. I'll take care of her."

Pushing his chair away from the table, the man called daddy disappeared up the stairs.

A short time later, Mitzi, clutching the strange woman's hand, struggled to keep up as they climbed steep steps. Upon reaching the landing, the redhead pointed to a boy sleeping on a cot in the room directly ahead. "That's Willard," she said matter-of-factly. "He's in first grade. You can call him Willy. And over here . . ."

Mitzi hardly had time to take in the boy's features before the redhead whisked her away to a room across the hall. Standing at the side of a crib, her face level with a sleeping toddler's, she heard, "That's Janice."

In due time, Mitzi would come to know Janice as her half-sister. Years later, when old enough to comprehend a baby's gestation period, she would do the math. "Janice is eight months my junior. Something's amiss."

"And this is Karen over here," the redhead stated, pushing her toward the double bed across the room. "You'll sleep with her." Twelve years hence she not only slept with this stepsister who upped her in age by eight months, but she also mimicked her behaviors. Had to. The redhead

121

demanded it.

"You better have your plate cleaned by the time Karen finishes hers or else . . ."

From day one, the redhead indoctrinated Mitzi into her *or-else* philosophy. Obedience was paramount. If she ignored, ran, dallied, or didn't hear, she could expect slaps to her face, hair yanking, shoves to the floor, kicks to her shins, violent shaking, hours of chair sitting, to bed with no dinner or whatever else her stepmother devised at the time. All punishments were peppered generously with scathing putdowns.

Mitzi, too young to have a sense of time, had no idea how long she had endured the redhead's abuse before the man called Daddy dumped her near-naked, badly beaten body onto his older brother's doorstep. Years later, her aunt Rachel confided, "That night, your father sped away faster than his balding tires could stir up dust. But not before I got into his face and screamed, 'That bitch of yours. If she were here right now, I'd kill her.'"

The next morning, Mitzi, lifted atop the kitchen's round oak table, stood still as Aunt Rachel, back from an early downtown shopping trip, pressed one new dress after another against her bare chest. Gramps, sipping saucer-cooled coffee, looked on.

"Too big," Aunt Rachel said, her eyes inviting gramps' input.

He, a man of few words, merely stated, "Well, if ya have ta, take 'em back. Get 'er some that'll fit 'er."

"My poor Aunt Rachel. Each time I landed on her doorstep, she'd trot downtown by bus, again and again, until she figured out the right shoe and dress sizes for me. I guess she had no other choice since I came clothed only in stinking underwear. Had she paraded my black-and-blue body before store clerks, a lot of heads would've turned. Still, not a soul would've said anything. In the 1940s, not much was done about *suspected* child abuse.

"And dear gramps. He proved to be my best buddy. Always, I could count on him to sneak me a cookie whenever Aunt Rachel said no. On sunny afternoons, we'd walk hand-in-hand to the corner drugstore where he'd treat me to candy or an ice cream cone. His small mining pension paid for everything—treats, teddy bears, dolls, dresses, shoes, even the ribbons for my hair. He outfitted me completely every time the man called daddy left my filthy, near-naked, badly beaten body on his brother's doorstep.

"Yes. The drop-offs were a nice reprieve from the never-ending cruelty of the redhead. But then, after I turned seven, after the big auction, after the man called Daddy moved his blended family far, far away, they stopped."

The big move . . . Mitzi recalled it all. Men moving furniture from house to yard. Vehicles strewed up and down the lane. Strangers hauling away whatever they won by outbidding others. All-day, *Sold* and *Stay out of the way* rang in her ears. By late afternoon, every stick of furniture, not destined for the trailer hitched behind the car, was gone.

"We spent the last night in that ten-room house sleeping

fitfully on the hard kitchen floor. Creaking noises, echoing from empty room to empty room, scared me. The whole house seemed haunted. Sooty bricks. I had no idea what was happening until three weeks later when we landed in the cold, cold Land of Icebergs, better known as the North Pole.

"Seems cousin Martha, who had married a reindeer farmer in Sleigh Valley, put the bug in my father's ear. She wrote, saying coal mines in Rudolphtown, west of North Pole Village, were going full bore. Kentucky's were cutting back. Thus, we pulled up stakes and headed north. What a shock. Howling winds and subzero temperatures greeted us. No trees. No grass. Just ice boulders and white, white snow as far as the eye could see."

Back in Somerset, Kentucky, Mitzi remembered attending a one-room country school situated on a weedy lot. A potbelly stove kept the classroom warm and also dried mittens. Outside, a long-handled pump pulled drinking water up from the ground. Two outhouses, or *privies*, stood on the hill behind the school—one for boys, the other for girls. At recess, primary-grade kids explored whatever nature had to offer outside while older students played cards with the teacher.

In Rudolphtown, teachers said *elfins* instead of *children*. The primary school—grades first through fourth—had two classrooms on the main level, plus drinking fountains, indoor bathrooms and a coal-fed furnace in the basement. At recess, elfins, anxious to stretch muscles, played with glee on swings, monkey bars, a merry-go-round, and an ice slide.

When Mitzi started second grade in the new land, the redhead forbade her to play on the ice slide. "It'll wear out your snow pants," she said. But Mitzi did play on it and got away with it because stepsister Karen, who also loved the slide, didn't tattle. Other rules though—controlling, crippling rules—challenged her to find creative ways to get her needs met.

"No, bohunk, I won't sign for you to have a library card. You're not good enough to have one." Stepsister Karen had one. But that was different. One grade higher than Mitzi, and considered *a good girl*, she *deserved* to have one.

The next time her classmates filed out to the mobile library, Mitzi, approaching her teacher, made up a lie. "I have a library card. May I go?"

With a sweep of her hand, Miss Hartson motioned for her to join the others. Giddy with excitement, she ran through the cloakroom and out the door. Back she came within the allotted time, clutching *Beauty and the Beast*. Not daring to take it home, she read it during free time. The next week she didn't return it to the mobile library. She did, however, sneak out *The Little Lame Prince*.

A week later, sitting rigid in her seat, Mitzi watched Miss Hartson trailing a finger along a row of books. Pulling *Beauty and the Beast* off a shelf, she asked, "Who put this library book here?" The room grew silent. Mitzi, paling, feared her teacher would march over and grill her with eyes telepathically demanding, "Fess up. I know you did it."

125

Thankfully, she didn't. Rather, she laid the book aside and went on with her lesson.

However, the sack lunches in the cloakroom . . .

During morning recess, Mitzi often edged her way to the school's front entrance. Beyond doors leading into the cloakroom, on an eye-level shelf, lay an enticing feast— yummy sack lunches. Heisting a treat was easy. All she had to do was tiptoe in, open a bag, grab something, run outside, hide under the front steps, and devour her loot.

One morning, opening the door to the cloakroom, Mitzi spotted Miss Hartson leaning cross-armed on a high windowsill ledge, inset above a row of coat hooks. Knowing she wasn't supposed to leave the playground, she steeled herself for a harsh reprimand.

"Mitzi. What a surprise. Come in. Join me. So nice . . ."

Miss Hartson, ushering her in with *unexpected* kindness, eased Mitzi's fear. Her teacher's forthcoming attention made her feel important. Still, longing to get on with her mission, she wished she would leave.

RING . . . RING . . . RING . . .

Mitzi's ears perked and her eyes widened. "Yes. My teacher has to leave to answer the phone. Soon I can get something to eat." Watching the swinging doors to the classroom close behind Miss Hartson, she, thrilled to have the cloakroom to herself, ran to the shelf crowded with sack lunches.

Choosing the closest bag at eye level, she unraveled its top and thrust her hand deep inside. Her fingers, meeting something smooth, round and hard, tingled with excitement. Taking a peek, her mouth started salivating. Anxious to bite into her prize, she began lifting the biggest, shiniest red apple she had ever laid eyes on from the depth of that bag. Up, up, up she pulled it, but she never got it out. From out of nowhere, something mighty powerful gripped and shook her arm, forcing her to drop the beauty back into the sack.

A second later, fright evident in *thief* Mitzi's eyes collided with victory shining in *detective* Hartson's eyes.

Shame drew color to Mitzi's face. She lowered her eyes to her *shoe station*. Trembling, steeling herself for a harsh reprimand followed by at least ten wickedly painful wooden-paddle swats, she waited. Surprisingly, when Miss Hartson opened her mouth, she expressed no anger. All she said was, "What's your telephone number."

Mitzi tearfully mumbled, "We don't have a telephone."

Dragging her feet home that afternoon, she didn't know which she dreaded most: telling her stepmother or having her teacher contact her. Sadly, both had to happen.

Not long after attending the requested parent-teacher conference, the redhead added *you thieving bastard* to her repertoire of despicable invectives. It, and others, such as *Shithead, you'll never amount to anything. Numbskull, get the hell out of my sight. Ya stupid idiot, can't you do anything right? Bohunk, where the hell are you? You good-for-nothing nincompoop, sneaky kraut, dimwit, moron, lame brain, lying thief, low-life scumbag . . .* All said from morning 'til night, with the intent to destroy her self-esteem.

<>•<>•<>

The third grade was different. Stealing stopped at school and started at home.

Thank goodness for snow pants, especially baggy-legged ones with ankle-hugging cuffs. Everything went down them. The man called Daddy's razorblade packet. The redhead's sewing kit and prized *Wonder Bread* desk calendar. Willy's pocketknife. Janice's *Little Black Sambo* book. Karen's cutout dolls. And almost daily, bread snitched from the kitchen table to appease Mitzi's hunger. It all went to school via her cuffed snow pants.

Most of her stolen treasures she crammed into her desk. The miniature desk calendar, she proudly gifted to Miss Ness, her third-grade teacher. The bread, she dug out of her snow britches and devoured on her way to school.

Days when the redhead's watchful eye kept her from snitching bread off the breakfast table, she would sneak into greenhouses on her way to school, grab an apple or pear from a dwarf tree and then run like crazy. Later, after the fruit was harvested, she discovered back-alley trashcans held sustainable food. Burnt toast. Bruised apples. Half-squeezed oranges. Bits of scrambled eggs. Cold, greasy bacon. Whatever wasn't smothered with bitter coffee grounds appeased her stomach.

"I never got caught doing that," Mitzi said, "but stealing greenhouse tomatoes on my way home from school . . .

Wow. What a daring *Peter Rabbit* venture that was. I'd climb the fence, sneak into the greenhouse, pick a couple of ripe tomatoes, and then I'd skedaddle out of there fast, hoping no one had spotted me. I pulled that off day after day. And like most thieves, over time, I let my guard down. Dilly-dallying in that greenhouse, I'd devour those tomatoes as soon as I picked them."

A grin spread across Mitzi's face as she recalled the day she was squatted down between two rows of pots, mouth sucking a tomato bigger than her face.

"Pants! Sooty bricks. Here it is sixty-some years later and those *farmer-in-the-dell* pants are still imprinted clearly on my brain. I can still see them, rolled up a time or two, lollygagging just shy of the toe tips of two hefty boot. From out of nowhere they appeared, and they scared the hell out of me. Caught red-handed, I inched my eyes up those pant legs. Up, up, up, past suspenders, past an open shirt collar, to the stern face of a very old man. I must've been a sight. Me, a dirty little urchin with tomato juice dribbling down my chin. And him . . . I probably scared him more than he scared me."

" 'So, you like my tomatoes, eh?' the old man asked in the gruffest, meanest voice I'd ever heard. Fear constricted my throat. I said nothing. Fiddlin' nutcrackers. I could hardly breathe, let alone cough up an answer. Still, I kept my eyes fixed on his stern face. To my amazement, his lips broke into a wide grin. 'So, you like my tomatoes, eh?" he repeated. "Well, help yourself. Eat all you want.' Short and sweet. That was it. He turned and moseyed away. And me? Well, I sat there dumbfounded, staring at his pant legs waning in the distance. After that though, knowing I could down as many tomatoes as I wanted, I ambled fearlessly into that greenhouse. Each time I did, I'd look for that kind old man. Sadly, I never saw him again."

In fourth grade, the stealing moved back to school.

One fall day, returning from *at-home lunch*, Mitzi burst into her classroom to the chatter of two classmates seated at the reading table, finishing their sack lunches. Scoping out the room, she saw something unusual lying on her teacher's desk—a waded green ball.

"Money!"

Her eyes rayed wider than sunflower pedals thirsting for warmth. "Could it be a dollar? A whole dollar. Yes. Yes. I think it is. Why . . . why I could buy candy. Lots of candy. And . . . and then I could share it with some elfins. And then maybe they'd be my friends. Oh, I've got to get that dollar."

Mitzi's overwhelming desire to possess that wadded green ball propelled her into fast-track thinking. "To get that dollar, I've got to trick those two elfins into believing I'm just playing."

Wasting no time implementing her hastily devised plan, she positioned her feet between two rows of desks. Arms out, hands braced on opposite desks, she swung her legs forward. Hop. Hop. Hop. Hop. Hop. Up the aisle, she flew.

Upon reaching her teacher's desk, she scooped up the wadded dollar, did a three-sixty, and skipped down the aisle with the intent to hide her booty outside. And then . . .

CLANG . . . CLANG . . . CLANG . . .

"Oh, no. The bell." Mitzi hadn't expected the bell to ring. Now, she couldn't run outside because there in the doorway, letting elfins in, but not out, stood Miss Ness.

Panic set in. Hardly able to think, yet knowing she had to find a hiding place for *her* dollar before Miss Ness called the class to order, she darted her eyes around the classroom.

"Where, oh where can I hide it?"

After questioning Balinda about money missing for her pictures, Miss Ness announced, "Okay, class, we're going to find that dollar if it takes all afternoon." In an army-sergeant voice, she issued one order after another. "Remove everything from your desks. Empty your pockets. Shake out every book. Take off your shoes. Yes, take off your socks too." Up and down the aisles she marched, inspecting every book, shoe, sock, and sweater pocket.

Dollar searching ate up the afternoon. The wall clock said two-forty-five. Still, no dollar was found. Disappointed, Miss Ness ordered, "Put your things back in your desks. It's nearly time to go home."

"Oh, how smug I felt back then. In a few minutes, I thought I'd be walking out the backdoor with that dollar. But then I turned in my seat and there stood Miss Ness towering over me. So many years ago. I can still see her standing there, hands on her hips, toe-tapping the floor, eyeing me suspiciously. And me? I figured the best way to look innocent was to smile. So, I did.

"'Come with me,' she ordered.

"Grabbing my hand, she pulled me down the aisle, beyond the reading table, and into her office. As she shut the door, I lowered my eyes to the chair in front of me. Upon it lay a box of greeting cards.

"'Off with your jumper,' Miss Ness said, pulling it over my head.

"I remember fighting trembles, hoping for a way out. Ironically, my teacher gave it to me when she turned to lay my jumper aside. Moments later, relieved, I watched her pudgy fingers exploring my blouse pocket, trying to ferret out a dollar that was no longer there.

"As for me, I thought that would be it. It wasn't. She proceeded to undo all my blouse buttons. Off it came. Next, much to my chagrin, she did the unmentionable."

Mitzi felt her body tense. The long-ago scene of Miss Ness stretching out the waistband of her underwear and peering down both her front and backside was indelibly printed on her mind. Afterward, Miss Ness, her voice sounding overly suspicion, said two words: "Get dressed."

Glad to be done reliving that scene, Mitzi slumped back in her chair. "Whew. I can hardly believe I chose to endure an embarrassing strip-search rather than fess up. But given how needy I was, and the abuse I was experiencing at home, it makes sense that I complied without making a fuss."

Recalling what she did next, Mitzi smiled. Back at her desk, waving her hand in the air, she shouted, "Miss Ness, Miss Ness."

"Yes."

"Maybe the dollar flew out the window."

At that moment, the dismissal bell rang. Almost as if it were bred into them, the entire class rose and turned to face the cloakroom doors. Dutifully, Mitzi waited for Miss Ness to dismiss her row. From where she stood, she could see the crumpled dollar under the greeting-card box on the chair in her teacher's office. Anybody could see it. It was so visible. But nobody did, except her.

The next morning, dragging her feet to school, Mitzi had one thing on her mind: retrieving that dollar. That is if Miss Ness hadn't already found it. As she neared the school, she expected to hear elfins laughing and chatting on the playground, but only fall's whistling wind fell upon her ears. Entering the cloakroom, seeing wraps hung on every coat hook except hers, she assumed she was late. With a heavy heart, she shed her winter wear and hung it on her assigned hook.

Rather hesitantly she pushed her way through classroom doors. Her classmates could hear her coming and she could hear them twisting in their seats. They all saw the downcast look on her face, and she saw a sea of stoic faces directing judgmental stares her way. Embarrassed, casting eyes to the floor, she hung back. No one said a word. They didn't have to. She knew they knew she, *the lowly White trash girl* standing forlornly before them in shabby dress and run-down shoes, had committed the cardinal sin, *stealing*. And not just once.

Hearing footsteps, she lifted her head to see Miss Ness making her way to the reading table at the back of the room.

"Mitzi, I found the dollar you stole yesterday and stuffed under the card box in my office. Now, come. Come over here and sit down on this chair."

Mitzi's wobbly knees slowly carried her to the sentencing table. Turning sideways to sit down, she glimpsed her classmates. All, facing backward in their seats, sat breathlessly, waiting for the drama to unfold.

"Give me your hand," Miss Ness ordered.

Twenty-nine students looked on as their teacher pressed ten little fingers of a fourth-grade thief—one by one—onto a black inkpad. No one so much as sneezed as she sequentially rolled each digit onto a white sheet of paper. Right-hand fingers left to right. Left-hand fingers right to left.

"See this envelope?"

Mitzi, looking into Miss Ness' eyes, nodded yes.

"When that ink dries, I'm going to mail your fingerprints to the police department, and then . . ."

And then the elfins kept staring and time marched on.

Four years later, the summer after eighth grade, Mitzi's stepbrother Willy cornered her in an upstairs bedroom when no one else was home. Mustering more energy than she thought she had, she struggled free from his exploring hands and ran downstairs and out the backdoor. His attack was the last straw. If she stayed, she knew he would pursue her until he managed to overpower her. Of course, the hammer would fall on her head, not his. The redhead would accuse her of seducing her firstborn. She would label her a slut and that would give Willy a license to pursue her again and again.

The family she ran to—they had five children under age eight—said she could stay one week. "Who else will take me in? Perhaps my dad's cousin, Martha, in Sleigh Valley. Will she and her husband Earl open their home to me?"

Remembering past visits to their reindeer farm—Martha heaping generous portions of meat and vegetables onto her plate, Earl filling her glass again and again with fresh milk, playing hours on end in the hayloft, feeding reindeer, going for sleigh rides—recalling all that, plus Martha's sweet smile and Earl's playful teasing, she reasoned, "Since they never had any children, maybe, just maybe . . ."

Six days into her week's stay, on a Friday, she called Martha and blurted into the receiver, "Hi, this is Mitzi McCully, Pete's daughter. Can I come live with you?"

"Well, I don't know. I have to ask Earl and he's out tending the reindeer."

"But I have to know right now."

Martha must have sensed desperation in her voice because not more than a minute later, she capitulated without seeking Earl's consent. "We'll make a run up to get you on Sunday, after church, between two and three o'clock."

Mitzi knew she was going to a good home. What she didn't know was Martha and Earl went to see her father the day after she called them. During their visit, Earl managed to pull him away from the redhead long enough to ask permission to *unofficially* adopt his daughter.

Two days after she had begged them for a home, Martha and Earl escorted her into their farmhouse kitchen. As she stared at Martha's welcoming feast—her first meal as their *unofficial* daughter—she heard Earl saying, "You can stay as long as you're *good*." When Martha said, "Eat all you want," she, drooling over the spread on the table, decided instantly, "I will stay, and I will be *good*. Super good."

Mitzi popped out of her daydream, saying, "*Good*. I tried being good all my life for my stepmother. So, when Earl said that, I decided I'd aim for perfection. I'd show him. I'd be good beyond redemption."

CHAPTER 12

"Still going strong up there, eh?" Mitzi mumbled, distracted by Santa's boot-clopping. "Yeah. I know. This sunshine has got a hold on you. And knowing you, you'll be daydreaming up there a couple more hours. Well, guess what, sweetheart? I'm doing the same thing down here."

Leaning back in her chair, closing her eyes, she focused on the word *good*. "Whew. I sure worked hard to meet what I believed was Earl's *good-girl* expectation. Trouble was, to me, pleasing others was what being *good* was all about. So, I went out of my way to please Martha and Earl, all their friends and relatives, my friends, and even my teachers.

"Did I vent any anger? No. In my quest to be *perfectly* good, and to keep those around me happy, I stuffed it.

"Did I know my bowing to everyone's beck-and-call was turning me into a people-pleasing robot? No.

"Did I realize I was putting others' needs before my own? No.

"Did I see that everything I did was feeding into my faulty perception of *good*? No.

"Did I know my flawed thinking was short-changing me? No.

"Sadly, I had been so browbeaten, and was so needy, I willingly sacrificed my own needs to be accepted."

The word *good* drew Mitzi decades forward to a scene in her cottage with Santa, to when she had had it with her humdrum *good* life.

She saw herself rocking back and forth, angrily jabbing her darning needle into one of his holey socks. Stressed to the hilt, depressed about life passing her by, she ranted, "I'm done with always trying to be *good*. I'm fed up with enslaving myself to others. And holy walrus turds. I've got to shake this *I'm-not-good-enough* feeling. And perfection? Why do I get so hung up on that!"

Blasted icicles, Mitzi Claus, chimed in her nattering Tomacita. *I'd say it's about time you did make some changes. Like maybe stop being afraid to try new things. And . . . and stop ragging on yourself.*

"Yeah. What've I got to show for my life? Nothing. Fiddlin' nutcrackers. I've lived my whole married life in this cottage getting good at doing what? Darning socks and baking pies? Pugh. Aren't those great accomplishments."

Mitzi's ho-hum, humdrum lifestyle hadn't bothered her much until she started watching *The Oprah Show*. On it, she saw so much of herself in Oprah's guests. But they, unlike she, had made great strides in their lives. Through Oprah, many were telling their stories to the world. Stories of how they were breaking old patterns, treading new waters, taking charge of their lives, and viewing themselves as worthwhile in their own right.

Seeing similarities in her life and many of Oprah's guests, Mitzi suddenly realized she didn't know much of anything beyond baking pies and darning socks. All her life, taking pains to please others—and since marrying Santa, waiting on him hand and foot—rarely did she take her longings or needs into consideration.

Thinking about how she readily succumbed to her self-inflicted, near-slave role in her quest *to always be good*, anger, a lifetime of fermenting anger churned her whole being as she wove . . . No. No. It was more like as she *jabbed* her darning needle between and betwixt worn threads of Santa's holey sock.

Looking up, she spotted him coming through the front door. The next thing she knew she was shoving her darning ball, his sock, her darning needle—the whole kit 'n caboodle—under his Soweto nose, and shouting, "Do you see this sock?" Through a sliver of a needle anchored haphazardly in his half-mended sock, she funneled a lifetime of suppressed anger and frustration at him.

"See this sock," she screamed, shoving it into his nose, nearly jabbing him with her needle. "It's the last one I'm ever going to darn. Do you hear me? The last one. I swear to the four winds on Saucer Plateau, I'll never, ever darn another one again for the rest of my life. Do you hear me? Never."

Mitzi couldn't remember what else she had said as she chased Santa around the cottage that day. She did remember his suggestion that she take a vacation—alone—had lessened her anger. The idea intrigued her. Not so much the getting away part but rather *the freedom to do it alone.*

"Taffy tarnation. I haven't taken a trip *alone* for what? Thirty-two years? And why not? Well, that's clear. It's because when I married Santa, cousin Martha told me my place was by my husband's side. 'Always put him first,' she said, 'and he'll take good care of you. And don't be fretful. A man has enough problems at work without having to come home to a nasty tongue.' Dumb me. I took her advice literally. Yeah. I let it feed right into my faulty belief that to be liked, accepted, even loved, I had to *always* be good."

Above Mitzi and the control panel, Santa, having reached the point in his daydream where he suggested Mitzi take a vacation, *alone*, remembered thinking, "Whew, I must've said what she needed to hear." Breathing a sigh of relief, he watched her hand, still clutching his sock with her darning needle anchored in it, dropping limply to her side. He rubbed his nose, inspected his fingertips. "Good. No blood. Just perspiration. Guess I can thank my snowy-white whiskers for that small miracle."

Mitzi, sighting Santa staring her way, knew he was daring her to play *who's gonna outstare who*—his usual tactic to counter her funks. Rather than biting the bait, she threw her head back and stomped down the hall, muttering, "A vacation. A vacation by myself. Just me alone. Not a bad idea. Think I'll start packing right now."

Santa, having second thoughts, groaned. "Oh, no. Why did I add that *getting-away-from-me* part? How will I get along without her? Sooty bricks. I don't know how to cook. Or sew. Or wash clothes. Or grocery shop. Or . . . or anything. All I know is toymaking and . . . and managing money. Money. She'll need money. But what should I give her? How can I set a limit when I told her to go wherever she wants and for as long as she wants? Blasted icicles. Guess if I have to, I have to."

Yanking his debit card from his wallet, he made his way to their bedroom. "Here," he said, throwing it on the bed. "Take this. It's good at any North Pole National Bank and the code is 7268 or SANT on the machine's keypad. So, go ahead. Take it. I'll get another." Stalling, he reiterated, "As I said. Go wherever you want. Do whatever you want. Take as long as you want. But please, remember one thing."

"What's that?" she asked, her tone sarcastic.

"Just remember that I love you. Okay?"

Her response, a cold stare, cut deep.

Mitzi, having nothing better to do while waiting for the ruckus above her and below her to stop, stayed with her daydream.

Emptying one hanger after another, she hurriedly packed before losing her nerve. Suddenly, Santa was in the room, throwing his debit card on the bed. His words, giving her permission to go, did not match the tone of his voice which she interpreted as: "Please, dear. Please, please stay." In response to him giving her free reign to spend as she pleased—despite apparent pain at seeing her go—she directed a cold stare his way, letting him know she wasn't about to be swayed by his weepy voice or sad eyes.

"How cruel I must have appeared back then. There I was, dashing about, collecting essentials for my alone journey. Sadly, I treated him like he was nothing more than a rickety old clothes rack standing in my way."

Santa, still marching around the platform, remembered the agony he felt while watching Mitzi pack. With her lips zipped, he, head hung low, looking sadder than a whipped pup, dragged his feet back to the living room.

Plopping into his recliner, needing something familiar to hold, he leaned toward a nearby shelf and grabbed a jar of soot from his prized collection. Often, he compared samples from his latest world-wide Christmas Eve run to those gleaned from chimneys on previous treks. Sometimes, he would even figure out the kind of wood people used as a heating source. Now, with despair rendering him helpless, the jar served only as an object to stare at. As he spaced emotionally, his body went limp. His mind though kept reeling.

"Never in my wildest dreams did I see this coming. If only I hadn't suggested she take off like that. Dancin'

Prancer. Now, what am I to do? I can't take care of this place. I can hardly take care of myself."

Carpet-muffled footsteps interrupted his thoughts. He looked up. Sighting Mitzi—suitcase in each hand—stepping briskly down the hall, he sighed wearily. He wanted to say something. But what? What words had the power to stop a determined woman? He didn't know. He longed to reach out, to grab her, to pull her close, to calm her.

She whisked by.

His eyes welled with tears. Her shunning was more than he could bear. Still, he watched her every move: hesitating; bending a knee; setting a suitcase down.

He placed the jar of soot on his side table. Sliding forward in his chair, teetering on its edge, he waited expectantly, hoping she would turn around.

"Come on. Can't you see my pain? My heart is breaking. Please change your mind. Please. Please stay. At least, look at me."

She reached for the doorknob.

He cringed inwardly. "Please, please, turn around."

She didn't.

His heart sank.

She stooped slightly to pick up her suitcase.

He held his breath.

With not so much as a glance back at him, she stepped across the threshold.

WHAM . . .

He jumped.

Her slamming the door on their lives—happy lives as far as he was concerned—left him feeling desolate.

Tears streamed down his cheeks.

"She didn't even say goodbye. Oh, what did I do to upset her? Wasn't I a good husband? Didn't I give her everything she wanted? I thought she was happy. She always seemed to be happy. So, where did I go wrong?"

CHAPTER 13

While Santa and Mitzi were reliving old memories on Saucer Plateau, the crowds below, egging each other on, upped their cheering each time they sighted Santa rounding the platform.

By now, most teen elves, but not Hunter, had hooked up with their friends.

"Pietro. Pietro. Where are you? It's not like you to stand me up. Are you staying away because Shelly is with me?" At long last, sighting him off in the distance, running toward the Victory Trees, Hunter expelled a sigh of relief.

"Hey, Pietro," he called, waving frantically. "Hey, man, I've been lookin' all over for ya? How come you're so late?"

Pietro, tripping over his own feet, fell into Hunter's arms. Too out of breath to say anything, he pulled back and playfully punched his arm.

Hunter found this annoying. The way he handled it depended on his mood. Today, with Shelly looking on, he raised his dukes, inviting playful sparring. The two, facing off, looked like an odd Mutt-and-Jeff pair: one short and squatty; the other tall and slender.

Pietro envied Hunter's rock-hard physic. He longed to be his mirror image. "He's lucky. Nobody teases him like they do me. Look at him. He's slim as an eel. And me? I've got this fat gut. And my dad, he calls me *butterball* right in front of my friends. That's annoying. And embarrassing."

Each time it occurred, Pietro would downplay his father's insensitivity by jokingly saying to friends, "Hey, what can I say. It's in the genes." Afterward, knowing he could eat whatever he wanted in his family's restaurant, he would gravitate to the pastry counter. Sinking teeth into a Danish role or a piece of scrumptious pie seemed to deaden his emotional pain. At least, for a little while. And if one pastry didn't do the trick, he could always eat another, and another. Sometimes he would stuff himself until he felt numb.

"Hey, man, come on. Tell me. Where've ya been? And how come you're so dang out of breath?"

"I, uh . . . I got stopped *[gasp]* by uh . . . See, uh, my old man, he, *[gasp]* he waylaid me just as I was about to uh, to skip out. And I had to *[gasp]* to stay and help him."

"Today! What was so important that it had to be done today? I mean, what'd he make you do?"

"Uh, the Candy Man . . . Oh, hi, Shelly. I, uh . . . I, uh, mean, Mr. Jasselton."

Shelly laughed. "It's okay, Pietro. I know everybody calls my dad *the Candy Man.*"

"Yeah. Well, the Candy Man, he uh, he set up a meeting this morning at our house with some restaurant owners."

"For what?"

"Hey, bozo. Whadaya think? To get some food over here. Ya know. In an organized fashion."

"Wow. That's some insight."

"Yeah, well, the Candy Man said with this warm weather and the beautiful view up there, he figured Santa would probably spend a few hours daydreamin' before giving his speech and . . ." Pietro stopped midstream. Cupping hands over eyes, scanning Saucer Plateau, he grinned. "Yep. Just as I figured. He's doin' just that, huh?"

"Uh-huh." Hunter grinned knowingly. He, Shelly, and those within hearing distance nodded agreement.

Pietro, popping a devilish grin, went on with his story. "Yeah. Everybody knows how easy it is for Santa to slip into a daydream. So, gettin' back to Vic Jasselton and my dad. They and some others met at our house this mornin' to figure out where to set up food wagons over here. Ya know. To make it handy for everyone to get some chow. And I, uh . . . I just finished helping my old man set up his."

"So, where'd he set up at?" Shelly asked, sweeping her eyes over the meadow.

"Way over on the other side of the mountain, next to your dad's candy stand."

She looked at him as if to say, "Why?"

Pietro, reading puzzlement in her eyes, didn't hold back. "Hey, I don't want my old man anywhere near us." Turning to Hunter, he said, "And you, bozo. You owe me big time."

"Whadaya mean, 'I owe you?'"

"Because I told my old man if he wanted my help, Hanna's Hamburger Wagon had to get the spot next to the Victory Trees. See. Over there. They're setting up right now, near *your* so-called tribe's tree."

"You're kidding me. Right?" Hunter's eyes lit up like neon signs. "Wow. That means I get my wish. A hamburger and French fries on Christmas Season Blessing Day." Doubling fists, jerking elbows back, he shouted, "Yes. Yes. This is my lucky day. And hey, man, I could kiss you. But trust me. I won't. Hey. What the . . ."

Glimpsing Shelly talking with her brother, giving him a side hug, he pulled a frown. "Hmm. Jordan doesn't look like he's afraid of her. They look like they're having fun." Noticing Pietro's dumbfounded look, he surmised he, too, was baffled by their friendly interaction.

Grabbing Pietro's arm, he blurted out what he had intended to say before getting distracted. "Hey, amigo, know what? For making it possible for me to get a hamburger today, you can keep that five-spot you owe me. That okay with you?"

"Yeah, man. Thanks." Pietro, eyes popping, thrust his chin to where Shelly stood side-hugging her brother. "Hey, bozo, would ya dig that. I ain't never seen them getting along. Shelly's never been nice to her bro. Never. Hey, man, what'd ya do to that gosling?"

Hunter, standing tall, answered nonchalantly, "Just kissed her. That's all."

<>•<>•<>

CHAPTER 14

Santa, still daydreaming, moved around the platform like a car set on cruise control. In a world of his own, he had no idea Mitzi, sitting below, was reliving her version of what they had both dubbed as *Mitzi's Charade*.

After slamming the cottage door, ramifications of what she was about to do hit Mitzi. "Am I really going out into the world by myself? Alone? Oh my gosh. What have I done?" Doubt, overshadowing her initial determination, played havoc with her thinking. "Dare I? Or, should I say, 'How dare I?' Sooty bricks. I don't think I can do this."

Heart pounding vehemence, knees going rubbery, plus guilt riddling her thoughts, signaled panic was setting in.

Keep it together, girl. Keep it together.

"Yeah, right. You keep it together."

Listen, girl, you better start breathing in slower than you're breathing out. And get rid of that should *rubbish in your head.*

"Easier said than done, you nattering Tomacita. But okay. I'll try it." Balling her fists, scrunching her brow, Mitzi confronted the *blathering blitz* with a string of commands . . . "Good riddance. Get Lost. Scram. Leave me alone. Butt out."

Her efforts proved futile. Rather than letting up, the scoundrels lashed back with: "*You should* not have done that. *You should* be ashamed of yourself. *You should* go back in there. *You should* beg Santa for forgiveness. Then again, maybe *you should . . .*"

"But I, uh, I . . . I . . ." Indecisiveness foiled Mitzi's attempt to defend her actions. Breathing hard, glaring at the door, she envisioned her feet straddling its threshold—one foot, inching its way toward *her* Santa; the other, itching to explore the world. The possibility of having both familiarity and an adventure into the unknown didn't occur to her. She felt she had to choose. And choosing wasn't easy. She pictured herself slipping back inside, melting into the comfort of Santa's arms, crying, asking for forgiveness. Another part of her, however, wanted . . .

Hey, girl, it's either now or never. Make up your mind.

"Now or never, huh? It's . . . It's just . . . Okay. I'm going." Her gumption restored, Mitzi tightened her grip on her suitcases and marched herself down to Dearborn Bus Station. Once there, she purchased a ticket to Kringleland.

"By tomorrow I'll be on a plane, heading to . . . Sooty bricks. I haven't thought that far ahead yet. And I'm still not sure about all this." Closing her eyes, she envisioned herself plucking petals off a daisy, much like she did when longing for her birth mother as a child. Only this time, instead of chanting, "Does she love me? Yes. She loves me," her lips spewed, "Shall I go, or shall I not go? Shall I go, or shall I not go?"

Fret over making a major decision took centerstage.

"Maybe I should tear this ticket up and go pour my heart out to Shooting Star. Get her opinion on all this. She's a consultant and a good friend. She'll take time to listen to me. But is it fair for me to bother her, especially now, with her recovering from that nasty snowmobile accident and all? Poor girl. She doesn't even know if she'll ever walk again, and . . ."

The loudspeaker blasting, *Now boarding at gate three for Kringleland,* forced Mitzi's hand. "I'm going," she said crisply. Rising to her feet, she joined the throngs heading for gate three.

Boarding the bus, sliding into a window seat, she mulled over many questions. "So, where do I go after I get to Kringleland? I certainly don't feel like going on a tourist binge. Hmm. Should I stay in a hotel for a few days? Maybe even a week? Do some shopping and then go home? No. I want to do something different. But what?" A flurry of snowflakes pulled her eyes to the window. She stared at them, hoping they would spark some ideas. To her chagrin, their only effect was hypnotic. Blinking hard, she said, "No help there."

Tilting her head back, she started reading the array of ads plastered above the bus windows.

"Snowmobile parts . . . Sorry. Machinery is not my thing. The best shampoo . . . Right. I'll stick with mine, thank you. Sable's Department Store . . . Ah, those are spiffy-looking shoes. Computer software . . . Fiddlin' nutcrackers.

Computers are so foreign to me. Let's see. What's next? Trade school . . . Hmm, trade school." Reading on, Mitzi's eyes sparked with interest. "Want to make some changes in your life? Courses at Vixen Vocational Center will change your course of life forever." As the ad's meaning sank in, her excitement had her bouncing in her seat.

"School. That's it. That's what I'll do." As her lips broke into a grin, a soda-fizz feeling filled her chest. "School. Yes. School it will be. Holy walrus turds. Elfins take vacations *from* school. But for me? I'm gonna spend my vacation *at* school. Now that's a switch."

Is that what you want, girl?

"Yes. It sure is."

Mitzi, bursting with excitement, fought the urge to broadcast her decision to the whole bus. Rather than making a fool of herself, she sat quietly, paying attention to the whirl going on in her head.

"Wow. What a way to escape my humdrum life. Instead of flying off somewhere and spending Santa's money on stupid stuff, I'm going to invest in myself. I'll take some classes. Hey. I can brush up on those office skills I learned in high school but never got to put to use. Yes. Yes. Yes. School, here I come."

To further shore up her decision, she rationalized, "I know Santa won't expect me or even want me to do this. But . . . come to think of it, he did say, 'You can go anywhere you want. Do whatever you want. Take as long as you want.' So, in a way, I already have his blessing."

Mitzi, floating on cloud nine, not only pictured herself in a learning environment, but she also started thinking beyond school.

"So, what will I do afterward? Get a job? Become a nine-to-five professional woman? Hmm. I wonder what Santa would say if I did. Guess I'll cross that iceberg when I come to it. Now, ain't this something. In one day, I've made two major decisions. Wow. That's what I call 'taking the bull moose by his rack.'"

Well, kudos to you, girl. You're finally taking charge of your life.

Mitzi ignored her nattering Tomacita's dig. Tired, deciding not to fight sleep's invasion, she closed her eyes. Soon, the drone of the bus motor, plus the musical ditty coming from a passenger's transistor radio—*Let your fingers do the walking*—began pulling her into la-la-land. She drifted off mumbling, "First, I must change my identity, change my i-den-ti-ty, cha . . ."

As sleep took hold, little did Mitzi know her subconscious, at the moment, was re-routing her last thoughts to her dream center.

The theatre lights dimmed. Mitzi, sitting in the last row of the balcony—with every seat before her empty—wondered why the stage had dark streaks raying out from front to back. Lifting her binoculars, panning over them, they flared into columns of names, all in alphabetical order. "That's odd. The stage looks like a page from a telephone book."

The musical ditty, *Let your fingers do the walking*, pulsed in her ears. "Where's that music coming from?" A draw of her ocular lenses across the stage produced nothing. "Hmm. there's no orchestra pit?" Next, running them up a side curtain, she spied a baton dipping to and FRO. A closer look had her saying, "That's not a baton. That's a radio antenna. And it's conducting an orchestra that isn't there."

Two ballet dancers, cued to enter when the radio's antennae dipped their way, pirouetted onto the telephone-page stage. Up, down and across, they cavorted in sync with the advertising ditty, *Let your fingers do the walking*. Mitzi, enthralled, watched them contorting their bodies into snappy thumb-finger movements. "Wow. Ballet dancers. Each pretending to be a hand. How poetic and expressive is that!"

When the music ended, the male dancer bowed low. To his right, his partner stretched her arms back. At the same time, she extended her right leg forward, gracefully lowering her slipper to a name in one of many columns on the stage floor.

Mitzi, lifting her binoculars for a better view, zeroed in on her selection. Finding the name appealing, she tumbled it off her tongue until she had it memorized.

"Next stop, Kringleland. We'll be pulling into Snowcap Hotel in a few minutes, folks."

The bus driver's announcement roused Mitzi. Like many passengers, she stretched and yawned herself to wakefulness, then checked her watch. "Hmm. Almost ten. Glad we're finally here. These old bones of mine are aching for a good bed." Sluggish and cold, she stood in the aisle, waiting her turn to exit the bus.

Stepping off, she pulled her parka's fur collar up around her face to appear less conspicuous. "No way do I want any elf recognizing me and messing up my plans." Minutes later, suitcases in hand, she approached the lobby.

"Name, please," the perky desk clerk greeted, giving her his most professional smile.

Mitzi didn't hesitate. The name from the telephone-page stage was still fresh in her mind. "Ponseta," she said, tensing her vocal cords in an effort to disguise her voice. "Elf Laura Ponseta." Intentionally avoiding the clerk's eyes, she picked up a pen and scribbled her fictitious name on the hotel's registry.

"No way do I want any elf finding out I'm here on a self-improvement journey. So, until I complete it, I'm going to think, eat, sleep, and be Elf Laura Ponseta. It'll be my own private secret. But I probably should let Santa know I'm okay, especially since I didn't even say good-bye to him."

Scoping out the lobby, she spied a postcard rack at the far end of the reception counter. Wasting no time, she purchased a pre-stamped one and quickly penned a short note.

My dearest Santa,

Just want you to know I'm taking a different kind of vacation. I'll be home when it's done. When that will be, I don't know. Yes, I'll remember that you love me, and I love you too. Mitzi

Spying a Penguin Courier mailbox near the revolving door, she deposited it, then ran to catch the elevator, held open by another late-night traveler.

"Well, here goes." Feeling somewhat lightheaded, she reminded herself to breathe. "I can't believe I'm doing this. To think, I'm going to sleep in a strange room tonight. Alone for the first time in thirty-two years." Briefly glimpsing the other woman in the elevator, she wondered if she, too, was seeking reprieve from a humdrum life.

CHAPTER 15

The next morning, waking in unfamiliar surroundings, Mitzi sat up with a start. A few blinks later she threw back the covers and swung her legs over the side of the bed. While stretching and yawning, the reality of yesterday's actions hit home.

"Oh, what in taffy tarnation have I done?"

Santa's face, in his frantic state, flashed before her eyes.

"I can't believe I nearly shoved my darning needle up his nose. And not just once, but, but . . . Oh my God, how many times did I do it! Fiddlin' nutcrackers. That was ghastly of me. And this school idea. It's probably stupid. Oh, whatever possessed me to run off like that? I must be losing my mind."

Losing your mind? Girl, you're insane. Oh, go ahead. Hightail your fanny back home. Beg Santa's forgiveness. Go on. Get. Go home and let your passive side reign.

As her nattering Tomacita played havoc with her thinking, Mitzi scoped out the room. A ceiling-to-floor mirror, dominating the opposite wall, made the room look huge. Her clothes, which she had thrown helter-skelter the night before, lay strewn on the floor and across a desk and chair combo. "Hmm. That wall-mounted TV there in the corner . . . Good place for it. Easy to view from this bed. And those wall hangings. Typical. Yeah. It's all typical hotel stuff." Her circular glance around the room ended at the nightstand beside her bed. On it, an arm's length away, she spied the telephone. For a long moment, she stared at it.

Yes. Go ahead, you yellow-bellied snow goose. Call the desk clerk. Find out when the next bus leaves for North Pole Village. Run back to the same old, same old. Go on, girl. Get it over with.

Under the weight of indecisiveness, and guilt, Mitzi's shoulders sagged.

"Dumb me. What I did last night was stupid. Really stupid. And poor Santa. I shouldn't have . . ." Reaching for the phone, sighting her aged body in the wall mirror across the room, her hand, rather than grabbing the receiver, flew to her gaping mouth. "Holy walrus turds. Is that what I look like? Why it's been . . . it's been forever since I've taken a good look at myself."

The aged reflection greeting her eyes was enough to quell her nattering Tomacita. She did not like what she was seeing. "Yuck. You're a mess, Elf Mitzi Claus. Why you're more shriveled up than a 99-year-old mistletoe berry. And your hair? Land of Icebergs. It's so dull and witchy looking. Sister, you don't look old. You look ancient."

Mitzi wrinkled her nose in disgust. Scrutinizing the whole of herself in the mirror, she couldn't believe . . . No. It was more like she didn't want to believe that that drab, shriveled-up mistletoe berry image looking back at her was what she had allowed herself to become.

"I look so dowdy. And my hair. Dancin' Prancer. It has no luster." Pulling fingers through it ignited a desire to recapture its vibrant luster, its bounciness, and her youth. She grabbed a clump and turned it upward. Split end after split end met her gaze. "My wedding-day pact with Santa . . . Why did I ever agree to never, ever cut my hair?"

Reluctantly, she set her eyes back on the mirror.

"Fiddlin' nutcrackers. What's . . . what's happening?" Like mist being usurped by sunshine, her old-lady reflection fast faded from the glass. In its place, a supple beauty—a young bride—filled the frame. She couldn't see her face. But oh, those cascading curls.

"What gorgeous hair. Wow. The way it flows down the back of her gown . . . It's so beautiful. I wish I had . . ."

As the bride in the mirror turned, exposing her face, Mitzi's hands flew to her parting lips. Wide-eyed staring, she stumbled over her next words. "Oh . . . O-o-oh. My-y-y. God. Why . . . why that's . . . It's me. In . . . in my wedding gown. But . . . but how . . . how can that be?"

Before her startled eyes, Earl, cousin Martha's husband, materialized. His weather-beaten, leathery face tugged at her heart. "Oh, Earl, you were the best father ever. And even though you weren't my bio dad, I loved you dearly."

His image, dissolving into a mist, left her saddened. A second later, as Santa's young face, framed by his signature-white hair and well-trimmed beard, came into sharp focus, her eyes turned sparkly.

"My gallant sweetheart. Oh, you were so young, so handsome in your red tuxedo. Red. It reminds me of your favorite saying. 'I like red, no matter what color it is.'" She giggled softly.

In the blink of an eye, the scene changed to Santa slipping an arm around the young bride's waist. Mitzi again drawing hand to lips, gasped loudly. "Oh, that long-ago day. Santa, you saw that I was shaking, so you put your arm around me. And me? I was so nervous I never heard a word the minister said. Oh, why am I being gifted this glimpse back in time?"

Who cares! Just enjoy it, girl.

"Yes. I am enjoying it, you nattering Tomacita."

Still, she, a bit spooked, couldn't help but look around the room for a ghostly presence.

Hey, dummy. Ain't no ghost gonna let you see him . . . or her.

"Yeah. Right." Breathing a little easier, she turned back to the mirror.

A bit giddy after viewing the next scene—the minister turning and saying to Santa, "You may kiss the bride now."—she wiggled on the bed. "I know what you're gonna do-o-o. You're gonna zero in on my e-e-ear instead of my li-i-ips." As Santa fulfilled her expectation, the mirror panned over the attending guests. Their giggles delighted her.

Unexpectedly, an elderly gent seated in the front row blurted, "Oh my, I think Santa needs some lessons in love." Again, the whole sanctuary burst into laughter.

Drawn into that long-ago moment, Mitzi chuckled.

"Holy walrus turds. I'd forgotten all about that."

Looking on, she anticipated Santa would . . . No. She knew precisely what her gallant sweetheart was about to do. True to form, the mirror showed him pushing aside her beautiful curls. Holding her breath, she watched him whispering into the young bride's ear.

"My love, your hair is more beautiful than Northern Lights dancing across a midnight sky."

"You're such a romantic," she said, "and I like it."

"Promise you'll never, ever cut your gorgeous hair?"

Mitzi nodded agreement along with the young bride.

"Yes. I promised that all right. I wanted to please him so much I willingly agreed to it. And I was so insecure, I feared if I didn't watch my Ps and Qs, if I didn't do everything he asked, he'd reject me."

As quickly as it had appeared, the bride-image faded from the mirror. Watching memories disappear, seeing her old-lady image resurfacing, Mitzi's smile waned.

"That was a dumb pact I made with Santa. And so long ago. Funny. Back then, it didn't seem dumb. Yeah. I willingly agreed to it. Guess it just proves how submissive I was then, and still am. Oh, how I wanted to please him. Holy walrus turds. It wasn't just him I wanted to please. It was everybody. How sad. I was sure hooked into believing nobody would like me if I risked being real. Yeah. I was downright afraid I'd be rejected if I failed at anything."

Mitzi flung her head back. Jokingly she said to her mirrored reflection, "Well, now, you drab old hag, are you going to spend your morning crying over those gray hairs, or are you going to do something about them?"

Taking charge of her life for the first time *in her life*, she turned away from the mirror, picked up the phone, and pressed zero. To the operator, she spoke in a voice echoing new-found spunk. "Operator, connect me with the hotel's beauty parlor. Please."

An hour later, strolling into Crystal's Hair Styling Salon, Mitzi felt like a teen elf primping for her high school prom. This was especially true since she had never experienced the magical touch of a trained beautician. While waiting for her turn, she flipped through a hairstyle magazine. Just as a confident young elf approached to take her under his wing, a short hairdo with curly ringlets caught her eye. "This is what I want," she said crisply. "And I want that auburn color too."

Watching the beautician snipping off her dull, gray tresses, Mitzi let out one gasp after another. By the time the hair on her head—what was left of it—matched the picture she had chosen, her excitement had her heart beating wildly. Staring at her *new 'do* in the mirror and impressed by the way the color accented her eyes, she coolly remarked, "Looks great. And . . . and my eyes. They look like . . . Why they look like they're full of life now."

Bolstered by her *new 'do*, she trotted off to Vixen Vocational Center. Under the fictitious name of Elf Laura Ponseta, she enrolled in a business refresher course, a displaced homemaker's class, a computer class, and an assertiveness training class. When the counselor urged her to take the latter, she thought, "I better not question him. I probably need that one more than the others."

Moving through her self-improvement journey, Mitzi not only conquered her fear of trying new things, but she also started seeing many old incidents in a new light.

One day, arriving early for her assertiveness training class, her mind drifted back to what her high school classmates had coined about her for their graduation memory book. At the time, their conceived ditty, *Elf Mitzi McCully, she thought she couldn't, but she could,* seemed odd to her.

"I thought what my classmates penned about me was stupid. But how right they were. All these years, I not only thought I couldn't do many things, but I also held back from trying anything new. I was afraid others would judge me as *not okay* if I didn't achieve perfection at whatever I did. Dancin' Prancer. I've been a prisoner of my own worries. All that time wasted. Well, not anymore. I'm not wasting one more minute. I'm done trying to meet others' expectations. I'm done being afraid to take risks."

To fill her evening hours, Mitzi joined a fitness club. Workouts, along with consciously eating better, melted away many pounds. She started feeling more vibrant and sleep came easier. To outfit her *slimmer* figure, she sought a wardrobe consultant. Learning spring colors went with her skin tone, she went on a shopping spree that would have sent Santa spinning like a top.

"Elf Laura Ponseta, you look dazzling," she said, taking stock of her slimmer figure in the department store mirror. "Wow. You look twenty-to-thirty years younger. Bet Santa will never recognize you."

Even though taken aback by her mirrored reflection, Mitzi felt something was not quite kosher. Scrutinizing her face from every angle, she finally figured it out. "It's these kinky, wire-rimmed glasses." Setting hands on hips, flinging shoulders back, she lectured away. "Say, spectacles, you might've gone well with my dull, gray tresses, but you sure play havoc with my *new 'do*. Sorry, but you're about to get booted out of my life."

Not wanting her new look to *look* off-kilter, Mitzi made an appointment with an optometrist. At her office a few days later, she chose blue-tinted contact lenses. "Might as well go mod all the way. Be a little different." Catching the doctor's dry smile, she felt she was being sized up. "Hmm. Does this doctor think I'm a crazy old lady?"

A dig from her nattering Tomacita quickly brought her to her senses. *Hey, girl, you gave up being perfect. Remember? So, don't go thinking you have to act a certain way to please this doctor.*

"Perfect I'm not. But this is the *perfect* time to practice what I've learned in my Assertiveness Class."

To counter any residual uncertainty, Mitzi lifted her head high and threw her shoulders back. Catching the optometrist's eye, she suspected her own eyes were broadcasting, "Yes. I know. My remolded stance is telling you I'm an assertive woman, huh?"

Three days later when she picked up her new contacts, the optometrist surprised her by asking, "Would you mind if I kept your old wireframes?"

"Mind? Be my guest."

"Thanks. You know, most people won't part with these things when they're this old."

"Really. Well, I'll have to say, they are old. I got them from my second cousin Martha. See. Whenever I had my eyes checked, I always had new lenses put in them. I'm a little sentimental about them, but change is in the wind. It's time I let them go."

Mitzi, cognizant of Santa's boots thumping overhead, remembered leaving the optometrist's office and heading for the nearest North Pole National Bank to make a cash withdrawal. Staring at his debit card, she felt a pang of homesickness. She missed Santa. Missed him terribly. Still, she would not let herself think about him, except when using his debit card. Self-preservation she called it. Her way of coping without him.

Call him. Call him, her nattering Tomacita badgered.

"Hey. I thought you were on my side in this. So, no. I won't call him. If I were to do that, I'd never finish what I've started. Besides, I know him. If I call, he'd pressure me to come home and this old gal's no quitter."

Before her nattering Tomacita could rattle her cage with any more homesick thoughts, she slipped the card into the bank machine and withdrew enough cash to cover her coming week's expenses. As she tucked it back into her wallet, even though she said, "Out of sight, out of mind," her thoughts lingered on Santa and his debit card.

"Why didn't I ever get a debit card of my own? Stupid me. I just relied on him to give me cash for everything. Well, if I ever get a job, I'm going to open an account and get one. And hey, even if I don't get a job, I can still do that. I'll just tell Santa I want a monthly stipend to spend as I see fit. After all, homemaking is a real job."

CHAPTER 16

Santa, set on milking every second of the unusually gorgeous day, kept circling the platform like a robot programmed for automation. Approaching each post, he would raise his hands and then wave like crazy. Moving on, picking up where he left off in his daydream, he found the words, *different kind of vacation*, on Mitzi's postcard puzzling.

"Mitzi, what in taffy tarnation are you up to? Are you hiking across Siberia? Riding an elephant on some African safari? Did you join a commune in the States? And what do you mean by, *I'll be home when I'm done*? Done! Done with what?"

At first, Santa, passed his days worry-free. He assumed two weeks of resort pampering would subdue his wife's needle-jabbing, ornery attitude. Then she would return, ever so happy to resume wifely duties. As weeks passed, worry consumed him. When crossed-off calendar days leaped over a second and into a third month, he was more than beside himself. He jumped every time the phone rang and ran to check the mailbox each evening after work.

The days dragged. Worry consumed him. His stubborn nature, plus believing Mitzi's leaving was his fault, prompted him to keep her disappearance under wraps. The seventy-fourth day though, as he circled the date on his calendar, he exploded.

"Enough is enough!" BAM. Down went his fist, rattling everything on his desk. The aftermath of that blow pulsed through his arm. He winced. However, his pain paled in comparison to his glut of bottled-up anger. Oh, how he yearned to let his fist fly, to scream at the top of his lungs; but not wanting to alarm Malka, his office manager, he held back. "No. Now ain't the time to blow your stack, mister. Not at your toy factory. Ya gotta keep yourself in check."

Feebly attempting to halt that which he couldn't, he sucked in and spewed out what seemed like every air molecule in the room. It didn't work. Both his mind, racing out of control, and his gut, blasting his breakfast with acidic juices, were sabotaging his efforts.

Anger, coursing through his veins like a herd of elk gone amok, pushed him to scream, "Mitzi, where in taffy tarnation are you? Disappearing for two and a half months is not okay. Taffy tarnation. If you were planning to leave me for good, why didn't you tell me? What are you anyway? A yellow-bellied snow goose?" Pausing, he gulped his latte, which he had taken to downing each morning to calm his nerves. "Okay, Lady Snow Goose, just what kind of moose malarkey are you up to? If you think you're coming back here and making me believe resort hopping is all you've been doing, you're crazy. Icebergs would have to turn into gushing geysers before I'd believe that story. I'm not stupid.

I know you. You're up to something." Hesitating, he chugged more coffee, then let his worries rip again.

"Mitzi, are you dying or something? Oh, don't tell me you've got cancer or some other life-threatening disease. Fiddlin' nutcrackers. I'm your husband. You're supposed to share things like that with me. And if it's not that, then what can it be?" He tipped his cup, tapped its bottom. Realizing it was empty, he resumed his grumbling.

"Sure downed that fast. Hmm. Gulping twenty ounces of caffeine in what? Less than ten minutes. Should've known better. Now I've got the jitters." Boy, did he ever. He couldn't stand still. Nor could he keep his mouth shut.

"Mitzi, have you hooked up with some weirdos? Holy walrus turds. Much as I hate to think it, that could happen to you. Especially since you're so gullible. Yeah, with your willingness to do anything to please anybody, I could see that happening. Oh, what if some weirdos have conned my Mitzi into drinking and using drugs?" He shuddered.

"Or, maybe you've found yourself a new lover." As those pitiful words left his lips, his thoughts, along with his anger, spiraled into the unthinkable. "Taffy tarnation, Mitzi. You better not be supporting some gigolo with my money."

Knock, knock.

Startled, eyeing the door, he said in a civil tone, "Yes?"

"Santa, are you all right in there?"

It was Malka, his office manager. The lady who had applied as a fill-in eleven years ago. The lady who agreed back then to stay until he found someone permanent.

169

"I have lots of experience," she stated during the interview. "I taught school for twenty years down in the USA under the name of Marlene. I did that because lots of people there didn't like Jews . . . at least not then. But I'm not hiding it anymore. I was born Malka and I'm gonna be Malka. And just so you know, I'll only be here for six months, uh . . . until my husband's grant to study glaciers at Blitzen University runs out. Then we'll be retiring to my home state of New York. I've been wanting to move back there for years. Uh . . . my family lives there."

Six months later when her husband's grant ended, he got it renewed, year after year. And she stayed on, year after year.

"Are you all right in there?" Malka repeated, this time with more concern in her voice.

"Yes, Malka I'm fine. Believe me. I'm fine."

"But all that racket. What were you yelling about?"

"Oh, uh, I just stubbed my big toe soldier. That's all."

"Not quite the truth," he mumbled, moving away from the intercom. "But how can I tell her or anyone else my wife is on a *different* kind of vacation. That she'll be home when she's *done*. If I tell anyone that, they'll think I'm crazy. Holy walrus turds. They might even think I did away with—"

"Okay. What are you mumbling about now? Is it something I need to hear?"

Started by Malka's voice, Santa looked down at the intercom. "Fiddlin' nutcrackers. I forgot to hit the off switch." Caught off guard, he groped for an acceptable answer. "Oh, I'm, uh . . . uh, I'm just thinking out loud about, about how to, uh . . . uh, about how to improve the design of one of my toy scooters."

"Really?"

The schoolteacher tone in Malka's one-word reply told Santa he hadn't fooled her one bit. Still, refusing to leak a word about Mitzi's disappearance to her, or anyone else, he, holding fast to his little white lie, said tartly, "Yes. Really."

"Uh, are you sure it's just your *big toe soldier* that hurts?"

"Yes, Malka. But it only hurts a little bit. Believe me. It'll be fine. Sorry for the racket. Guess it brought out the worst in me, huh?"

"Yeah, well . . . it sounded pretty bad. Now, how about an icepack for it?"

"No. No. That won't be necessary. It'll be okay."

After that little episode, Santa made sure he didn't raise his voice until after he left his toy factory at quitting time. Then half running, half walking, he would cut loose with lonely-man sorrows. Nearing his lane huffing and puffing and dragging his feet, his wishful anticipation always turned into desperate pleas.

"Please, God. Let there be light. Just a little light in the kitchen window or . . . or at least a postcard in the mailbox."

Sadly, his supplications would go unanswered. He would find no postcard in the mailbox. Neither would he be greeted by light pouring from any cottage window. Night after night, disappointment sliced his hopes to shreds. And always, stress, weighing heavily on his shoulders, turned the climb up his porch steps into a monumental task.

Once inside his hauntingly quiet cottage, knowing he had to eat, he would force down a TV dinner while staring at the television. Sometimes, when drawn to his and Mitzi's faded wedding picture, hanging over the fireplace mantel, he would lament, "Mitzi, my beautiful Mitzi, what did I do to make you leave me? Did you get tired of my long whiskers? I told you before we married, 'Don't ever buy me a razor.' Is it my weight? You know I have to store lots of calories for my Christmas Eve trek. Maybe you're sick of living with a guy who looks different every year. Yeah. That's it. Isn't it? That's got to be it. Why else would you stay away so long?"

At times, he would speak defensively.

"Sooty bricks, girl. I can't help it if sometimes I'm Caucasian White. And sometimes I'm Indian Red. And sometimes I'm Asian Yellow. And sometimes I'm Chicano Brown. And then again, sometimes I'm African Black. It's not my fault my momma came from Black, White, and Brown lineage and my poppa was a combination of Red and Yellow. Then when they married and made me, Mother Nature mixed all their colors into some weird DNA concoction that produced me. Me! A frickin' freak of nature. It's all her fault. She cursed me for life."

Many nights, he would stare at his Soweto nose in the mirror and growl like a grizzly bear. "Nose, why do you have to change every year? Why can't you be like everyone else's nose? Why can't you just stay the same?"

Deeper and deeper he would descend into self-pity.

"Tell me, Mother Nature. Why me? Why did you make me different from every other living soul on the face of this earth? You know you could've given me an Indian nose, Asian eyes, Hispanic skin, and Nordic blond hair. Whacky walruses. I'd have been the happiest elf alive if you would've just mixed a little of this and a little of that into one *stay-the-same* package. But no. You had to conjure up these weirdo genes that, in one dip of your magic wand, change my whole appearance every year. Tell me. Why on my birthday do you have to rearrange my face and turn my skin into an entirely different color? Why did you do this to me? Huh? Why did you curse me for life? Why did you make me into a frickin' freak of nature?"

At this juncture, he would stomp his feet and yell, "It's not fair. It's just not fair."

Following whining, came demanding arrogance and a full-blown pity party.

"Yeah, I know. Everybody loves me. Nobody makes fun of me ever, huh? Hey, if that were true, why's my Mitzi gone? Tell me. What happened to that undying love and devotion she vowed to give me *forever and ever* on our wedding day? Hey, Lady Nature, why don't you tell me that? You won't, will you? That's because you haven't got the guts to show your face."

As if half expecting to glimpse a little old lady holding a magic wand in hand, climbing porch steps, he would peer out the window. "There's no such person," he would remind himself. "She's just an illusory figment that most folks blame bad weather on. And one my poppa used when I was a little elfin to explain why I woke up looking different every year on my birthday."

Despite this logical reasoning, he would go on and on with his guilt-laying trip.

"Listen, Lady Nature. Do you know how much I've wondered what the elves and Mitzi *really think* of my yearly racial changes? They don't say it, but I bet you a gazillion snow crystals they're all thinking I'm a frickin' freak of nature and it's *all* your fault."

As always, his ranting would bring on more and more tears until exhaustion drew him into a fitful slumber.

Now, lying in bed on the seventy-fourth night since Mitzi's departure—totally convinced his wife could no longer handle his racial changes—he moaned pitifully into his pillow. "Hon, did you get tired of living with a freak of nature? Is that why you're staying away? Oh, please. Don't let it be that. Please don't think of me as a frickin' freak of nature. Please, Mitzi. Please come back. Don't you know how much I miss you and love you? Don't you understand? I love you more than anything. You're the most precious gift I've ever had. Oh, Mitzi, I don't think I can go on without you. I'm so miserable. Please, Mitzi. Please. Ple-e-ease, come home."

CHAPTER 17

Mitzi, sitting at the control panel, clicking fingernails on chair's arms, was unaware both she and Santa were reliving the same events, each from their perspective.

"Shimmering icicles. He's sure into a long daydream. Well, if he can keep it up, so can I. Let's see. Where was I? Ah, yes. I had just completed classes at Vixen Vocational Center and was packing to go home."

Closing her eyes, she envisioned herself standing in her hotel room, beaming with pride for not only doing well in all her classes but also for getting through the whole ten weeks without a single elf in Kringleland recognizing her.

"Am I ever anxious to get back home and just be Mitzi Claus again," she said as she tucked her certificates of completion into a suitcase side pocket. She had planned to take the evening bus home. That, however, went by the wayside when Luba Zemlic and Molly Pollard, friends from her displaced homemakers' class, pressed her to attend the dinner celebration following their graduation ceremony. Truthfully, she longed to, but couldn't find the courage to tell them she wanted to skip the hoopla to go home to a husband she had led them to believe was dead. Reluctantly, she agreed to join them, even though it meant postponing her departure until morning.

"How could I tell those two I'm Santa Claus's wife when I told them, and everyone else, that I'm a widow?"

While stuffing shoes into a Ziploc bag, the question her assertiveness training instructor had asked on the first day of class popped into her head. "And why are you here, Elf Laura?" Instantly, she stated the lie she had rehearsed. "I'm here because my husband died in a mining accident four months ago, and uh, I need to figure out how to move on with my life."

Mitzi had felt pleased with pulling that off. Now, she felt frustrated and trapped. "I've lived a lie for ten weeks. Oh, why in taffy tarnation did I start this charade?"

Annoyed at questioning her motive, she threw her hands into the air. Her bag of shoes swung about, almost bopping her on the head. Glancing from shoes to bed, she heaved them toward the open suitcase. Overshooting her target, she watched them rolling off the far side.

"Why'd I lie? Why did I lie? Oh, why *did* I lie?"

Stomping around the bed to retrieve her shoes, two childhood *lying* incidents vied for her attention. In one, she had gotten away with lying. In the other, she had been helplessly drawn into her stepmother's scapegoating web; a web in which telling the truth would have cost her dearly.

The incident in which she had gotten away with lying, happened when she was eight years old.

Awakened by hunger in the middle of the night, she was heading for the kitchen to raid the breadbox when . . . FLICK.

In reaction to bright light filling the hallway, plus her stepmother's harsh voice—"Bohunk, what the hell are you doing out of bed?"—she pulled her elbows to her sides, crossed her hands over her bare chest, and stared down at her feet. Fear, intermingling with night's chill, set her to shivering. Her skimpy underwear, permeated with the stench of squalid living, afforded her no warmth. Feeling trapped, trembling, she could do nothing but stand in the submissive position expected of her. She dared not move a muscle. Her mind though was racing like crazy.

Setting her eyes on the hemline of her stepmother's *warm* flannel nightgown, she quickly made up a lie. "I . . . I must've been sleepwalking, Mommy."

Stiffening, steeling herself for a cuffing that would likely send her flying, she closed her eyes and waited. At the least, she expected a hard slap across her face along with some harsh reminders of her unworthiness while being dragged by the ear to the small bedroom she shared with five blended siblings. When that didn't happen, she dared a peek. Her stepmother, she could see, had caught sight of her father stirring in bed. As she watched him shifting sleepy eyes from daughter to wife, her heart thumped wildly.

Hoping to prevent explosive fireworks between them, she haltingly repeated her lie. "I . . . I guess . . . I guess I must . . . must've been sleepwalking, Mommy."

In the silence that followed, she prayed her father

177

wouldn't get up. If he did, they would fight, and that would seal her fate for the following afternoon.

Just like Pavlov's dogs salivated every time they heard a bell, Mitzi trembled whenever her father and stepmother argued. It was a given. After they fought, after he left for work, the redhead would go ballistic; and like a tornado that holds back nothing, she would tear into *her step-brat* with a vengeance.

While envisioning a hellish scenario of hair-yanking and face-slapping, Mitzi heard, "Get back to bed." The redhead's directive, like music to her ears, sent her feet scampering.

She had gotten away with lying. Two years prior though, back in Somerset, Kentucky, at age six . . . a *forced-lying* incident landed her in a no-win situation.

CHAPTER 18

"I did not start that fire. Mommy, please. Please believe me. I did not start that fire. I'm not lying. Honest. I didn't start it." Despite Mitzi's persistent claims of innocence, the redhead, as usual, processed her truth as lies.

Late August 1947 . . . the midday heat was overly oppressive.

Mitzi's father, Pete McCully, lunch pail in one hand, sloshing water bucket in his other, headed for his old Model-T Ford parked under a tree bordering the barnyard. Weeds, dry and brittle, crackled underfoot as he approached it. Propping hood, unscrewing radiator cap, he could see it needed water. "Least ya ain't bone dry," he uttered. "Know I've been pushin' my luck keepin' ya this long, but money's tight. Can't afford to have ya blow on me now."

Pete's shift at Stonega Coal and Coke would start at four o'clock. Living in the country, quite far from work, two-thirty was his usual time to head out. Today, needing to stop at Joe's Junk Yard to scrounge for a used radiator, he was leaving earlier. Two hours later, muttering, "Just my luck. He didn't have one," he arrived at the mine with barely enough time to don coveralls and lantern hardhat before stepping into the pully-operated elevator and descending a hundred feet or more down the shaft into *coal* blackness.

Pete knew this mine better than the back of his hand. At age twelve, after his father incurred a broken back in a mining accident, after two company men hauled him home over cobblestone streets in a mule cart, after one grabbed his arms and the other his legs and dumped him at his front door, after a month of fine neighbors contributing food from their larders . . . after all that, reality hit. Daddy would never be able to work again.

For the survival of the family, Pete McCully, twelve, and brother Tom, fourteen—much against their father's wishes—applied for work in the mines. Both lied about their ages, claiming to be sixteen and eighteen respectively.

Now, twenty-two years later, thirty-four and stoop-shouldered, he walked with a drag. And too, when a *sickly child*, he was twice pronounced dead by Dr. Jones. His "I don't feel good" kept him home so much, he only made it through the second grade. Lacking smarts, he could advance no further. Knowing he had to feed seven mouths, eight counting his own, he worked overtime whenever he could. Since World War II ended though, rarely did the opportunity arise. Lately, Stonega was cutting hours.

As he worked his shift, coupling and uncoupling coal cars, plus greasing their squeaky wheels, he had no inkling of the fire or his wife's intention to incriminate his daughter.

<>•<>•<>

Why her stepmother picked such an energy-draining day for yard cleanup Mitzi did not know. Searing sun and high humidity had already zapped the energy produced from her meager lunch. Her stomach screamed for nourishment and her mouth felt drier than a dust-throbbing desert.

Water . . . She guzzled it whenever she could get it. And to get it, she had to buck her fear of the dark, plus her fear of getting caught. Often, her dehydrated body would push her to rise in night's still hours. On such occasions, she would sneak downstairs, push a chair against the pantry sink, climb up, grab the pump handle, and then pump and drink until her stomach could hold no more. During the day, when the redhead wasn't looking, she drank milk, juice, liquid of any kind, from cups left unattended by younger half-siblings. When sentenced outside for long, hot hours, she would scour weeds for tin cans holding rainwater.

Mitzi, her mouth drier than a sun-bleached clamshell, drooped like a wilted flower. She couldn't clench her thirst until the opportunity arose to sneak some water. As for hunger, weeds she would normally eat were growing abundantly at her feet. But under her stepmother's watchful eye, she didn't dare stoop to pick any.

Of the four kids directed to collect and throw rubbish into the loose-stone firepit—which lay a mere *stone's throw* from the house—she was the only one not whining. She didn't dare. She could tell the other kids' bellyaching was getting on the redhead's nerves. As Mitzi expected, it wasn't long before she caved. "Oh, go on. Get in the house. I'll be in as soon as I light this fire. Not you, bohunk. You're not finished yet. You get around to the other side of the house and pick up all the trash over there. All of it. You hear? Go on. Get. And be quick about it."

Dutifully, Mitzi did as she was told. A short time later, rounding the northeastern corner of the house, intending to deliver her armload of trash to her stepmother, she stopped short and stared. Flames, bright red flames raying out from the loose-stone firepit, tongue-licking dry weeds, met her eyes. Immediately assessing the situation as bad—very bad—she sprang into action.

Dropping her armload of trash, she ran up porch steps. Bursting through the screen door, she screamed, "Fire, Mommy, fire." Frantically she tugged at the redhead's arm with one hand while pointing toward the door with her other. Again, and again, she screamed, "Fire, Mommy, fire." The redhead, tending her baby of one year, repeatedly shoved her away. Mitzi, astute enough to know at the tender age of six that disaster was looming, refused to give up. Repeatedly, she screamed, "Fire, Mommy, fire. Fire, Mommy, fire."

The redhead, assuming her step-brat was referring to the fire she had lit earlier, said to Willy, "Go outside and see what the bohunk is yapping about."

Seconds later, Willy came flying through the screen door, screaming, "Ma. Ma. The whole field is on fire."

After Willy peddled five miles to the nearest neighbor to call the fire department, after Karen, Mitzi and Janice

182

worked the child bucket brigade from the handpump over pantry sink to the field in flames, after the coal shed burned to the ground, after fire crept to within yards of the tinder-dry farmhouse, after the firetruck *finally* arrived at sundown, after a late peanut-butter-and-jelly dinner filled tummies, after little ones were tucked into bed . . . after all that, the redhead ordered Mitzi to stand in front of her.

"You bastard, you started that fire. Didn't you?"

"No, Mommy. I didn't. Honest, I didn't."

The redhead, grabbing and squeezing her arms, yelled, "You lying son-of-a-bitch. Look at me. You did start it."

Mitzi, her restrained arms hurting, sobbed, "No, Mommy. Honest. I didn't start that fire. No, I didn't—"

"Don't 'NO' me, you lying son-of-a-bitch. You did."

"No, I didn't. Honest. I'm telling the truth."

"You lying bastard, you were the only one out there. So, you started it. And since you did, tomorrow morning you will stand in front of your daddy, and you will tell him you started that fire. And if you don't, I will give you such a beating, you'll be sorry you were ever born. Do you understand me? Huh, shithead? Answer me. And stop that blubbering before I give you something to really cry about."

Mitzi, fighting hard to hold back sobs, nodded yes.

"Good. Now, you bastard, get to bed."

Mitzi woke the next morning dreading her fate. The time between her early awakening and her father's rise dragged.

When he finally came downstairs, the redhead waited until he finished breakfast before summoning her.

"Mitzi, get out here."

Head down, dragging bare feet through a hallway running from playroom near the front door to kitchen at the opposite end of the house, she approached her father. Glimpsing him—coffee cup in hand, leaning against the cold cast-iron cookstove—she looked into eyes eking despair. The redhead, standing beside him, giving her a contemptuous look, yelled, "Come on. Stop your stalling. Get the hell over here."

That morning, with cruel threats looming over her, a browbeaten little girl—eyes aimed at bare feet—slowly approached her daddy. She did not want to lie to this man whom she hardly knew. But it was either spit out the lie or endure the beating promised by her sinister stepmother.

Standing before her father, who slept and ate at the house but never so much as acknowledged her existence with a *Hi*, she heard her stepmother saying sweetly, "Now, tell the truth. Tell daddy who started that fire. Tell daddy the truth. Come on. Tell daddy the truth."

The truth? The truth would bring wrath upon her head.

After *Tell daddy the truth* registered in her head for the fourth time, she, fully aware of the fate promised if she failed to meet her stepmother's expectation, reluctantly forced the expected lie up her throat.

"I started the fire."

Her barely audible lie slid softly off her parched lips.

Even so, she knew the man called *daddy* had heard it because no other sound in the room competed with it.

A moment later, she glanced up at him. Despair, outlining his haggard face, seemed to be sucking the will to stand erect from his shoulders. Reading sadness in his eyes, she knew the lie she *did not* dare *not* tell, for fear of being beaten unmercifully, had pierced his heart.

Sneakily glimpsing her stepmother's face—now turned to her husband's—Mitzi immediately understood her bloom of gloating satisfaction. Her father's emotional pain was giving her joy. At that moment, Mitzi realized her intent had not only been to scapegoat her, but to also pierce his heart, to convince him his firstborn child had committed this horrific deed. And he bought it.

The next thing Mitzi caught sight of was her stepmother's hand motioning her to get out. Thankful for the dismissal, she hurriedly pushed her way through the kitchen screen door. As she burst forth into stifling heat, she believed in the eyes of the man called Daddy, she would, from that day forth, be viewed as a very, very bad girl, never, ever to be trusted. Moments later, sitting alone on a porch step, steeped with the pain of entrapment, she dropped her head to her knees and cried her heart out.

"Back then, I lied to survive," Mitzi reminded herself as she shook off feelings associated with that memory. "But why did I lie in my classes for ten weeks?"

Dropping shoes into the suitcase, she rationalized, "But I wasn't lying. I was pretending. And it must've been okay for me to do so because my husband does it every Christmas Season. When he goes out into the world, does he tell anyone he's the *real* Santa Claus? No. He even lets the whole world believe his symbolic color is *always* White when it's not. So, if he can pretend for a whole lifetime to be something he's not, surely no harm can come from me living a lie for a measly ten weeks."

Done with that spiel, Mitzi jerked the closet door open. All but two hangers were empty. One held her navy blue suit for her morning bus trip home, the other her casual black slacks for the evening's farewell dinner. She pulled her slacks off the hanger and laid them neatly across the bed.

"I wonder what Luba and Molly would think if they found out I was playing this charade." On her way to the bathroom to shower, she resolved, "I'll tell them who I am after I get back with Santa. That is if he'll take me back. It's been ten weeks. Stupid me. I should've called or at least sent him another postcard or two. But if I had called, most likely I would've caved to his pleas to come home. And receiving more postcards from the same place . . . Why he would've then known I had never left the Land of Icebergs."

Later, at the farewell dinner, when Mitzi shared her intention to leave for North Pole Village in the morning, a startled Molly Pollard blurted, "What! Elf Laura, you're leaving us? Why? Why are you going up there?"

"Well, I have family there," she answered, deliberately

keeping her response vague.

"Are you coming back?" Luba Zemlic pressed.

"I'm not sure." And she wasn't. For days, she had been plagued with vacillating visions. On the one hand, Santa greeting her with open arms. On the other, him exploding with anger and rejecting her. So, to everyone's probing questions, she kept her responses vague.

"I'm just going up there to visit some family. I might look for a job. Maybe I'll stay. I don't know. Right now, I'm keeping my options open."

Around midnight, shortly after returning from her graduation gala, she, pajama-clad, stood near the window, gazing into the vast starlit sky. "Santa," she said, "tomorrow I'm going to give you the biggest surprise of your life."

Minutes later, pulling back bedcovers, she prayed this would be her last night sleeping alone. "Please, God. Please. Let him greet me with open arms in the morning." As she slid into bed, she felt her body trembling. Whether induced by night's chilly air or from fear, she did not know. "It's fear," she concluded, pulling herself into the fetal position. "I'm afraid tomorrow . . . I'm afraid I might be rejected by the person I love most dearly. Hopefully not, but . . ."

The nocturnal hours passed slowly. She tossed and turned. Sleep eluded her. Far into the night, she fretted. "Will Santa like the new me? What should I say to him? How can I explain what I've done to myself? How will he react? How will he handle all my changes? Will he be pleased? Will he be proud of the new me? Or, will he bellow angrily, 'Get out. I never, ever want to see the likes of you again.'?"

Mitzi's anguish kept her in a frenzied state. Sleep came fitfully. As dawn approached, tension from worrying the night away pressed her to leap out of bed. She dressed quickly. Stuffing PJs into the suitcase, she said, "Oh, I can hardly wait. I'm going home."

Unable to go anyplace until the bus came, she paced the floor. A glance at her suitcases found her checking and rechecking to make sure she had packed everything. "Shimmering icicles. I can't stay in this room another second." Still, she lingered, sweeping her eyes across the room one last time before heading for the elevator.

To the desk clerk, who suggested she take advantage of their free continental breakfast, she said, "Thank you. But I think I'll skip breakfast. My stomach is way too queasy to handle food. Especially this early."

Mitzi found herself pacing the lobby, checking, and rechecking the time. "Dancin' Prancer. That bus won't arrive for another hour yet. Maybe if I read, time will go faster." Sinking into a plush leather chair, she picked up a travel magazine. Flipping through its pages, she scanned its words; however, the ability to comprehend their meaning just wasn't there. All she could think about was getting on that bus and going home to *her* Santa.

CHAPTER 19

Mitzi paid no mind to Santa's boot-clopping overhead. At this point, she hoped he would keep daydreaming a little while longer; at least, until she finished reliving the best part of hers, which, never in her wildest dreams did she expect or plan to do. "This, I'm going to enjoy." Chuckling, she leaned back in her chair, closed her eyes, and surrendered to fate's twist.

"Last stop, Dearborn Station." As intended, the driver's booming voice roused those who were snoozing. "And hey, folks, looks like we're gonna have us a decent day."

"Yes, it does," Mitzi said, spotting a small fleet of wispy-white clouds in an otherwise clear sky. "Hmm. I'd say it's a great day to come home to my sweetheart." Her words rang true even though her eyes conveyed concern about her upcoming face-to-face encounter with Santa.

Meandering through the North Pole bus terminal, she felt like an unwelcomed prophet. Again, and again, she waved at familiar faces. Many, in turn, nodded politely, but none smiled recognition. Some reticent glances she construed as, "Lady, I don't know you. So, why are you waving at me?"

"Hmm, nobody seems to recognize me."

Of course, silly. Nobody here knows Elf Laura Ponseta, her nattering Tomacita poked.

"Well, that being the case, I think I'll stroll down to Santa's toy factory and see if I can fool him before going home. Yeah. That oughta be fun. Except, no way do I want to lug these heavy suitcases around with me. Let's see. What can I do with them? Ah, I know. I'll stash them here in a locker."

Minutes later, a locker key pinned to her inside purse lining, Mitzi started hiking to Santa's toy factory. Upon arrival, she butted a shoulder against its heavy door and heaved with all her might.

CRE-E-EAK . . . CRE-E-EAK . . .

Slowly its old hinges gave way to her efforts. Stepping across the threshold, her eyes went straight to the elevator at the lobby's far end. Its cage-like interior—facing a rider-operated, accordion-action gate—screamed antiquity. Even so, the old, paint-peeling monstrosity still worked. Today, that was all that mattered. "Run. Run. Catch it," she demanded of her legs. Run, run, her legs did run. Catch it, they did not.

"Prancing Dancer. I missed it, and this thing takes forever to come back down."

Peering through the iron gate's negative spaces, she scrutinized two cables traveling in opposite directions. One pulled the elevator up, the other acted as a counterweight. As soon as they stopped moving, she pushed the up button and cocked an ear. Only faint *I'm-not-going-anywhere* clicks responded to her finger tapping.

"Blasted icicles. Some toymakers must be loading the dang thing up with cargo. Oh, why doesn't he install more elevators? Modern ones?"

Running her eyes around the lobby, the *new Mitzi*, disgusted with the drabness of the whole space, started pacing and venting. "This place is a mess. Look at it. Only one bulletin board. That's all that breaks the monotony of these walls. Why there's nothing esthetic, or inviting, in here at all. Hmm. Some plants and a few pieces of artwork would brighten it. Yeah. I can make that happen."

To abate boredom, she stopped in front of the bulletin board. "Hmm. Might as well see what's going on around here." Her eyes glazed over several production quotas, a worker of the month picture, bowling leagues schedules— all stuff of interest to Santa and his toymakers, but not to her.

Through a drawn-out yawn, she had just said, "Bor-r-ring," when a notice in big red letters jumped out at her.

"Red. Hmm. Santa's favorite color. Of course. Red to attract attention. Well, it's got mine." Zeroing in on it, she read aloud, "Wanted, regional production coordinator for Santa's toy factories. Applicants must apply in person. Schedule an appointment with Malka, Santa's office manager." She reread it silently, then said, "Well, blow me down an iceberg slide. I believe that's the job Santa was

talking about creating before I left. Betcha I could do it."
Imagining that unlikely possibility, her fingers flew to her
lips and her eyelids expanded tenfold. "Do it? Why, Mitzi
Claus, you wouldn't dare."

*That's right, Mitzi Claus. You wouldn't. However, if you as
Elf Laura Ponseta were to apply . . .*

"Yes. If I went in as Elf Laura Ponseta, why that would
put a whole different spin on things. I bet I could pull it off,
but . . ."

Her nattering Tomacita, quick to take advantage of her
pause, interjected, *You want that position, don't you? Admit it.
Hey, you've got the skills, so, why not go for it?*

"Nah. I better not. I *should* just be a *good* wife and go
home."

Should? *What gives with that, girl? And* good? *That word
enslaved you for the better part of your life. Girl, you need to stop
playing those old tapes. Listen. You don't have to prove you're*
good *to anyone, and neither do you have to live by* should. *But if
you want to be a so-called* good wife, *then so be it. Go home.
Forget what you've learned these past ten weeks. But don't do it
simply because you think you* should. *On the other hand, if you
want to take a risk, for taffy tarnation, take it.*

Mitzi, overwhelmed with the pros and cons of her
mental tug-a-war, hopscotched her eyes from bulletin board
to elevator, to factory door, to bulletin board again. "Dancin'
Prancer. This is hard. I'd like to apply for that position, but I
miss Santa, and I feel bad about staying away so long."

Girl, wake up. Stop piggybacking guilt with familiarity and all its comforts. Stop letting your past influence your thinking.

Mitzi, dander flaring, fingers curling into tight fists, shot back. "I've got to go home and clean my cottage. Maybe make Santa an apple pie. Yes. That'll please him."

Please him! Is that what you want? Girl, you're hopeless.

"What do I want? What do I want?" Mitzi stared at the clunky door she had pushed so hard against a few minutes earlier. "Shimmering icicles. That took muscle power to open. Now, to plug in some brainpower. Gotta make a decision."

Yes, you do, girl, and you haven't got all day. So, what's it gonna be? Are you gonna launch your life in a new direction or are you gonna go back to the way you were?

At this juncture of her mental tug-a-war, a question posed by her assertiveness training instructor—one that caught her off guard—popped into Mitzi's head.

"Laura, what do you do to take care of yourself?"

Automatically, the words, "I do things to please others," flew off her tongue.

Her instructor's comeback: "But that's not taking care of you, now is it?" forced her to take a hard look at the way she habitually ignored her own needs. Thinking on it now, she set her eyes on the old elevator bidding entrance. "Let's go for it, Elf Laura," she said, running with zest. Ignoring her stomach's queasiness, she pulled the accordion-action gate back and stepped inside the old box.

As the elevator slowly rose, a mixture of fear, anxiety, and excitement set her heart palpitating. Quickly, she gave herself the once-over. "No runs in my pantyhose. No lint on my pantsuit. Hope my hair looks good enough."

Hey, girl, you need to rethink that last remark. Replace it with, "My 'do looks just fine." *And add,* "I look fine too."

"Yeah, yeah. I know. I've got to stop worrying about every little thing. But this is risky and . . ."

The elevator's arrival on Santa's floor prompted Mitzi to zip her lip. Pulling back the old box's see-through gate, she stepped out onto the worn, red carpet. Heading toward Malka's desk, she mumbled, "Okay, Mitzi girl. Remember. You've got to think, talk and be Elf Laura Ponseta."

CHAPTER 20

Malka lifted her eyes from her proofreading task to size up the woman approaching. Ever mindful of her appearance, she tuckered a strand of silver-gray hair behind her right ear then greeted cheerily. "Good morning. May I help you?"

Mitzi cleared her throat. Despite feeling a flush creeping up her neck, she managed to disguise her voice and respond calmly. "Hi. I'm Elf Laura Ponseta. And, uh, I'm here to apply for the Production Coordinator position posted in the lobby. Are you still scheduling interviews?"

"Actually, interviews were supposed to end yesterday. But, no need to worry, my dear. Santa hasn't taken that notice down yet. So, I can schedule a time for you."

"That's kind of you. So, uh, when may I see him?"

"Let's see." Malka flipped through his appointment book. "Hmm. Looks like he has an hour free this morning. At nine o'clock, to be exact. So, you could see him then. Or, I see he has some time on Friday. In the late afternoon, at three-thirty. So, what would work for you? This morning or Friday afternoon?"

"I'll take this morning. I'm from Kringleland and—"

"Oh, you live in Kringleland. My husband teaches there. At Blitzen University. He's head of the department that's doing some kind of research on glacier ice."

"Really," Mitzi said, feigning surprise.

"Yes. He was supposed to retire ten, no eleven years ago, but every year, the U.S. government renews his grant." Malka, turning on the drama, rolled her eyes, spread her lips into a smirking grin, and threw back her shoulders, all while expanding her cavernous lungs with a hefty intake of air. On the tail end of a long exasperation, she said in a deep, frosty voice, "I daresay, I think it's just an excuse to keep us from moving back to New York City. Uh, that's where my family lives."

Mitzi, smiling knowingly, simply said, "Hmm. I know how that goes. Uh . . . can you tell me if Santa's come in yet?"

"Yes, he has. And even though it's a bit early, I suppose I could buzz him. What's your name again?"

"Elf Laura Ponseta."

Mitzi, realizing she had passed her first test, breathed a sigh of relief. Malka, whom she had known for years, had shown no sign of recognizing her.

During the interview, Mitzi couldn't believe how oblivious Santa was to her facade. With him accepting her as Elf Laura Ponseta, she hadn't the courage to say, "Hey, sweetheart, can't you see? It's me. Mitzi. Your wife."

"Elf Laura, how did you acquire all these skills?" Santa asked with great respect.

"Oh, I've been organizing my husband's business affairs

for years."

"You have?"

"Yes. My husband always bounces new ideas off me."

"I'm amazed at how much you know about toy production. You seem to know more than any other elf I've interviewed."

"Oh, toy production has always fascinated me."

"Really." Santa's eyes lit up. "Fascinated you, huh?"

"Yes. For years."

As Santa leaned back in his chair, Mitzi sneak-peeked his eyes "Ut-oh. He's checking me out from head to toe." She held her breath. "Surely, he knows it's me. He must know." Clutching her chair's arms, she braced herself for the inevitable.

"My eyes. They'll give me away. At every masquerade party, he's always been able to pick me out. No matter what, I've never been able to fool him. He's always said, 'Hon, your eyes give you away every time.' And today? Oh, I feel so vulnerable. I have no mask. I have nothing to hide behind, except . . . except for my new contacts and this curly hairdo. Watch. He'll realize I'm playing him, and then he'll explode."

"I've made up my mind," Santa announced, rising from his chair. Volleying arms forward, grabbing both sides of his desk, he stared pointedly into her eyes.

She, stiffening, looked away. The way he was ogling her, she expected him to say, "Mitzi, is that you?" He didn't. Instead, he shocked her by saying, "The job is yours. When can you start?"

Uncomfortable with *his eyes* drilling hers, Mitzi leaned back in her chair and lifted *her eyes* to the ceiling. She parked them there partly out of fright and partly because she didn't know what else to do with them. "I can't hide them. I need them to see. But he keeps seeking them."

Her worse fear—*My eyes will give me away.*—gnawed at her. Still, she kept trying to read his, knowing he was bent on reading hers. All through the interview, sneak-peeking his when he wasn't seeking hers, she could tell he was trying to take in the whole of her without being obvious.

Clearly, he was being obvious.

Mitzi knew her husband. She sensed his loneliness. She also suspected he was on to her. At one point, believing he knew, she had clutched her chair's arms to prepare for his rage. However, when he offered her the job, she realized he hadn't recognized her at all. Perplexed as to what to do next, she pulled a tissue from her purse and started kneading it.

Despite her desire to yell, "Santa, sweetheart, it's me. I'm so sorry. I know I've put you through a lot," she sat tightlipped, wrestling with her thoughts. "I can't believe he offered me the job. But . . . but dare I take him up on it?"

"You do want the job, don't you?" Santa asked, his eyes telling her he was eager to hear her answer. "Or, do you need some time to think about it?"

"Job?"

The word echoed in her head like a yodeler's voice in the Swiss Alps.

Job . . . Job . . . Job . . .

She struggled to regain composure. Initially, she intended to say no. But surprisingly, when her lips parted, out came, "Oh, yes. Yes, sir. I do want the job."

"Well then, tell me. When can you start?"

"Is tomorrow morning okay?" Dazed, actually shocked she had agreed to take the position, she rose from her chair and extended a hand to seal the deal.

Santa grasped her hand, not tenderly as her husband, but firmly as a businessman. "Yes, tomorrow morning is fine." Seeking her eyes, he added, "Oh, there's one more thing. I forgot to mention you'll need to check in here every day for the next two weeks so I can train you. After that, we'll set you up in Mistletoe Office Building. Oh, uh, it's just a few blocks from here. Does that sound okay to you?"

"Sounds fine to me," she said, heading for the door. "See you in the morn."

"At eight-thirty sharp," he returned.

"On the dot," she shot back.

Minutes later, playfully bouncing her feet down Santa's toy factory steps, excitement poured from her lips. "He hired me. Yes. He hired me. I got the job. Yes. Yes. Yes. He hired me. But, but . . ."

In the blink of an eye, somberness, like a menacing black cloud, overshadowed her elation.

"I can't believe it. My husband didn't recognize me. Hmm. Have I changed that much? Oh. My. God. What if I can't pull this off? Wait a minute. Elf Laura, *you* told him I

199

wanted the job, so, you have to do this for me. You have no other choice but to help me swim through this pickle stew. And you've got to do this without messing up. No way can you let Santa see *me* in *you*. You got that?"

CHAPTER 21

Santa, still daydreaming, checked his watch. "Shimmering icicles. I've been hiking around this platform for more than two hours. Oh, well, if the elves have the energy to keep cheering . . . Hey, that's great. Just hope they won't run out of steam before I finish."

Resting longer than usual at the Sleigh Valley post, Santa spoke as if the crowds could hear him. "Yeah, I can keep up with you. But luckily for me, I get to take four breathers every time I go around this thing." Re-energized, moving on, he visualized himself sitting in his office, reflecting on his interview with Elf Laura Ponseta.

"What a relief. No more interviewing and I know that elf will be a cracker-jack worker. She sure knows her toy stuff. But where'd she come from? I know every elf in this Region. At least, I thought I did until she walked in. Sooty bricks. I've always had an excellent memory for names. But hers . . . Taffy tarnation. Where has she been hiding all these years? And how could a smart elf like that live in my homeland without me at least meeting her? Fiddlin' nutcrackers. If I had, I would've put her to work years ago. Ah. Maybe she's an immigrant. Nah. She can't be. She knows too much about our toy production. Wait. That gal . . . Hmm. She did look a lot like Mitzi did thirty years ago. Except . . . except for that short hairdo and those surreal blue eyes. If it weren't for them, and her voice, I'd have sworn she was my Mitzi."

Santa, perplexed by the sudden appearance of this stranger, who in many ways reminded him of his wife, thought about the two times during the interview when he had looked deep into her eyes.

"Her eyes are so like Mitzi's, but she can't be Mitzi. Mitzi's eyes are hazel, and that applicant's eyes are blue. The deepest sky blue I've ever seen. I swear. She even walks like Mitzi. Maybe . . . Could she be? Nah. She can't be. Mitzi's too shy and accommodating, and that woman is anything but. Besides, my Mitzi's a homebody in the truest sense.

"And . . . and, my Mitzi would never pretend to be somebody else. She's too honest. Still, if it weren't for that gal's blue eyes and short hairdo, I would've sworn she was my Mitzi. But then Mitzi hasn't been that slender in what? Twenty, thirty years? And she'd never break a promise. She'd never cut her hair. No. I know my Mitzi. She'd never break our wedding-day pact."

Santa slid forward in his chair and propped his chin on upturned palms. For the longest time, he wracked his brain for a memory of Elf Laura Ponseta. Try as he might, he couldn't pull forth one smidgen of information on her.

<>•<>•<>

Nearing the next platform post, Santa thought back to how his pulse had quickened every morning when the time clock clanged 8:30 a.m. He knew Elf Laura was punching in. Always on time, she brought certain magic, making life worth living again.

Before hiring her, his work interest had plummeted. Often feeling blue, he would spend hours staring into space, sometimes switching back and forth from the good times he and Mitzi had shared to worrying about her present welfare. Day's end often found him grumbling, "Sock darning and home-cooked meals I can do without. It's sitting in that empty cottage night after night, missing my Mitzi, that's the pits."

He missed many things about his wife. Things he had taken for granted. Like good home cooking. Now, he was enjoying another woman's company—not in his cottage each evening, but in his office every day. And he loved it. Still, loving it scared him. At times, he even felt guilty. He often wondered what Mitzi would think if she knew how much he loved working with Laura.

Love!

Thinking about love and all its complications—especially if he were to slip up with Elf Laura—scared the Ghost of Winter out of him. Often, he would say, "That woman, whom I've yet to find any information on, is an employee and nothing more. But why, why does my heart tug every time I look at her? There's something extraordinary about her. Almost familiar. What it is, I do not know, except . . . except she sure reminds me of my Mitzi. If it weren't for those deep blue eyes, I'd have sworn she was my Mitzi. And too, her voice is different. Not Mitzi's at all. Hmm. Might Elf Laura be related to my Mitzi? Now, how funny would that be? Yeah. Ha, ha. A distant relative of Mitzi's working right under my nose and me not knowing it.

"Fiddlin' nutcrackers. I should've never hired her. But I had to. I knew the moment she walked in she was right for the job. On the other hand, if I hadn't, maybe that stupid moose dream wouldn't be haunting me every night."

Santa wasn't stupid. He knew there had to be a connection between his fondness for Elf Laura and the dream that had been haunting him since the day he hired her. Night after night, an adult moose, standing at least sixteen hands tall—not including its antlers—appeared in his dream. Everything about the animal spelled moose, except his snorting snout. That frightened him. Not that the beast was ugly. He wasn't. But his twinkling eyes, Soweto nose, and snowy-white whiskers—all mirroring his own— were a little too much. So uncanny was the resemblance, he referred to him as Santa Moose.

Once a roaming-free creature—before being shackled to a cart—Santa Moose would stubbornly weld his shanks to the ground whenever his peddler owner needed to make an important delivery. It made no difference how much his owner prodded him to move, he refused to budge. Sometimes he would stand rigid for the entire day.

His stubbornness frustrated one peddler after another. To be exact, a total of fourteen in less than three years bartered him away. Each, in succession, settling for less money than the previous one.

Even though he was strong and could pull quite a load, Santa Moose's reputation plummeted. Word about his stubborn streak traveled far and wide. One day, an old woman peddler, the spitting image of Mitzi, purchased him for three cents. Three cents! What a comedown. A good working moose was worth at least seventy dollars. Santa Moose, believing a value of nothing was a sure-fire ticket to independence, chuckled. "Freedom is just around the corner. I'll soon be living a carefree life. Yahoo."

Each night, after falling asleep, the same scenario unfolded. Santa Moose, assuming Mitzi Peddler would get frustrated with his stubbornness and set him free, boasted to a moose friend passing by, "Hey, Homer, pretty soon I'll be roaming free, doin' whatever I please."

His friend, slowing a bit, yelled back. "Yeah. Right. And how ya gonna eat? How ya gonna defend yourself?"

"Eat? Defend myself?"

His friend's comeback not only squashed his zeal, but it also put the kibosh on his plan. "Yikes. How will I make it in the wild tundra? For years I've been pampered with fresh moss and all the fodder I can eat. If I screw up and she sets me free, I might starve to death. Or, worse yet, some hunter might shoot me. Holy walrus turds. I'd be a goner."

Haunted by these fears, Santa Moose didn't mind Mitzi

Peddler tricking him into doing her bidding by dangling a clump of fresh moss over his head. He loved fresh moss and he willingly did anything to get it. Day after day, eyeing that moss, he would trot on and on from morning until nightfall, concentrating on catching and sinking his teeth into it. So fierce was his determination to get it, he never realized crafty Mitzi Peddler was guiding him right where she wanted him to go.

Santa, upon awakening each morning, could not unravel the meaning of this dream. "Does it have something to do with my feelings for Elf Laura? Is my conscience reminding me I'm a married man? Is it telling me I'd better not fool around with another woman?"

Ever since hiring Elf Laura, he found himself wrestling not only with this dream but also with a gamut of lovesick emotions as well. Sometimes he would catch himself dreaming what it would be like to be married to Elf Laura instead of Mitzi. That frightened him. Still, he couldn't bring himself to admit his feelings for Elf Laura were much like those of a man falling in love.

Repeatedly, he fought to keep his lovesick feelings in check. Often, he would scold himself. "Listen, Mr. Soweto Claus. Even though you go home to an empty cottage every night, you're still a married man and don't you forget it."

Forgetting would have been easy if . . . nightly, he didn't have to contend with that darn moose dream.

<>•<>•<>

CHAPTER 22

On the last day of Elf Laura's training, Santa entered his office grousing up a storm.

"Mitzi, where in taffy tarnation are you? When I suggested you take a vacation for as long as you like, I didn't expect you to be gone forever." Halting abruptly, he stared at his calendar—the one he was using to mark off days since his wife's departure.

"Holy walrus turds," he said, slamming his latte down on the corner of his desk. Fortunately, its lid was on tight. "As of today, it's been three whole months since you flew the coop." Plopping onto his swivel chair, elbow-propping his chin, he stared straight ahead. Glazed eyes, along with pouty lips, clearly broadcasted his foul mood.

"What if something's happened to her? What if she never comes back? What if she divorces me?" Fear of being served divorce papers loomed over him like a storm cloud weighted down by a ton of hailstones. Lately, whenever some briefcase-toting elf walked toward him on the street, his fear of being served rose from the slightest to the highest possibility. "Surely that couldn't happen to us. Or could it?"

The sound of footsteps drew him away from troubling thoughts. Grabbing his latte, taking a sip, he stared

207

longingly at Elf Laura strutting into his office. "She's so fit and trim." Setting his cup down, he cracked a smile. "Bet she forgot to punch in. Or was I so deep in thought, I missed hearing the time clock? Oh, Laura, what I wouldn't give to spend some *alone* time with you away from this office." Knowing that last thought could lead him down a path he would later regret, he pushed it out of his mind. He couldn't stop his melancholy though. It, pulling chin to chest, morphed his eyes, his lips, his whole face, into a pout.

Mitzi, approaching his desk, commented on his haggard look. "Santa, you look so down in the cranberry bog. Is something bothering you?"

"No. Nothing's bothering me. Nothing at all." Dropping his eyes, he picked up his latte and downed a few gulps.

"Hey. That cranberry-bog look tells me something's troubling you. Come on. Fess up. What's wrong?"

Mitzi, pert and alert Mitzi—alias Elf Laura Ponseta— skidded to a halt in front of his desk. Looking expectantly to him, she waited for a response.

"Shows that bad, huh?"

"Sure does. And I know we won't accomplish much today if you don't get it off your chest."

"Well," he timidly admitted, "it's my wife."

Mitzi's brow shot up three notches. Deciding to play along as though she knew nothing, she spoke in a subtle tone. "Your wife? Is she sick or something?"

"I don't know. I mean, she could be. Then again, maybe she's really happy. Happier than she's ever been."

"Santa, you're not making any sense. Can't you tell whether your wife is sick or happy?"

That did it. After three months of bottled-up frustration running amok in his head, he shot up from his chair and yelled at the top of his lungs, "I can't when she's not around, and I haven't heard a word from her in three months."

His yelling pulled Mitzi's hands to her ears. Fighting a pang of guilt, she drew in enough air to effectively fire back an exaggerated, yet believable response. "Three months. What a long time to be without your wife."

"Yeah. And for all I know, she could be dead or dying. Or . . . or lying unconscious in some God-forsaken place."

Santa, now pacing behind his desk, threw his hands into the air. Realizing he was swinging them around, sort of out of control, he quickly pulled them down and shoved them into his pants pockets.

"I know she's using my debit card to get cash, but . . ."

His stalling bought Mitzi time to think. "He's frazzled. And something deep inside is pushing for release." Saying nothing, just watching, she noticed him retracting tight fists from his pant pockets. That cinched her prediction. "Yes. My prophecy is right on. He's going to explode."

Santa, anger getting the best of him, mumbled, "I've got to hit something. Something right now." BAM . . . He let his fist fly. BAM . . . BAM . . . BAM . . . BAM . . . BAM . . . After repeatedly hammering the corner of his desk, setting everything on it rattling, he glared at Elf Laura and said with warbled emphasis, "But, as to *where* she is or *what* she's doing with *my money*, I haven't the slightest clue."

Taken aback by his angry outburst, although expecting it, Mitzi jumped. "Should I give up this crazy charade? No. Such a revelation in his state of mind wouldn't be good. I'd better not say anything. At least, not yet. Best to keep up this act a little while longer." Faking surprise, she said, "You haven't heard from your wife in three months? What happened? Did you two have a big fight or something?"

"No," he answered, his voice much lower since getting some physical release. "We didn't fight. I mean, she hardly ever got mad at me. Sometimes I'd get *really* angry at her. Especially when she'd put herself down. But her getting mad at me? No. Never. Maybe that was the problem. She was always sweet and lovable and . . . and agreeable, until one evening when I came home from my toy factory."

"Until you came home from your toy factory? What on earth did you do to make her leave?"

"I have no idea. I mean, I don't remember doing anything. All I know is, she started complaining about never doing anything but darning my socks. Then when she almost jabbed her stupid darning needle up my nose, I . . . I blurted out the first thing that popped into my head."

"What did you say?"

"I told her to go take a vacation. By herself." Santa said this with reluctance as if he was ashamed to admit it. "Grant it. I didn't expect her to leave so willingly. Just like that. POOF. She was packed and out the door."

"Why didn't you stop her?"

"Why didn't I stop her? How could I? I was the one who suggested she leave. I even gave her my debit card. Dumb me. She's free. She's got her plum pudding and can eat it too. *Alone.* Or . . . or, she could have a new lover. No, no. I don't want to think that. But who knows? She could turn into a floozy dame or—"

"Or, she could be afraid to come home," Mitzi interjected, shrinking back slightly.

Santa's voice rose. "Afraid to come home! Why would she be afraid to come home? She knows I love her. That was the last thing I told her before she walked out." Plopping down in his chair, seeking something to busy his hands, he picked up a paperclip and started uncurling it.

Mitzi, although startled by his outrage, managed to say, "What . . . what if she's changed? Maybe your wife's afraid you'll not like what you'll see when she comes back."

Santa's nostrils flared. "Listen here. I don't care if she's turned into a monster. I don't care if she yells and screams at me every day. I don't care if she never, ever darns another one of my holey socks. I just want her home because . . . because I love her. And I miss her. I . . . I miss her terribly."

"You do, huh?"

Like a locomotive running low on steam, Santa, through labored breathing, said, "Yes, I do."

Sighing, he looked down at the mutilated paperclip in his hand. "Stupid me. Why did I blurt out the story of my wife's disappearance to this elf, of all elves?" Despite embarrassment reddening his face, he glanced up to check

211

Laura's reaction, only to see her walking away.

"Listen, Santa," Mitzi said, moving toward the desk she, as *Elf Laura,* was using. "Women's intuition tells me your wife knows you love her, and she loves you too. Just wait. She'll pop in one of these days. Probably when you least expect it. So, keep the faith. Okay. Just keep the faith."

"Faith. My faith is running out."

Mitzi jumped.

Santa, noticing, said with sensitivity, "I'm sorry. So, sorry. I kinda lost it, huh? Please. Please, forgive me. I mean . . . Fiddlin' nutcrackers. I don't know what came over me."

"That's okay. Better to get it out than to sit on it."

As she spoke, Santa watched her leaning over, clutching her desk. He also detected sadness in her voice. Sadness that tugged at his heart and prompted him to make his move, despite knowing he shouldn't.

"Look, Laura, I probably won't be the best company, but how about dinner tonight to celebrate your graduation from this training? I could make reservations at Snow Goose Restaurant. How about it? Hmm? I promise I won't load you down with any more of my troubles."

Mitzi answered in a voice hinting nervousness. "Santa, I'm sorry. I can't."

"Why not?"

"Because I have a special celebration planned for tonight and to do it, I, uh . . . I need to ask you for something."

"What's that?"

"Well, I know I might be pushing it a bit, but I was

wondering if . . . Uh, could I leave a couple of hours early today? Maybe have the whole afternoon off? See. I'd like to go home early to prepare one of my husband's favorite meals. It's gonna be *private*. I mean the two of us having dinner together. Just him and me. He doesn't know anything about it. Uh . . . I, uh . . . I plan to surprise him."

"Hmm. That sounds like a reasonable request. Besides, you've been such a fast learner, we'll probably wrap up early anyway. And I'm all for couples having alone time together."

Santa said this with zest, although secretly he longed to be included. Also, the word *private* tore at his heart. "Yeah. Private time with a woman. How long has that been for me?" As he tried pushing that thought out of his mind, he eyed Elf Laura longingly. "Oh, her husband. He's a lucky man to have her for a wife. Her asking for time off to cook *him* a special dinner . . . Guess I should be happy for them. But I'm not. I'm jealous. And I'm miserable. And I'm lonely. Terribly lonely. But I'm not gonna let her know that."

Opting to weigh his misery against Laura's happiness, sent Santa tumbling over self-pity falls.

"What moose-pucky luck. While she's pampering him, I'll be forcing down a tasteless TV dinner. Then I'll sit there staring at the TV, trying not to worry about my Mitzi. Yeah. I'll try not to worry, but I'll worry long into the night. And Elf Laura and her husband? Bet they'll be cuddling and keeping each other warm all night long. And me? Yippy. I get to sleep in a cold bed all by myself. And when I fall asleep, that stupid moose dream is gonna haunt me until my alarm goes off in the morning. Frickin' fiddlesticks. Why do I always get the short end of the icicle?"

As the morning ticked by, Santa noticed Elf Laura seemed unusually high spirited, like a horse anxious to get on with a race. "Bet she's glad the training is ending. Not me though." Sadly, for him, the prospect of her leaving triggered flashbacks of Mitzi walking out three months earlier, something so painful he visibly shuddered.

For the rest of the morning, operating under a veil of gloom, he forced himself to concentrate on finishing Elf Laura's training. A few minutes before noon—masking his melancholy with a smile—he stood at the door bidding her goodbye.

"You've learned well, Laura, and I'll miss your cheery smile. But I suppose we'll see each other now and then."

"Oh, we'll probably see a lot of each other. And I want you to know I'm ever so grateful for all you've taught me. Thanks so much."

"You're most welcome," Santa said, gripping her hand, pressing a key into it. As she looked quizzically from it to his face, he met her eyes with a smile. "It's for your office suite on the fifth floor of the Mistletoe Building. Right now, it's just a bunch of empty rooms. So, your first assignment is to order some furniture and office supplies. Oh, and decorate it to your heart's content. And hire yourself an office manager."

"Nice," Mitzi said, throwing her arms around his neck.

Her hug caught him by surprise. Relaxing, closing his eyes, he, without thinking, lifted his arms to embrace her. Her closeness, her tenderness awakened emotions that seemed to be screaming, "Come on. Get with it. Caress her cheek with your soft whiskers. Run your fingers through her curly ringlets. Kiss her, ya old codger. Kiss her."

Such thoughts set off an internal alarm. Like knights dueling, his logical side began sparring with his emotions.

"I have to keep myself in check. My reputation is at stake." Still, with her nearness awakening his passion, he felt his self-control waning . . . fast. Too fast. Opening his eyes, connecting with hers, he said without thinking, "Oh, Laura, you're so beautiful."

For a moment, Mitzi studied his eyes. She had willingly succumbed to his tender touch. She wanted more but felt she had to pull away. "Thanks, Santa," she said, lowering her eyes as if embarrassed. "That was a sweet compliment. But I'm sorry. I have to go. Remember. I've special plans with my husband tonight."

Santa, longing for closeness, kept gazing into her eyes. "Oh, I shouldn't be feeling what I'm feeling right now, but your eyes . . . Beautiful. Beautiful. And oh, so-o-o penetrating. Penetrating! Mitzi's eyes are penetrating." For a moment, his emotional rollercoaster veered toward the belief that Elf Laura was Mitzi. That is until his integrity stepped in and put on the brakes.

"Stop that. Wishful thinking isn't going to change anything. And understand this, mister. Even though Laura's eyes are penetrating like Mitzi's, it doesn't make them Mitzi's. Besides, the eyes you're gazing into are blue. A deep-sea blue. And Mitzi's eyes are hazel. Always have been, and always will be."

Feeling like a warrior defeated in battle—no less by this woman's husband whom he had yet to meet—Santa, resignedly dropped his arms to his sides.

Mitzi, long perceptive to Santa's emotions, noticed a subtle shift in his mood seconds before he loosened his grip. She, herself, feeling uncomfortable, turned and fast-trotted over to the elevator without looking back. On her way, sighting an empty chair at Malka's desk, she, drawing hand to mouth, gasped. "Oh, Malka, what would've you thought had you witnessed *Elf Laura* and Santa hugging just then?"

Santa, emotionally raw, managed to blink back tears until *Laura* enclosed herself in the old elevator and hit the down button. Then the dam broke. Tears, along with head chatter, flowed freely. "Oh, I'm so miserable and she seems so happy *[sniff, sniff]*. Fiddlin' nutcrackers. If Mitzi never comes home *[sniff]*, will I ever find happiness again?"

Stepping back into his office, he said wistfully, "Sure wish that moment didn't have to end. But then, it's best it did." Still, his desire for more pulled him across the room to a window facing the street. Sighting Elf Laura bouncing down his factory steps, he brightened. Thoughts of their embrace kept him staring until she turned the corner.

"Oh, that hug felt so good." Trembling at the thought of what could have happened, he scolded himself. "Listen, ya old bloke, you're a married man. So, you better get all thoughts of courting that woman out of your mind. You're not going to be unfaithful to your wife no matter how long she stays away. Hear! Besides Elf Laura is married. Oh. My. God. She's married." His eyes bulged disbelief as if that fact was sinking in for the first time.

"So, why in the past two weeks didn't she say a word about her husband? Not a word since the interview. Not until today. He must be an important person. Dancin' Prancer. Why don't I know a thing about the Ponseta family?" He scratched his head, hoping that would stir his memory. Much to his dismay, it didn't.

"Might as well complete her training report even though right now I've less energy than a polar bear in hibernation." Dragging his feet over to his desk, he searched through his computer for the right form. "Shouldn't take me more than five minutes to complete it. Then what? Humph. Guess I could hop an iceberg and head south. Meet up with a polar bear for dinner. Yeah. Right. Wouldn't that be fun?"

Ripe with self-pity—much like a cranberry left behind in a vast bog after the others had been harvested—he felt abandoned and angry.

"You cheated me, Elf Laura Ponseta. You cheated me out of an afternoon of wit and laughter. Now I have no one to spin tales with for the rest of the day. Anyway, who wants to keep company with an old, roly-poly Santa Claus? For sure, Mitzi doesn't. Probably no one else does either. Yeah. Everybody wants my toys, but does anyone want me? No. That's because I'm a frickin' freak of nature. And another thing, Elf Laura Ponseta, if you hadn't asked to leave early today, I wouldn't be doing this report until after five." Momentarily halting his grousing, he looked down at his clenched fists. They seemed to be saying, "Go ahead. Pound your desk again."

"No," he resolved. "Ain't any use pining for someone I can't have. Gotta let it go."

As his fingers flew over the keyboard, he boasted, "I can type faster than I can chimney hop on Christmas Eve. There's not a person alive who can type faster than me."

That remark drew him back to his high school days when selecting classes for his senior year. "Typing. Gotta take that. It'll be an easy credit and a sure-fire way to be around lots of girls because that's a class mostly they take."

The school had only been in session one week when his typing teacher, Ms. Gardner, became concerned about him being a distraction to other students and her teaching efforts. Her unease pushed her to say to principal Fields, "I've never seen anyone pick up the skill so fast. He's good, but also a showoff. Can we give him full credit and move him to another class? One he knows nothing about."

"Full credit? Absolutely not, Ms. Gardner. He's not getting full credit if he doesn't put in his time."

Later, after school that day, Mr. Fields, upon hearing a commotion coming from the typing room, ran to investigate.

At the door, he stopped cold, stared, rubbed his eyes, and stared some more. What he saw struck him not only as odd but also as incredible.

In the third row's first seat, sat Santa, hunched over a manual typewriter, pecking away like crazy with only one hand. A young brunette, he noticed, was holding his left hand while rubbing his back with her other. Another student, with long blonde tresses, was running her fingers through his snowy-white hair. And of all things, he was blindfolded. A dozen or so other elves were prancing around, trying their best to distract him. Their attempts, he could see, weren't fazing him at all.

Mr. Fields, asserting authority, marched over and yanked Santa's paper from the typewriter. As he did, a hush fell over the room.

Santa, knowing full well who had walked in, slumped down in his chair. The others, taking advantage of their principal's focus on Santa's paper, slithered away. Reaching the door, they ran.

Santa, realizing the gig was up, removed his blindfold. Not knowing what else to do, he stared at the floor and waited.

As Mr. Fields scrutinized Santa's *errorless* typing, befuddlement cut deep, deep valleys into his forehead. Clearing his throat, he thrust an arm toward the door and said one word. "Go."

The next day, when called to the office, Santa assumed he was in serious trouble. To his surprise, he was awarded full credit for his typing skills and assigned to another class, one in which he had to work doubly hard to pass.

"Done," he said, smiling smugly. "What that principal didn't know is I can think about anything while I type."

At that moment, he pictured Elf Laura, and her *unknown* husband, clinking wine glasses, toasting their happiness . . . both enjoying a blissful evening together. The image spoiled the moment.

"Blasted icicles. Some guys get all the breaks. Bet she'll serve him roasted turkey bird with all the trimmings, including cranberries. Or maybe a nice ham or . . . or prime rib. And I bet she'll spoil him with a homemade apple pie too. And what do I get? Nothing. Nothing but a tasteless TV dinner. Fiddlin' nutcrackers. I'd go home in a minute if my Mitzi was there making me a pie."

Weariness, taking its toll, showed in Santa's sagging shoulders. Knowing his wife would likely still be gone, he decided to lollygag around his office until six. Going home any earlier to a wife-less cottage was just too painful.

CHAPTER 23

Like the Energizer Bunny, the elves kept going and going. Somehow, their shouting mania evolved into a game nobody had planned. The rules were simple. When you see Santa rounding the platform, shout like crazy. As he walks away, hush up. Rest your lungs for the next go-round. It was a grand game for all, especially for little elfins.

Santa, breaking from daydreaming, peered down at the crowds. "Still cheering me on, huh?" At the next post, he expressed his gratitude. "Fiddlin' nutcrackers. All of you going strong like that . . . It means I can stay with my daydream. Have to say though, I didn't expect this. But it's nice. Hopefully, I'll finish before you wind down."

Marching wearily across the platform, bent on getting through his daydream before the crowds ran out of steam, he shouted, "Yes. Do keep it up so I can play out *Mitzi's Charade* to the end." Picking up where he left off, he saw himself, head resting on forearms, fast asleep, snoring.

Jethro, the night janitor, finding Santa slumped across his desk, snoring loudly, nudged his shoulder. "Santa, Santa. Come on. Wake up." Hearing a moan, he stood back, crossed his arms, and waited for sleep's hold to break. It didn't. Instead, one groggy *Huh?* followed by throaty snores, signaled he needed to try again.

"Come on, Santa. Ya gotta wake up."

Santa lifted his weighty head. Glimpsing Jethro with a half-opened eye, he let out a moan. "H-u-u-uh." Plop . . . Instantly, loud snoring overpowered the room's silence.

Frustrated, Jethro upped his voice and put more oomph into shaking his shoulder. "Santa, come on. You've gotta get out of here. It's lockup time."

That did it. Bolting upright, Santa yelled, "Lockup time!" Squinting, he turned to his wall clock. "Ten after six. It can't be that late. Can it?"

"Afraid it is. Had you a nice little snooze, huh?" Jethro, smiling, watched Santa funneling his next words through a stretched-out yawn.

"O-o-oh, I wasn't suppo-o-osed to fa-a-all asleep."

"Yeah. Well, ya did."

"But I've never fallen asleep on the job before."

Jethro, fast-walking out the door, waving *bye* over his shoulder, yelled back, "Happens to the best of us, Santa. Betcha you've been wearing yourself out working and worrying lately."

"Working? I don't know about that. But worrying? Yeah, I've been worrying all right. Worrying about where in taffy tarnation my Mitzi is."

As Jethro disappeared down the hall, Santa rose to his feet, mumbling, "Mitzi, Mitzi, are you ever gonna come home?" His eyes, although edged with tears, didn't spill.

"I hate this, lady snow goose. Since you disappeared, I do nothing but worry about you. Whacky walruses. What do you want? Are you hoping I'll file for divorce? Give up on you? Believe me. I've thought about it. Only it's been more like . . . like I've feared you'd have someone serve me.

"I'm lonely, Mitzi. Night after night in that cottage . . . sitting by myself . . . It's getting to be too much. And if Elf Laura . . . If she wasn't married . . . Hey. I was only a dream away from making advances at her. Good thing that stupid moose dream kept me in check. If it hadn't, I would've made a moose-ass out of myself. Sooty bricks, Mitzi. I'm having a helluva hard time and . . . and loneliness is the pits. And my patience is running thin. Fritterin' fiddlesticks. When I said to take as long as you want, I didn't mean forever. Honestly, I don't know how much longer I can take this . . . this being alone. I've given you space, Mitzi. I haven't tried looking for you. But this is ridiculous."

Santa bemoaned all this and more as he navigated around his desk, filling his briefcase. At one point, gripping a stack of papers, shaking them in the air, he ranted as though Mitzi were standing in front of him. "See this. It's stuff to keep my mind occupied after dinner. *Stuff* to distract me from worrying about the *no good* you're likely up to."

BOOM . . . BOOM . . . BOOM . . .

Mindful of his heart racing, he pulled a hand to his chest. Its rapid throbbing warned him to knock it off. With less intensity, he said, "Glad that's done. Now, to get some fresh air. Pronto."

Grabbing his parka, he flipped off the light switch and headed for the elevator. Along the way, he stomped his boots, as if trying to sluff off anger.

On his ride down, his emotions plummeted from heights of rage to depths of self-pity. A few moments after exiting the old monstrosity, he stepped into night's Arctic air, primed to lament.

"If only I was as lucky as Elf Laura's husband. He has her. And tonight, I betcha he'll get something like prime rib or honey-baked pork chops. And what do I get? Chicken and dumplings? Turkey and cranberries? Meatloaf and baked potatoes? Baked ham and sweet potatoes? Yeah. I wish. Taffy tarnation. A working guy should have more to look forward to than just tasteless TV dinners and cranberry-bog loneliness every night. It's not fair."

As usual, he nursed his poor-me feelings all the way home until . . . "Fiddlin' nutcrackers. Blasted icicles. Dancin' Prancer. Holy walrus turds. Bushwhacked penguins. Frickin' fiddlesticks. Yelpin' seal pups. Taffy tarnation. Wha-a-at . . . What in Elk Tundra . . ."

Off in the distance, down his cottage lane, he saw it. "Light!" Several windows, pushing brightness into the inky night, met his startled eyes. His excitement spiraled. His feet skidded to a stop. His jaw dropped. His eyes nearly popped their sockets. Caught off guard by the unexpected, he blinked and blinked. "Can it be?" Reluctant to accept what his eyes were seeing, he pleaded, "Please, God, please.

Please don't let me be dreaming. Please, please. No tricks."

Suddenly, everything seemed surreal, as if he were an actor in a play about to step onto a stage that had just popped up before him.

He rubbed his eyes. He stared and stared. Fearing disappointment—that someone other than Mitzi had stopped by to surprise him—he held back from accepting what his eyes were shouting. "It's real, man. It's real." As he teetered between disbelief and "Wow, this is wonderful," he felt, and heard, something giving. An explosion. His voice screaming, "Mitzi. My Mitzi. She's home at last."

Trembling as the earth does in the throes of an earthquake, he pressed his wobbly knees into action. He took a few steps. Then doubt slackened his pace. "No," he resolved. "This old moose ain't gonna get all lathered up over nothing. I probably left those lights on this morning." Still, a few seconds later, having to find out—and right now—he hastened his gait.

With the get-up-and-go of a twenty-year-old, he sprinted up porch steps. Bursting through the front door, his sniffer, assaulted by a spicy aroma, gave him a reason to pause to catch his breath. Smiling, pulling a hand down his beard, he drew in another good whiff of the sweet smell. "Ah, apple. My favorite pie. She's here. My Mitzi. She's home at last."

Into the nearest chair, he dumped his briefcase. That act, plus his excitement, nearly sent him tumbling head over heels. After steadying himself, he raced to the kitchen, shouting, "Mitzi, Mitzi. Hello, hon. Am I ever glad you're ho-o-ome . . . What? What the . . ."

The sight before him—bursting his happy bubble—pushed his eyelids to their outer limits and turned his face twenty shades of gray. His lungs, working overtime, pumped labored breaths up his throat. Frazzled, he lacked the wherewithal to know he was on the verge of hyperventilating. Gasping for air, he looked aghast at the woman standing before him . . . a woman he knew as Elf Laura Ponseta, *not* his wife. The sight of her—in his cottage, cooking, using everything dear to *his Mitzi*—was beyond his comprehension.

"What kind of joke is this?" Unable to make sense of it, he flinched inwardly. The woman before him, whom he had grown fond of the last two weeks, whom he had taken care not to overstep his bounds and who had made his heart flutter every time he looked at her, was standing not more than ten feet away from him—in his kitchen—holding a fresh-baked pie between two potholders.

"What? What is Elf Laura doing here in *my* kitchen?"

His trembling lips, intent on speaking, couldn't. He kept his head level while his eyes, like yo-yos, shot up and down the length of her figure. He took in her every move, from her hands setting hot pie on a cooling rack to the flirty smile she was directing his way.

Eyeing her stepping forward with outstretched arms, and winking at him no less, he stiffened. Then he exploded. "ELF LAURA PONSETA . . ."

His booming voice brought her feet to a halt. It also wiped the smile from her face. "What are you doing here in *my* kitchen, wearing *my* wife's apron?"

At that moment, his voice inflection matched Papa Bear's in *Goldilocks and The Three Bears*. However, there was a big difference between that fairytale and what he was experiencing. That story was fiction. What was happening *now* in his kitchen was real. Too real.

Elf Laura, still beckoning him with outstretched arms, took another step toward him.

He, scared silly, pulled back. Disbelief scrunched his forehead into a scowl. In shock, forgetting to breathe, his face flipped from ghostly white to beet red. Then gasping for air, drawing hand to chest, he clutched his coat lapels. A shiver coursed through his body and chills, sweaty chills, turned his skin clammy. Physically, he was a mess.

As he exhaled, he sought plausible answers for his confusion. "This elf refused my dinner invitation and then asked to leave early to fix a special dinner for her husband. So, why, why is she here in *my* kitchen, using everything *my* wife holds dear? And where's *her* husband? Sooty bricks. What would he think if he knew *his wife* was standing here in *my* cottage flirting with me? And Mitzi. What if *she* were to walk in now? God, please. Help me swim through this pickle stew. Give me some answers. Tell me what to do. And make it fast."

Sweat turned from beads to coursing rivulets on Santa's brow. Feeling crazed, as crazed as a dolphin caught in a fisherman's net, he began doubting his sanity. "Oh, what in taffy tarnation did I do after falling asleep? Blasted icicles. I don't remember doing anything. Am I in the middle of a crazy dream? Oh, God, please. Please let me be dreaming."

Wanting Elf Laura to be gone, he shut his eyes and willed her to vanish like a bad dream does upon awakening. A second later, opening and casting them to where she stood, he was forced to accept—albeit unwillingly—that she, still beckoning with outstretched arms, was no dream.

"Dancin' Prancer. Does this woman ever have gull! Why, why . . . How dare she take over my wife's kitchen?"

He struggled to come up with an answer. His gut, sensing he couldn't, seemed to be shouting, "Run, Santa. Run." But he couldn't run. He could only move back one step at a time. And as he did, Elf Laura, sexily sashaying toward him, matched each of his steps with one of her own.

Backward stepping into the living room, with Elf Laura still in pursuit, a light popped on in his head. "Ah, I've got it. Since learning my wife's gone, this dame schemed all day to take her place. That's it. She didn't want a dinner invitation. No. That wasn't good enough. She decided to move in. Holy walrus turds. She thinks she can take over *my* cottage and, and *me* too. And all that talk about her husband earlier today . . . That had to be a ruse."

To dodge her clutches, he stepped behind his recliner. Feeling safeguarded by the chair, he, voice modulated by tremors, tried reasoning. "For fiddlin' nutcrackers, Elf Laura. You . . . you know as . . . as well as I do that . . . that we're both married. And . . . and just because my wife isn't here, doesn't give you the right to . . . to barge in here and . . . and take over like this."

"Are you surprised, Mr. Soweto Claus?" As Mitzi spoke in her natural voice—something she hadn't done in three months—she watched Santa stiffening.

"What did you say?" Looking at her instead of paying attention to where he was going, he tripped on an area rug. Thrust forward, he grabbed the coffee table to break his fall. Holding on, allowing time for his wobbly knees to stabilize, he stared at its floral centerpiece. "These are Mitzi's favorite flowers. And that's Mitzi's voice coming from *Elf Laura's* mouth. But how can that be?"

Thrusting upper torso backward, he bolted upright. Too confused to say anything, he, hands now planted on hips, stared hard at the woman standing before him.

"I said, 'Are you surprised, Mr. Soweto Claus?'"

Again, reacting to Mitzi's voice, Santa's eyes rayed beyond their limits, his jaw dropped and the hairs on the back of his neck stood up straighter than upside-down icicles. "Am I going mad? I swear this woman sounds just like my Mitzi. And she called me mister and Soweto. Only Mitzi calls me mister and my ethnic nicknames."

Mitzi, eyebrows now arched like mountain peaks, said a third time, "Are you surprised, Mr. Soweto Claus?"

His posture—jaw dropped, eyes popping, fists compressed, chest bearishly heaving—struck her as funny. She couldn't keep it together. Doubling over, laughing fitfully, she said, "Oh, oh. The look on your face. If only I had a camera."

A scowl cut deep furrows across Santa's brow. "Huh? For sure, that's Mitzi's voice." He scrunched his eyes and jerked his head left to right. Despite past wishful thinking on the matter, the probability of Elf Laura and Mitzi being the same person was, at the moment, hard to swallow. "Is it possible? Might Elf Laura be my Mitzi?"

As if needing confirmation, he scanned her slender figure from head to toe. As he did, he felt transported back in time, to when they were both thirty years younger. Putting two and two together, it took him but a moment to realize he had been duped.

Fury exploded from every cell in his body. His mad side, rising in crescendos, showed in the swelling of his chest, the curling of his fingers, and the flaring of his eyes.

"I've been tricked," he screamed, "How could you, Mitzi? How could you do this to me? You . . . you—"

"Do what?" Despite feeling vulnerable, and nervous, Mitzi decided to employ her most reliable tactic: flirting. "It will calm him, I'm sure." Sensuously fluttering her eyelashes, then upping the ante with a coquettish smile, she, slowly like a cat on the prowl, sidled close to him.

"O-o-oh, o-o-oh," Santa moaned. The softness of her touch, her skin meeting his and the warmth of her breath seeping deep into his whiskers quickened his heartbeat. It also pulled the plug on his anger.

"Ah, closeness. Yes."

He wanted nothing more than to succumb to what he had missed for the last three months; but, at the moment, craving answers more than tenderness, he checked himself.

Determined to find out why she had stayed away so long, why she didn't write or call, and especially why she had tricked him into believing she was someone else, he pulled her hands down from around his neck. Stepping back, squaring his jaw, he nailed his eyes to her startled face. Slowly, in a dead-serious voice, he formed his words. "Why, Mitzi? Why? Night after night I sat in this cottage worrying about you. Why did you stay away so long? Why didn't you write or call? And, lady snow goose, I think you had some nerve playing this imposter game right under *my* Soweto nose. So, tell me. Why, Mitzi. Why? Why did you pull this charade on me?"

"Pretty good acting, doncha think?" she said, deliberately skirting the issue. Inching in closer, looking faintly apologetic, she smiled nervously. "Come on. Admit it. You didn't know it was me. Now did you?"

Santa, his ego bruised, threw her an icy stare. "Women," he said frostily.

"I do love you, you know," she said, unease cracking her voice. "And I didn't mean for it to go this far. But when I saw that announcement posted in your lobby . . ."

As Mitzi spoke, Santa studied her eyes. "Oh, they're so penetrating, so deep sky blue. No. No. No. This can't be."

What he saw twisted his heart into twenty million loops of agony. Anguish immediately constricted his airway. To her approach, he threw out his arms, sending her flying backward onto the sofa. His reaction startled him but didn't lessen his rage. Hovering over her, he bellowed angrily, "Lady, you're not my wife. I don't know how you found out Mitzi calls me Mr. Soweto Claus. That's our private secret. And yes, you do a magnificent job imitating her voice. But I'd swear to the Four Winds on Saucer Plateau that . . . that . . . that you're *not* my wife."

"I am too," she retorted, fighting back tears.

"Oh. No. You're. Not."

"Yes. I. Am. What more do I have to do to prove it?" she demanded, turning on him with a temper that matched his. "Do I have to tell you all our private secrets? Like the one on our wedding day when you *made* me promise to never, ever cut my hair. Do I have to tell you what you whispered in my ear then?"

Santa, still sizzling, thrust an arm out and waved an accusing finger in her face. "Lady, I don't know who you are, you . . . you conniving little snow goose. And . . . and I don't know how you found out so much about Mitzi and me. But, you can tell me every secret pact I've ever made with my Mitzi and I still won't believe you're my wife." He dropped his head, swung it from side to side in apparent disgust. Turning on his heel, he walked over to the picture window and stared blankly out it.

CHAPTER 24

"Hey, sweetheart, that old sun has traveled some distance since you went up there. So, what's it gonna be? Midnight before you come down?" After voicing that rhetoric, Mitzi, knowing she had no choice but to accept the situation for what it was, picked up where she left off in her reminiscing.

"Oh, I'm so excited and, and scared too," Mitzi said as she darted around her kitchen that first night home, putting last touches on her surprise dinner for her sweetheart.

Since leaving Santa's office, besides grocery shopping, pressing to find tapered candles and his preferred wine, ordering flowers from her favorite florist, and preparing a tasty meal, she—wanting ambiance—had hurriedly cleaned, plugged in air fresheners and set a table fit for royalty. She had worked feverishly against the clock. Now, with that clock's ticking eating up the dinner hour, she sat, worrying about Santa being a *no show*.

"The apple pie is just about done and he's still not home. Where is he?" Standing on tiptoe, leaning over the sink, she stared out the kitchen window. The inky night was too much of a contest. Even squinting, she could not penetrate its blackness.

"He's always home by five-thirty when it isn't the Christmas Season. I sure hope he didn't decide to stop by Pietro's Diner or Hanna's Hamburger Joint for a quick bite. Or, for a leisurely dinner at Snow Goose Restaurant."

Ding . . . Ding . . . Ding . . . Click.

Mitzi's shaky fingers grabbed two hot pads. Hurriedly she pulled the sweet-smelling pie from the oven. Hands full, she nudged the door up with the toe of her shoe. Aware its loud bang was followed by a muted sound coming from the living room, she froze. Her throat tightened. Her eyes rayed wide. Her lips trembled. Her heart fluttered.

The moment she had both dreaded and longed for was finally upon her. She hadn't anticipated how she would feel, how Santa would feel, or how they would play it out. Her lungs, demanding air, triggered a gasp. On the tail end of it, came the whispered words, "Someone's in the house. My sweetheart. He's home."

"Mitzi . . . Mitzi . . ."

Her name. Her real name. She hadn't heard it spoken in three months. No sooner had it enter her ears than there he was, standing under the archway in all his Soweto glory.

She stared at him.

He stared back.

She tried deciphering the look in his eyes. "He's shocked. No. He's confused. No. I think he's frightened. Or . . . or is he mad?" Somehow in the midst of her fluster, she managed to set the pie on a cooling rack.

Longing to hold him close, to soothe him, she stepped forward. Noticing terror in his eyes—him recoiling—she stopped short. In an attempt to calm him, she asked, "Are you surprised, Mr. Soweto Claus?" It didn't work. Rather, the sound of her *true* voice widened his eyes and unhinged his jaw.

Why she found his discombobulated look so funny was beyond her. She tried but couldn't squelch the laughter exploding from her lips. Seconds later, one glimpse of his fast-reddening face—a sure sign he was about to explode—was enough to snuff her giggles.

His cutting words, "How could you? How could you do this to me?" pierced her heart like a bevy of dead-on arrows. Thinking a huge hug after three months of absence would calm him, she wrapped her arms around his neck. Then drawing forth her best buttery voice, and batting her eyelashes, she asked, "Do what, sweetie?"

She remembered him loosely putting his arms around her and looking tenderly into her eyes. She expected him to draw her close, to kiss her. His hesitation alarmed her. When he shoved her onto the couch and yelled, "Lady, you're not my wife," her eyes filled with tears. However, she, determined not to crumble, held them back.

His refusal to believe her, to accept her, hurt deeply. But beyond hurt, his standing by the window, arms stiff, fists clenched, smoldering like a hot ember, and too stubborn to voice what he was thinking, had her mystified.

She, herself—with the pain of rejection so unbearable—

felt like running. Rather than acting on that urge, she forced herself to think rationally, to look to a probable future without him.

"Is it possible *the new me* has shocked him beyond acceptance? Have I changed that much? Maybe too much? Guess his rejection means I'll have to move out, get my own apartment. I could make it. I've got a job. No. Blasted icicles. I don't want to live alone. I want closeness again with the man I love."

Unable to tolerate his silence any longer, and determined to fight for their marriage, she, working to keep her voice level, asked, "Okay, Mr. Soweto Claus. Just what in taffy tarnation do I have to do to prove to you that I am Mitzi Claus, your wife?"

Fast ticking seconds turned into long minutes.

She waited.

He didn't move nor did he speak.

Ill at ease, Mitzi grabbed a couch pillow and crushed it to her bosom. "Is he going to answer me, or is he going to walk out? I hate this. But taffy tarnation, there's nothing I can do but wait . . . and hope."

CHAPTER 25

"She says she's my wife. Pugh. She's an imposter." These words played repeatedly in Santa's mind as he stared out the window, nursing his anger.

Holding to his stubborn nature, he resolved, "I'm done talking to this woman. She'll never convince me that she's my wife because my Mitzi's eyes are hazel not blue. And I know for a fact, no one can change the color of their eyes. Yes, my skin color changes yearly, but my eyes don't."

Passing minutes, along with chest-heaving breaths, played into calming Santa physically. That, in turn, helped erode his pigheaded thoughts. "Guess I have to tell her what I know. Otherwise, I've no just cause to kick her out. And I want her out like, like right now because I can't stand her playing with my emotions any longer."

Still operating on the fringes of anger, he whirled around and hurled his best gut-wrenching hurt and frustration at her. "You'd have to change the color of your eyes, Elf Laura Ponseta. You thought of everything but that, didn't you? And, Elf . . . Elf, whoever you are, you know as well as I do, you can't change what you've been born with.

Nobody can."

Anticipating a shocked look and a quick skedaddle from his cottage, he folded his arms across his chest and drilled his eyes into Elf Laura's. He expected her to crumble. But she didn't crumble. Neither did she look shocked. Nor did she look surprised. On the contrary, she looked rather amused.

Mitzi, rising from the couch, walked slowly toward him. Keeping a safe distance, she lifted her eyes to his. Purposely tipping her lips into a sly, smug smile, she emphasized every syllable of every word she spun off her tongue.

"You're absolutely right, Mr. Soweto Claus. I can't change what I've been born with. I wasn't blessed with racial and facial-feature changes like you were. Yes. I know I can't change the color of my eyes. But who says I can't cover them up, eh? Maybe tweak them with a little color."

Breaking from their stare, she leaned forward and cupped a hand under one eye. A moment later, standing erect, looking o-o-oh, so-o-o smug, she thrust her hand under his Soweto nose for his inspection.

"Contacts!" As Santa stared at the tiny saucer in her outstretched hand, his naivety slapped him in the face. "Stupid, stupid me. I should've known." Following this self-denigration, he clonked his forehead with his right palm. "They're such a deep blue. Why didn't I figure that out? Hmm. Guess I must've been too hung up on missing you."

Curious to see the difference, he lifted his eyes to inspect hers. Glimpsing one blue and one hazel eye staring back at him, he, still flabbergasted, shook his head in disbelief.

"Had you royally fooled, didn't I?" she said, grinning shamelessly.

"Royally? Yes. I guess you did," he answered, casting a penitent glance her way. "Contacts, huh? Blue contacts."

"My dear Mr. Soweto Claus, you might have been born uniquely different than anyone else in this world. And yes, your ethnic color magically changes every year on your birthday. But hey, you don't have the market on all the magic in the world."

Raising an eyebrow, taking in his reaction, she noticed he seemed too stunned to speak. As she leaned back to slip the contact into her eye, she heard him clearing his throat. "Ah, good. He's about to find his tongue."

"I never claimed I could corner the market on anything. But there's one thing I'd like to know."

"What's that?" she asked, putting her arms around his neck, her dreamy eyes connecting with his. This time he didn't pull away or push her away.

"I want to know who else was in on this little caper?"

"Who else, sweetheart? Sorry. I didn't seek the help of one little old elf in this whole Region." Pausing, she worked her fingers into his beard. After fluffing it a little here and there, she, eyes beguiling, lips pouty and voice syrupy, said, "Actually, sweetie, you were the one who put me up to it."

"Me!" Clasping her arms, holding her at bay, he yelled, "Bog wash. I didn't tell you to lose weight. I didn't tell you to cut your hair. I didn't tell you to stay away for three months. I didn't tell you to apply for that job. And I certainly didn't tell you to get those stupid contacts. Now, did I?"

Slipping from his grip, triggering a finger at him, Mitzi promptly threw the blame back on him. "Yes. You're right about all that. But did you conveniently forget, Mr. Soweto Claus, that it was *you* who made it all possible?"

"What! I made it possible?"

"Yes. By giving me permission to take a vacation for as long as I wanted. Remember?"

Mitzi, hesitating, sent him an indignant stare. Boldly stepping closer, pushing her face into his, she said in an even tone. "I think, my dearest, your exact words were, 'Go any place you want. Do whatever you want. You don't have to tell me where you go, or what you do, or anything.' And you made it all possible by handing me your debit card. And yes. I did do something different."

"But fiddlin' nutcrackers, did you have to become a completely different person? You know, I loved you just the way you were."

"Really," she said, her tone indignant. "Well, Mr. Soweto Claus, I might have been A. O. K. the way I was for you, but I was not A. O. K. the way I was for me. You see. I didn't like *what* I had become, or actually, *what* I had always been. So, I went on a self-improvement journey. And I learned a bunch about taking care of myself. Like holding my own and speaking my mind. And now, Mr. Soweto Claus, I like *myself* a whole lot more, but . . ."

Hesitating, standing on tiptoe, she pushed her nose up

to his. Fluttering eyelashes just short of his spectacles, she honey-coated her next words. "But more than anything else, sweetie, I like that you hired me as production coordinator under the name of Elf Laura Ponseta. Because if I, *Elf Mitzi Claus,* had applied for that job, you and I both know you would've found every excuse in the book *not* to hire me."

Santa, quick to protest, yelled, "What! You're still going to keep that job? Mitzi, you've got to be kidding. All my toymakers will have moose-malarkey conniption fits. Why I can hear them now. They'll say, 'What! You hired your wife for that position?' And they'll all be thinking, 'Why not me?' For sure, they'll accuse me of favoritism."

"So," she said, directing an indignant stare his way. "They can say whatever they like. And, listen." Pausing, she pulled her shoulders back and propped her hands firmly on her hips. In this stance, exuding the confidence of a high-powered attorney, she retorted smartly, "Let me remind you, Mr. Soweto Claus, you hired me because I have the skills. And, if you try firing me just because I happen to be *your* wife, I'll file a lawsuit with the North Pole Discrimination Board. And you can bet those flapping-red snow britches you're wearing there, I'll win too."

Santa, mulling over her huffy comments, scowled.

Mitzi, unwilling to back down, steeled herself for battle.

About twenty seconds later, after the reality of her words sunk in, Santa shook his head and smiled ruefully. "Mitzi, I can't believe you did this. I can hardly believe it's you standing there. How could you change so much? And so fast? Like you look like and even sounded like, until now, like a completely different person."

"Sweetheart, I worked hard and fast. And believe me, I never want to be the dowdy person I sadly let myself become. Not ever again."

Grinning with a hint of boyish pleasure, Santa stared at his newly *reconditioned* wife. "Well, I know when I've been had. Guess I'll just have to learn to live with the new you, huh? And also accept that you're a businesswoman now."

Mitzi thought a moment. Then spreading her lips into a victorious smile, she said, "Guess so, Mr. Soweto Claus. Yes. You'll just have to learn to live with *the new me* because no way am I going to let you slip through my fingers. So, face it. You're hitched to *the new me* for eternity and then some."

Her last words sent a flutter through Santa's heart. Smiling, reaching out, he gently tugged her hand.

She willingly fell into his arms.

Holding her close, planting a kiss on her forehead, he teasingly inquired, "What's for dinner, my love, besides that luscious-smelling pie? I am invited to dinner, aren't I? After all, I remember a gal named Elf Laura Ponseta asking her boss for some time off so she could prepare one of her husband's favorite meals tonight. Would she accept a dinner invitation to a nice restaurant from her boss? No. Can you imagine? He spent two weeks slaving away, teaching her everything he knows, and she refused. Guess she thinks more of her husband, Mr. Ponseta, than she does of her boss, Saint Nicholas Claus, huh?"

Santa remembered Mitzi snuggling in close, laughing.

Laughter. He loved hearing the laughter he hadn't heard for three months. At least, not as *Mitzi Claus*. Playfully he tickled her. "Hey, I can feel your ribs. Let's go put some meat on those bones."

Quick to respond, Mitzi shot him a look that clearly said, "Hey, buster, don't try making me into what I used to be."

He knew what her eyes were saying. And he liked it. Smiling, he wrapped his arms around her and drew her toward him. Her closeness set his heart throbbing. He needed no coaxing to kiss her, which he did passionately. Afterward, still feeling amorous, he slid his lips to her ear and whispered tenderly, "I'll always love you, my dear, no matter what you do to change yourself."

"Then you don't mind that I cut my hair?"

"Looks pretty good to me and feels nice too. And I must say, it sure makes you look younger."

"That was my biggest fear, you know. I was afraid you'd hate me for breaking our wedding-day pact."

"Mitzi, if there's one thing you've taught me, it's, 'I've got no right to run your life.'"

"And all the time I worked with you as Elf Laura Ponseta, you never suspected who I was?"

"Hon, as hard as it is on my *male ego*, I have to admit you did pull the moss over my eyes. And speaking of moss, I had this weird dream every night after that woman, *Elf Laura Ponseta*, began working for me. You were in it too. I mean, the old you. And now, I think I've got it all figured out."

With a snap of his fingers, he smiled the same way anyone does after solving a difficult riddle. "Yes. That clump of reindeer moss you were dangling over my head, *Elf Mitzi Peddler*, represented this little charade you were playing, didn't it? And I was stupid enough to stomp after it."

"Reindeer moss? Elf Mitzi Peddler? What are you talking about?"

"Ah. That's my little secret. But, maybe I'll share it with you while Elf Laura Ponseta has a *private* celebration with her husband tonight."

Mitzi laughed. "You'll never let me live this down, will you?"

"Listen, I'll tell you one thing," he said, pausing to kiss the tip of her nose. "No one, not one of my toymakers has ever pulled anything like this on me. Tell me. What did you do? Plan this caper for months?"

"No. It just came to me as I sat there on the bus."

"On the bus? What bus?"

"Come on," she said, pulling him toward the kitchen. "I'll tell you all about it while we eat. You are hungry, aren't you?"

"Am I hungry? Shimmering icicles. You're asking a man who's barely survived on TV dinners for three months if he's hungry? Oh, Lady Snow Goose, let me tell you. My mouth is watering for some of that hot apple pie and whatever else you cooked up out there."

CHAPTER 26

Santa's feet felt pretty good considering he hadn't sat down for quite some time. When he started his daydream, little did he know Jingle-Jangle mountain would quiver, on average, two to five times per hour. Its effect on his feet, so soothing, he ranked it up there with a professional masseuse's kneading fingers.

His stomach though was a different story. Desperate for nourishment, it was howling worse than a tornado descending on Kansas City. Knowing he wouldn't be eating until late evening, he tried appeasing it with a little pep talk.

"Yeah, I'm aware you're hungrier than a polar bear coming out of hibernation, but you're just gonna have to wait until tonight's feast. Then I'll fill you up good."

Weary at this point, he approached the Kringleland post with a drag in his feet. Leaning over the railing, he took stock of the commotion below. "Still going strong, eh? Ah. It sure does tickle me to see how much fun you're having. And oh, what a day this has been. Perfect for daydreaming. Just wish I had time to run through another. But, I can't let myself do that. Wouldn't be fair. Not after spending what? A little under three hours . . ." Pausing, glancing at his watch, his eyes flared wide. "Well, throw me down an iceberg slide.

245

I've spent nearly four hours daydreaming up here. Okay, Mr. Hum-Bow Claus, you've got to get on with your speech. So, just one more go-round to motion everyone to hush and that's it. And don't you dare start another one. Hear?"

On the lower platform, Mitzi's thoughts lingered on the blissful dinner she and Santa had shared on that long-ago night. When he winked at her and said, "Mm, yum, yum. This is so delicious and so much better than TV dinners," she knew he was overjoyed at having her home. And too, she felt confident he would soon forget the worry she had caused him. "He's so happy to see me, he'll . . ."

CRE-E-EAK . . .

The sound of wood stressing startled her. Lifting her eyes to interlocking beams overhead, spotting nothing amiss, she dismissed it with a shrug. About to lean back in her chair, she heard a faint thud, thud. Her spine stiffened. Cocking an ear, she listened intently. Recognizing it as Santa's boot clomping, she, relieved, sagged against her chair's back.

"Hmm. Am I imagining things? Probably. Think I need to relax. But . . ." She paused, looked up. "Taffy tarnation. What if those students didn't put that thing together right? Maybe they didn't use strong enough nails. Or . . . or what if they forgot to nail down some boards."

Now on the brink of hysteria, she yelled, "Hum-Bow, you better stop your daydreaming up there and get on with your speech before that platform comes crashing down."

She cocked an ear. Listened. His footsteps, getting fainter and fainter, never breaking their methodical clomp-clomping, let her know he hadn't heard a word she said.

"Wow. He's still going strong. For all I know, he'll likely spend a couple more hours up there daydreaming before giving his speech. And me? What can I do? Twiddle my thumbs? Dancing Prancer. I should've brought a book. Why I didn't is beyond me. Not good planning on my part. Should've known with this warm weather, he'd spend half the day up there daydreaming." She glimpsed the position of the sun, then spoke a little sharper. "Half the day? Better make that the whole day."

A sudden shift in her chair had her bolting upright. "Blasted icicles. There's nothing wrong with the structure of that platform. It's the mountain. It's . . . it's sha-sha-shaking a-a-and . . ."

As fault line flutters turned into serious grinding, the earth beneath her feet swayed like waves being churned during a furious thunderstorm. Glancing at the platform overhead, she cried, "Ho-o-oly wal-walrus turds. That cro-crossbeam. It . . . it just shi-shi-shifted. I-I'm sure of it."

Rat-a-tat-tat. Rat-a-tat-tat. Rat-a-tat-tat.

She jumped. "What's that noise?" Up, down, left, right, she jerked her head, searching . . . Catching sight of something rolling on the table beside her, she grabbed it before it could hit the ground. "A pencil. Just a pencil." Breathing raggedly, she said. "Am I getting worked up over nothing or what?"

Hey, girl. There's no time for denial. Face it. This is real. So, hold tight. More shaking will likely follow.

"O-o-oh, you-you *nat-nattering Tom-a-a-cita.* How I-I wish you weren't so-o-o ri-right."

Mitzi, determined to remain calm, and rational, hopscotched her eyes from one post to another, checking for damage. "Those things are planted in deep wells of cement and couldn't possibly topple. Or could they?"

Queasiness—much like seasickness—drew a hand to her stomach. And for good reason. The ground, again shaking, was playing havoc with her chair, her teeth, her everything. As it did, a feeling of doom swept through her, condensing all her emotions into one: fear. And it was blooming more terror than she cared to experience.

"Yi-i-ikes," she cried, looking up. "Tha-a-at pla-a-at-form i-i-is swa-sway-swaying . . . a-a-and a-a who-o-ole lot too."

Survival mode kicked in. Shifting to autopilot, she started reacting to shock while in shock. Her back stiffened, her hands gripped her chair's arms, her legs splayed, and her feet anchored her to the ground . . . all within one second.

"Santa, Santa," she yelled. "Are you okay up there?" She strained to hear. When he didn't respond, and her cocked ear failed to pick up any boot clomping, she hoped he had secured himself, but imagined the worse.

Feeling the ground swaying again, she feared for her life—and for Santa's—but knew she had to keep panic at bay. "Got-got to-to think rationally. Ca-ca-can't stay in thi-this chair. Got to do-o-o something to secure my-myself. Bu-bu-but how? An-and with wha-what?"

A quick scan of the area landed her eyes on a box overflowing with extension cords. Knowing what she had to do, she dropped to all fours and crawled over to it.

Moments later, right shoulder weighed down with a heavy cord, she crawled to the backside of the fireplace. Once there, she looped it through some ladder rungs—a fairly easy task compared to wrapping it around her waist and knotting it. Her shaky fingers pulled the knot as tight as the cord's stiffness would allow. Eyeing the swaying platform, praying it wouldn't come crashing down on her, she yelled, "Santa, I sure hope you had enough sense to secure yourself up there. If you ask me, you'd better get on with your speech. And make it short, so we can get down from here before this thing comes crash . . . or . . . or . . . just, just skip your spe-e-eech."

CR-A-A-ACK . . . RUMBLE, RUMBLE, RUMBLE . . .

All around the mountain, elves looked to the sky, searching for signs of an impending storm. To their eyes, the heavens appeared exceptionally clear.

CR-A-A-ACK, CR-A-A-ACK, CR-A-A-ACK . . . RUMBLE, RUMBLE, RUMBLE . . .

Hunter, quite concerned, kept scanning the sky for dark clouds. Within the heaven's blue dome—trimmed here and there along its rim with jagged mountain peaks—all he could see was a tight-knit group of cottony white clouds far to the south.

CR-A-A-ACK . . . RUMBLE, RUMBLE . . .

Many elves, feeling the ground shifting beneath their feet, started screaming, "Earthquake. Earthquake. Run. Run. Run for your life."

Other than darting hither and tither, seeking family and friends, most, in a state of shock, didn't know what to do. All feared not only for their own lives but also for Mitzi's and Santa's. Around the mountain, those trying to view Saucer Plateau, could not sight either of them. In the midst of this pandemonium, a young woman on the south side, binoculars aimed at the platform, thrust a hand into the air and yelled, "I see red. I see red. Way, way up there. It's . . . it's Santa's legs. I think. Yikes. They're dangling off the platform."

"Are they moving," came a concerned voice from her left.

"I don't think so, but I can't tell from here."

Hearing that news, many elves turned held-in breaths into mournful sighs.

"And Mitzi? Has anyone spotted her yet?"

"Sorry. I can't see her. Maybe someone on the other side has though."

The news, *Santa's down. Don't know if he's dead or alive. Haven't spotted Mitzi yet*, traveled around the mountain faster than an e-mail zipping over the Internet. In response, many frazzled tongues blurted, "What should we do? What should we do?"

The unknown set everyone on edge. Bickering erupted. It, in turn, played havoc with reaching a consensus on what to do. It also ate up precious minutes.

"Doncha think we should send up a rescue party?"

"I don't know. Do we want to risk losing *our* lives?"

"I know it's dangerous, but what about *their* lives?"

"Hey. If that mountain crumbles, we'll all be goners."

"Well, if it does, I'd rather die rescuing them than waste my time arguing with you."

"I say we wait until the shaking stops."

"No. We need to rescue them now."

"Not with all that stuff tumbling down."

"Stop being a whimper. Come on. Let's get moving."

"No. It's too risky. Besides, we have no medical equipment—"

"Hey. We can't just abandon them. After all, they're—"

"You're not thinking rationally. We need to . . ."

While voices escalated, and tempers flared, the inner earth's tectonic plates started grinding again. CR-A-A-ACK, CR-A-A-ACK, CR-A-A-ACK . . . RUMBLE, RUMBLE, RUMBLE . . .

Those rumbles—much more ear-piercing than previous ones—were followed by fissures breaking through the upper crust of snow and ice on the mountain's south side, quite close to the Blessing Day platform.

CR-A-A-ACK, CR-A-A-ACK, CR-A-A-ACK . . . Huge

251

chunks of ice, even rock, started breaking away from cliffs. CLATTER, CLATTER, CLATTER . . . BOOM . . . BOOM . . . BAM . . . CLATTER, CLATTER, CLATTER . . .

Mere seconds after the mountain stopped rumbling, elves turned their attention to the platform again. Word through the grapevine was, "Santa is still flat on his back with his legs dangling over the platform, and there's no sign of Mitzi yet."

Exercising its mighty jaws again, the earthquake's epicenter, apparently doing its bumping and grinding right under Jingle-Jangle mountain, birthed more fissures, which in turn, sent a lot of ice and rock tumbling. CR-A-A-ACK, CRACK, CRACK . . . BOOM, BAM, BOOM . . . CLATTER, CLATTER, CLATTER . . . Loose rubble ricocheted all over the mountain. When the rumbling subsided, someone shouted, "Jumpin' seal pups. Look. Look up there at the platform."

Eyes oriented upward. The exclamation, "What! How can this be?" spoken by many, echoed around the mountain. In the south meadow, elves gasped as the Krisville post, like a mere twig, snapped in two, flinging Santa high into the air.

Hardly able to comprehend the gravity of the situation, everyone stared in disbelief as he flew through the air like a limp red sock.

Suddenly airborne, Santa's lungs exploded. "YEE-OW-E-E-E. HE-E-ELP. HELP ME-E-E." His desperate scream splayed no further than the ledge he was falling toward. And his weighty body? It, landing with a thud, sent snow flying twenty feet or more into the air. Flakes, riding air currents at the weightless speed of goose down, settling layer by layer on top of him, made him look like a bowled-over snowman.

Elves, shocked, baffled senseless, stumbled about meadows, frantically crying, "Santa. What happened to our Santa? Where'd he land? Has anyone sighted him yet? And Mitzi? Any news about her? Oh, what can we do?" In the ensuing chaos, everyone kept asking questions. Questions no one could answer.

Santa, thankful for the soft, snowy landing and glad to still be alive, but aching all over, stayed still for a few minutes. Then lifting his head, shaking off wet stuff, his eyes met unfamiliar territory. His heart sank. He blinked and blinked.

"Where in taffy tarnation am I?"

Deciding to check his surroundings, he pressed a hand into the snow to gain leverage. His palm, rather than meeting a firm surface, went straight down. As his shoulder met snow, his fingers grasped for something but latched onto nothing. Thinking this odd, he withdrew his hand and peered down the hole his arm had just created. Seeing nothing but snowy landscape far below, the color drained from his face. "Holy walrus turds. I'm on a narrow ledge and

. . . and I'm so far up. Oh, I hope this thing is strong enough to hold me." Turning to explore hiking-out possibilities, his eyes met sheer cliffs. "Jumpin' seal pups. There's no way to get off this thing. I'm doomed."

Fright pumped a loud plea up his throat. "HELP, HELP. SOMEBODY, HELP ME."

Desperately hoping for a response, he cocked an ear, listened. Silence. Only deafening silence befell his ears. The sobering truth hit hard. Dropping chin to chest, he whimpered, "I'm too far up. Might as well save my breath. Nobody's gonna hear me. Taffy tarnation. I'll freeze to death in this sweaty suit. Yeah. The sun's going down and by morning, I'll be stiffer than . . ."

RUMBLE . . . RUMBLE . . .

The onset of an aftershock threw Santa forward, almost spilling him over the edge. "Oh, no. No, no. Please. Please stop. Please, no more vibrations."

Unlike the slight quivers he had welcomed earlier, these aftershocks were not wanted. Their coming one after another, each exceeding previous ones in intensity, terrified him. When they finally stopped, he hardly had time to think about securing himself when the mountain's next jolt came with a vengeance. Far more tumultuous than the others, it shot him straight up with what seemed like the thrust of a missile. Flying haphazardly through the air—mimicking an airplane with a clipped wing—his lungs exploded with frantic screams.

"OH . . . O-O-OH . . . HELP . . . I'M FA-A-ALLING . . ."

KER-PLUNK . . . THUD . . . PI-SHOO . . .

His descent into a deep, deep snowdrift was soft, but it created a stir that mimicked a raging blizzard.

"Wha-what?"

Santa aware a weighty force was crimping his legs toward his chest, reflexively linked his forearms over his head. This act bought him a bubble of air. In the ensuing seconds, he tried, but couldn't stretch a limb, though he could feel himself moving . . . slowly at first, then with immense speed.

"Dancin' Prancer. What's happening? Am I falling into a deep crevice? If I am, I'll never be found. No. I'm . . . I'm bouncing."

BOING . . . BOING . . . BOING . . .

"Oh, God, please help me."

Encapsulated in total darkness, Santa had no idea how much time had elapsed since he flew off the ledge. When the mountain shook a second time, he had reflexively shut his eyes. Now open, he desperately sought, but could not see, a speck of light. Light, elusive light—nonexistent now—sent his thoughts running rampant in the direction of doom.

"What happened? Did I pass out? Did I just come to? Am I dead or alive? Am I in purgatory? Am I stuck between Heaven and hell? Does earth still exist? Is my spirit being sucked into a *dark hole* somewhere in outer space? Oh, God, help me. Please, please help me."

With Santa's where-with-all usurped by total darkness, his anxiety quadrupled. "What's happening? I know I'm bouncing around in something, but what? Oh, uh, I can't [*gasp, gasp*] . . . can't breathe. Air [*gasp, gasp*] . . . There's no air. [*gasp, gasp, gasp*] . . . I can hardly [*gasp, gasp*] . . ."

Unbeknown to Santa, his compressed body now the core of a growing snowball, was racing helter-skelter down Jingle-Jangle Mountain's southside. And as it rolled, that snowball, licking up every *stick-able* snow crystal in its path, was not only growing exponentially on each revolution, it was also fast becoming a death trap. Sadly, he couldn't see anything nor could he move a muscle. He didn't know where he was going. And worst of all, he couldn't catch his breath.

"What's happening? Why am I being tossed about like a loose football?" Seconds before his airless tomb robbed him of consciousness, a meek "Help. Help." slipped off his lips.

CHAPTER 27

As the mountain swayed yet again, elves, looking up, sighted Santa flying through the air. From whence he came, they did not know. His landing, they could see, sent a geyser of snow gushing high into the air. While it was fluttering back to earth, a tiny avalanche—hardly worth worrying about—came from behind and flipped him over backward. Those below with binoculars, sighting this and expecting Santa to stand up, chuckled. However, when his body remained tightly knitted and started tumbling forward— drawing more and more snow to his sweaty suit with each revolution—not only did jaws drop, but also, shock slowed reactions.

"How can this be happening?"

"Wow. I sure hope he survives this."

"It doesn't look good."

"Yeah. That snowball is getting bigger and bigger."

"And . . . and he's trapped deep inside it."

"Our beloved toymaker is doomed."

"He's gonna die."

"Die? Don't say that. He can't die."

"But . . . but there's no way to stop that thing."

Before stunned crowds, that snowball-in-the-making,

with Santa entombed in its belly, kept bouncing down the mountainside. It, drawing more and more snow to its orb, and increasing in speed on each revolution, rolled haphazardly from ice boulder to ice boulder. Elves, standing stoic, dazed by the shocking phenomenon, seemed unable to do anything but express their observations and worries.

"Fritterin' fiddlesticks. It's so big and getting bigger."

"Yeah. And it's really picking up speed."

"Isn't there any way to stop it?"

"No. Nothing short of a miracle."

"It's moving faster than an avalanche."

"Can't anyone think of a way to stop it?"

"Believe me. If I could, I would."

"Hey. If we don't do something, Santa's doomed."

"Doomed. Oh, I can't stand to look anymore. I can't. I just can't."

For those watching from the south meadow, the on-coming tragedy was too much. Shocked, scared, stunned, dazed, numbed, bewildered—overloaded with all these emotions and then some—many, wholly mesmerized by its growing girth and ever-increasing speed, stood rigid as fence posts, staring at it barreling straight at them like a truck with no brakes. Not an elf realized s/he was standing on death's doorstep, playing Russian roulette with a loaded snowball until . . .

"Taffy tarnation. It's coming right at us. Yee-ow-e-e-e."

Thank goodness someone had the sense to scream. Just in the nick of time too. Fortunately, that scream broke shock's hold on the masses. Elf after elf snapped to. Screaming, trying to veer from that gigantic snowball's path, they took off in every direction.

"Yee-ow-e-e-e. It's going to . . . It's—"

"Run. Run."

"Go. Go. Go."

"Don't stop."

"Grab that little elfin. Quick. Scoop her up."

"Take my hand. Hold tight."

"Hurry. Hurry. Faster. Go faster."

"Move it. Move, move. Come on. Don't stop."

"That way. Go that way."

"No, no. Not that way. This way."

For ten to twenty seconds, pandemonium reigned. Elves pushed, shoved, yanked coat sleeves, swooped up little elfins, then scattered like mercury beads spilling from a broken thermometer. Whew. Miraculously all came through the human stampede with very few scrapes. That's not to dismiss, some barely escaped the path of that speeding orb.

SWI-I-I-I-I-I-I-I-I-I-I-I-I-I-I-I-I-I-ISH . . . THUD.

The ground, undulating like a giant tsunami wave, played havoc with everyone's equilibrium. Swaying this way and that, one elf after another toppled over like game pieces on a wobbly table.

PLOP . . . PLOP . . . PLOP . . . PLOP . . . PLOP . . .

By the volume of screams, it was evident everyone feared for their lives. Panic now superseded concern about Santa and Mitzi's welfare. Terrified, many yelled, "The world's coming to an end. The world's coming to an end. We're all going to die. This is the end. We're doomed."

In less than a second—faster than a TV screen blanking out after hitting the OFF button—the inner earth's tectonic plates halted their grinding. Relief hit the masses. Mouths ceased screaming. Eyes stared blankly. Cocked ears heard nothing but eerie silence. Then that gave way to . . .

"Oh, thank God. We're still alive."

The echo of those words, spoken by so many at the same time, rose around the mountain like the chatter of penguins welcoming spring.

With shock's hold broken, one by one, elves, cautiously, bravely, rose to their feet. Sighs of relief and gentle hugs reaffirmed life's preciousness. In the midst of this thankful communion, Hunter, among many, yelled, "That snowball. That giant snowball. What happened to it? Did anyone see where it went?"

Questioning eyes met questioning eyes. Shoulder shrugging and palm-up gestures indicated no one knew.

Then *hark!* One lone voice, Spice's—one of Santa's most trusted elves—lifted everyone's hope. "Hey, look. I just spotted it. It's over here. Inside the Victory Trees."

Sure enough, the massive snowball, with Santa still entombed inside it, had glided dead center into the Victory Tree formation. As it did, it tore down the crepe paper streamers woven across the entrance. It now lay wedged up against the Mediator Tree. The mighty Mediator Tree had achieved what elves feared couldn't be done. It had stopped that gigantic snowball.

Fortunately, the sudden impact loosened and sluffed off some outer layers of snow. Even so, a tangled mess of crepe-paper streamers, crisscrossing over and around the whole sphere like crazy zigzag stitching on a darned sock, held the rest intact. And Santa? Poor Santa. Everyone knew he lay trapped within its core.

Precious seconds ticked by as elves stumbled about, trying to orient themselves to what had just happened. In reaction to a shrill whistle coming through speakers, hundreds lifted their eyes upward to where Mitzi stood, clutching a microphone on Saucer Plateau. Seeing she was safe, many sighed with relief.

"You down there," she said with authority. "About a dozen or so of you strong elves get into those Victory Trees and dig Santa out of that snowball. And hurry. Be quick about it."

No longer did any elf worry about breaking Santa's edict: *No one is to ever enter the Victory Tree formation for any reason.*

Any reason? Pugh. They had just cause, and it was better than any reason. Santa had to be rescued. Those closest to the Victory Trees tromped right into his off-limits, sacred V formation.

Spice, taking charge, had already grabbed Hanna's hamburger flippers and hotdog skewers. "Now, remember," he said as he hurriedly passed them around, "only use the handle end of these skewers to do your digging. And be careful. We don't want to jab Santa with one of them."

Soggy crepe paper streamers and slushy snow flew helter-skelter as elves frantically dug into the snowy hull. Within seconds, one shouted, "Look, I've found the toe of Santa's boot." Knowing what that meant, all scooted to the other side and began tunneling like crazy, searching for one thing, and one thing only: Santa's Hum-Bow nose.

Mitzi knew Santa would need medical attention, and fast. Unfortunately, they had no transportation. Most locals had arrived on foot and those who came in from suburbs had left their snowmobiles, sleighs and skis, even their cell phones— as was required—in North Pole Village.

"I'll have to assign a strong elf to go for help. One who can run like lightning. But who?" From so far up, Mitzi couldn't recognize anyone. However, she could see one elf bending over, picking up a pair of skis.

"Skis!" She couldn't believe her eyes. Skis were the answer to an unspoken prayer.

"You, down there," she shouted into her microphone. "You, with the skis. Get them on your feet and ski over to the nearest cottage and telephone for an ambulance. And tell them to use the service road to get in. And . . . and be quick about it."

Mitzi's frantic voice startled Hunter. He glanced from where she was standing on high to the skis he had just picked up.

"She's asking me to go for help. Fiddlin' nutcrackers. I wouldn't've bombed over here on these things if Shelly hadn't acted so uppity this—"

"Hunter, Mitzi's talking to you. Are you going to go for help or not?"

Shelly's voice jarred Hunter to action. He dropped his skis and stepped into them. Turning to face her, he asked, "Will you snap my bindings, please?"

Stooping down to connect them, she surprised him by saying, "I'm sorry. I guess you were right about your feelings this morning."

"What? She's telling me I was right. And she's apologizing. I don't believe it. This girl, who Pietro said was a stuck-up snob, is apologizing? Stuck-ups don't apologize."

"Did you hear me?" Shelly asked, pushing for a response. "You were right about your feelings this morning."

"Yeah, well, my feelings didn't tell me something like this would happen to Santa."

"Will you forgive me?"

"Forgive you?"

Smiling shyly, Shelly reached for his outstretched hand. As he leveraged backward, she rose to his level.

Once standing face-to-face, he said, "Yes, of course, I'll forgive you. But only if you'll give me a shove to get started."

Hunter readied his ski poles. Glancing over his shoulder, seeking Shelly's eyes, he nearly lost his balance as she shoved him off, shouting, "Ready. Set. Here goes. Look out belo-o-ow."

CHAPTER 28

News of the Mediator Tree stopping the gigantic snowball traveled around the mountain faster than a meteorite. Like migratory elk, elves in droves headed for the Victory Tree area. Mitzi, watching the convergence from on high became alarmed.

"This is not good. I know everyone is concerned about Santa, but I've got to get them to make way for the ambulance. But how? What can I say? Ah, I know." Leaning into the microphone, being careful not to sound preachy, she said, "Attention, everyone. If you aren't helping with the rescue, please head over to Dasher Hall and start preparations for tonight's feast. Or, or . . . or go home."

She waited. To her surprise, no one budged. "Why aren't they moving? Ah, I know. They're scared. Scared Santa is dead. Oh, what if he is dead?"

A somber funeral procession flashed before her eyes. She felt her knees buckle. "No. No. No. You can't die yet," she screamed, stiffening her legs. "Sweetheart, you've got to be alive when I get down there."

Hey, girl, stop stressing yourself. Think positive. Hold yourself together. Say something that'll give these elves hope.

Heeding that nudge from her nattering Tomacita, Mitzi

took a deep breath. Leaning into the microphone, she spoke calmly. "Listen, all of you. I know you must be scared. Believe me. I am too. But we must have faith. Now, by the time Santa gets dug out of that snowball and examined at the hospital, he's going to be mighty hungry. And you all know how he likes to eat. So, please. Go start preparations for tonight's turkey feast. Oh, and whatever you do, don't forget the cranberries."

Casting an expectant glance toward the crowds, she waited for them to disperse. No one moved.

"Well, that approach didn't work."

Disappointed, she sucked in a deep breath to build momentum for her next command. To her surprise, before she could utter a word, one elf, heading toward Dasher Hall, thrust a fist in the air and started chanting, "Don't forget the cranberries. Don't forget the cranberries. Oh, whatever you do, don't forget the cranberries." The beat caught on. One by one, others fell in line, fist thrusting and chanting, "Don't forget the cranberries. Don't forget the cranberries. Oh, whatever you do, don't forget the cranberries."

As Mitzi watched one elf after another joining the line, she felt tension draining from her shoulders. Smiling, pulling back from the microphone, she said, "Well, I'll be. One elf induced the whole crowd to action. Good job. And whoever you are, you've got my gratitude."

Having diverted the elves to a useful task, Mitzi had one thing, and one thing only on her mind—finding out if Santa was still alive. Antsy to get off the mountain, she hurried down the path, chanting, "I must have faith. I must have faith." Still, with each stride forward, her fears mounted.

The moment she reached the clearing below Jingle-Jangle Mountain, she glanced over at the Victory Trees. An opening between some lower branches afforded a peek. Catching sight of a figure dressed in red, stumbling about, clearly disoriented, she, overjoyed, shouted, "Santa. Thank goodness you're alive." Seeing him on his feet, wobbling about, she shed not only tears of joy and relief, but also the foreboding dread that had laid heavy on her heart all the way down the mountainside.

The late afternoon's dipping sun, busily retracting the warmth of the day, reminded her to wick away tears before they froze to her skin. Dabbing scarf to cheeks did the job. Several deep breaths later, her gumption restored, she ran for her destination as fast as her legs would press through deep snow. Still, before reaching the Victory Trees, overexertion reduced her pace to a slow walk. As she got closer, on-coming lights, those of the ambulance, kept her from seeing an elf approaching. She jumped upon hearing his voice.

"Mitzi. Oh, Mitzi. Spice here. Sorry if I startled you. But I'm glad to see you. Come. We need your help."

"Why? What's the matter?"

"What's the matter? I'll tell you what's the matter. It's your husband. He's a stubborn moose. He keeps insisting he's fitter than a brand-new toy fiddle, and he's not."

"Yes. I can see that."

Sighting his tight fists, steely eyes, and set jaw—what she had long ago dubbed as *raging bull-moose posturing*—her heart sank. For a moment, she assessed the activity around him. Twenty or so elves circling him, on-the-ready to stop him if he tried to bolt, clarified for her why he was furious.

"You've got him trapped."

"It's for his own protection," Spice said, his voice defensive. "Actually, to be truthful, we did it because he seemed so discombobulated after we dug him out of that snowball. We'd say something to him and a minute or so later . . . Well, it was like nothing we said registered. And he keeps insisting he's gonna climb back up that mountain to give his speech. And I think you and I both know that would spell disaster. And if you ask me, he really needs to see a doctor. Good thing you sent that young elf to fetch an ambulance."

"Who was *that* young elf?"

"Hunter Swift Bear."

"And the elf who led everyone to Dasher Hall?"

"Oh, that was Shelly. Elf Shelly Jasselton. She has spunk and—"

"Thanks," Mitzi said hastily. Lifting a hand, signaling him to hush, she strained to hear what Santa was saying.

"All of you. Go on. Get away from me . . . Whadaya mean, hospital? Bog wash. Nobody's gonna make me go to the hospital on Christmas Season Blessing Day." Catching a glimpse of his wife approaching, he ordered, "Get rid of them."

"No. Now, listen to me. You've had a terrible accident and—"

"Fiddlesticks. That was nothing but a little joyride."

"Joy ride! You could've been killed."

"But I wasn't now, was I?" Crossing his arms, he glared defiantly at her.

Mitzi, meeting his stubborn gaze with one of her own, retorted, "Hey. Listen to me. Every elf here is trying to help you. We all know you're in pain. So, come on. Cooperate. You've got to go to the hospital."

"Oh, no I don't. What I've got to do is get back up there on that platform and give my speech."

"Mr. Hum-Bow Claus, either you walk into that ambulance, or I'll order you strapped to a gurney and carried in. It's your choice. Now, what'll it be?"

"Oh, all right."

Santa, wanting to avoid such humility in front of his toymakers, reluctantly stepped between two paramedics waiting to escort him. Midway to the ambulance, he turned around. Grasping his head, he made a scrunched-up, mistletoe-berry face at Mitzi. His behavior alarmed her. Not the face making. That she dismissed as normal. But gripping his head? She knew he only did that when he had a horrific headache.

The ambulance arrived at Sleigh Valley Hospital in record time. Dr. Swift, Santa's long-time ice-fishing buddy, met him at the door and had him wheeled into an examining room. Grabbing a metal instrument, he ran it from heel to toe on the sole of each foot. Santa laughed fitfully. "Ho, ho, ho. That tickles. What are you doing?"

"Just making sure your wires aren't crossed. Now, lie down here. I need to check you out a little more. Then I think I'll have my attendant take you to the next room to do an MRI."

Santa held back. Looking through the glass partition between the room he was in and the one housing the huge MRI machine, he pulled a hand down his whiskers and said dolefully, "You're gonna run me through that? Through something that looks like a convoluted railroad tunnel? You've kidding me. Right?"

"Afraid not. We've got to see if that tumble messed up your head. Or your back. Or, maybe a bone or two." Realizing his answer was not what Santa wanted to hear, he teasingly added, "Okay, ya old bloke. If you must know the truth, it's really to see if your head is full of snowballs."

Santa, thinking on that, said nothing.

Dr. Swift, noting his failure to match or exceed his sarcasm, pondered this oddity. "Hmm. What's with him? Has he lost his quick wit? He usually loves a good round of bantering, and he prides himself at being a master at it. So, why not today? Could he be afraid of the MRI machine? Is he claustrophobic?"

Deciding to try a gentler approach—much like he used with young elfins—he said more thoughtfully, "Come on, ol' buddy. There's no need to be afraid. This procedure won't hurt one bit. I promise. All you have to do is close your eyes and lie still while you're in there. Maybe do a little daydreaming. And in no time flat, it'll be over."

"I'm done daydreaming. Did enough of that today." Linking fingers behind his head, he leaned back and eyed the ceiling. "Doc, there's a big cobweb up there. In that corner. See it? Don't they ever clean this place?"

Dr. Swift, amused by Santa's avoidance tactic, smiled. "Hey, buddy. I know you're stalling. That you don't like hospitals. But listen. Besides all those scrapes and bruises you acquired on your roll down that mountain, you've got several nasty bumps on your head. You could have a concussion. Maybe a slow bleed in your brain. So, let's get some testing done."

Santa, tearing up, looked away.

Dr. Swift placed a hand on his shoulder. "Hey, ol' buddy, what's troubling you? Whatever it is, we need to talk about it before I buzz my attendant. Come on now. You know you can trust me."

"Well," Santa said hesitantly, "you'll probably think I'm sentimental, but I'm afraid you'll keep me here overnight. And then . . . and then the feast will be called off and . . . and that'll mean every elf from here to yonder will be disappointed. And . . . and . . . and me too. We'll all miss the merrymaking."

"Is that what's bothering you?" Dr. Swift swallowed hard to check a chuckle. Gripping Santa's shoulders, he looked him straight in the eye and said, "Hey, ol' buddy, you can stop worrying. The feast is still on."

"It is?" Santa brightened.

"Yes, it is."

"How do you know?"

"I know because a young man named Hunter got word from some young gal that orders were given to get it ready before you were ever dug out of that snowball."

"Orders! Orders from whom?"

"From your wife, of course. Why I hear tell her fast thinking saved your life."

"Really?"

"Yes. Really. And about attending that feast. You may on one condition."

"Condition! What condition?"

"You must invite me to be your honored guest."

"What! Honored guest? Why, you . . . you conniving old fox. You just want to be second in line, behind me, to get the choicest pieces of turkey." To drive home his point, Santa repeatedly finger-tapped Dr. Swift's chest. "Listen. That's not going to happen. Hear? I've never singled out anyone to be a so-called *honored guest* at any of my celebrations, and I'm not going to start now either. So, stop trying to roast your chestnuts over my hot coals."

Usually when Santa refused to listen to reason, Dr. Swift would capitulate. That is, he would as Santa's friend, but never as his doctor. As his doctor—despite Santa pulling every trick in the book to disarm him—he would firmly stand his ground. Today, he would rely on something Santa couldn't match or repudiate. Sound medical doctrine.

Knowing he had the upper hand, that he would win this round with Santa, Dr. Swift raised his brow and spoke with authority. "And I, Dr. Swift refuse to be moose whipped by any patient, including you, ol' buddy. So, as I was saying, I insist on being your honored guest if I am to release you. And I do have the authority to keep you here overnight. All I have to do is fill out a little paperwork and it's a done deal."

"So, now, it's blackmail, huh?"

"No. I just want to observe you closely for a few hours. You do have a slight head injury, which probably isn't anything to worry about. But, to be on the safe side, I'd like to stick by your side tonight. Keep a close eye on you. So, buddy, what'll it be, a turkey feast or gourmet hospital food? And, Mr. Saint Nickolas Claus, I know that you know what I mean when I say *gourmet hospital food*."

The standoff began.

Santa drilled Dr. Swift with an icy stare.

Dr. Swift buttoned his lip and sat down in his swivel chair. Purposely avoiding eye contact with Santa, humming as though he had not a care in the world, he, with an air of flippancy, repeatedly stroked his whiskers. It was his way of saying, "My dear friend, today, I intend to wait you out."

A few minutes later, interpreting the glare in Santa's eyes as "I'm not gonna give in," he picked up his medical chart and began doodling in its margins.

"Stubborn moose. You think you're gonna win this one.

Well, you're not. You should know by now that I know exactly what I have to do to break through that tight-lipped snow cave of yours. Yeah, ya old fool. You think that stare of yours will unnerve me. Well, today, that ain't gonna happen. And since you won't budge, you leave me with no other choice but to play my next card. Seems you've forgotten all the meals I've eaten at your cottage. So many, I know exactly what you like and dislike in the food department."

Emerging from his thoughts coughing, Dr. Swift got what he wanted. Santa's attention.

"Say, I hear tell tonight, besides the usual turkey, sage dressing and cranberries, they'll be serving fluffy, garlic-flavored mashed potatoes. And the green-bean casserole . . . it'll have twice the mushrooms the recipe calls for. And I hear tell they shipped in fresh ones for it. And there'll be corn pudding made with sour cream. Yum, yum. And for dessert, that favorite bakery of yours over there in Sleigh Valley . . . Well, they'll be supplying apple pie topped off, of course, with French vanilla ice cream. Oh, and there'll be cheesecake with strawberries too. Mm. Yum, yum. Won't that be finger-lickin' good?

"Now, let's see what's on this hospital menu for tonight's dinner? Hmm. It says here the main course is gonna be liver and onions, with sides of turnip greens and mashed rutabaga. And it looks like everyone gets a nice, tall glass of yummy prune juice to wash it all down. And for dessert? Oh, what can be more soothing on the tummy than some plain old lime Jell-O. Hmm. Sounds like the whole meal is nutritional. Why it's just the ticket for someone with a head injury. Doncha think?"

Glancing up from his chart, Dr. Swift spied a look on Santa's face only one word could describe. *Yuck.* Spreading his lips into a smirking grin, he almost said, "Good. I've won." Thinking better of it, he held his tongue.

Santa, reading his smug look, begrudging gave in. "Okay. Okay. You win because I ain't eatin' none of your yucky hospital food. Now, what was it you wanted?"

"To be your honored guest tonight. I'd like to sit next to you. Keep an eye on you."

"Oh, yeah. I remember." Santa, stroking his beard, said this even though he had no recollection of it. "So, are we done here?"

"No. Not until we do an MRI on you."

"An MRI?"

"Yes. An MRI. We just need to run you through that machine over there. Remember? We discussed it earlier."

"Ah, right. I, uh . . . uh, yeah. I remember."

Santa wished he hadn't answered with hesitancy. Dr. Swift, he feared, probably knew he was fudging it. He cleared his throat, then added, "Well, what are we waiting for? Let's get this picture-taking over with so we can go eat. I'm hungrier than a polar bear." To further make his point, he pushed his middle forward and said, "See this gut? When it's totally empty, I can get pretty nasty. So, watch your back. If I don't get some turkey and cranberries pretty soon, I just might eat you alive. GR-R-R-R—"

"Threats, threats, threats," Dr. Swift shot back, playing into his game. As he hit the buzzer to summon his medical attendant, he linked his eyes with Santa's and smiled reassuringly. But he, himself, didn't feel reassured. His best buddy, showing signs of forgetfulness, worried him.

"Oh, and one last thing before doing your MRI. I'd like you to sign this consent form, to give me permission to consult with Mitzi. Might not need it, but just in case—"

"That I don't mind doing," Santa said, grabbing the pen and form. "Mitzi's my right-hand gal. You've got my permission to tell her anything."

Comments concerning *Won't Tell, Part 1 of 3* can be posted on the site where this book was purchased by the person who purchased it. Doing so would be very much appreciated as it helps generate sales. Thank you.

WON'T TELL

PART

2 of 3

CHAPTER 1

"Is something wrong? Santa's okay, isn't he?" Mitzi asked, shedding her parka as she entered Dr. Swift's office. Her panicky look betrayed anxiety, as did her fingerplay on purse straps. Taking a chair, she eyed Dr. Swift warily. All morning, since receiving his call, she hadn't been able to focus on anything work-related.

Yesterday she woke at the crack of dawn consumed with *what-ifs* concerning Santa's ethnic secret. Today, a different set of *what-ifs* vied for her attention. "What if he has a brain injury? What if he can't work? What if he can't make his Christmas Eve run? What if he . . ." By the time she reached Dr. Swift's office, her worrisome thoughts had whipped her stomach into a spasmodic frenzy.

"Why'd you ask me here and not Santa?" she asked, perching birdlike on a chair across from him.

Before saying a word, Dr. Swift handed her Santa's signed consent form. Leaning back in his chair, eyeing her thoughtfully, he shared, "Santa said you're his righthand gal, that I can tell you anything. Thankfully, he willingly signed—"

"I can see that he signed it," she said, setting the form on

1

his desk. "So, let's get to it."

"Well," he began slowly, as was his nature, "something concerns me, and I, uh . . . I mentioned it to Santa last night when leaving the party, but, most likely, he forgot what I said a minute or two later. Mitzi, I'm afraid, until he gets over this—"

"Over this? Over what?"

"My dear, I know you're anxious, but please . . . trust me. I'll get there."

"Okay," Mitzi said, although it wasn't okay with her. She wanted him to get to the point; but long aware of his slow, methodical nature, she resolved to just listen.

"Now, where was I? Ah, yes. As I was saying, until he gets over this, Santa will likely experience a good deal of frustration. Even some confusion. And if you have some understanding of it . . . Well, what I'm about to tell you is . . . Oh, and, uh, I'd wager with him being so private about his yearly racial changes, he won't want anyone else knowing. So, it's probably best to keep this secret."

"Secret? Of course. But, Doc, you're scaring me. What did you mean when you said, 'until he gets over this?'"

<>•<>•<>

www.HavetPress.com

HavetPress@gmail.com